MARINE MOON

Rea Rahaman

WORKBOOK PRESS LLC
187 E Warm Springs Rd,
Suite B285, Las Vegas, NV 89119, USA

Website: https://workbookpress.com/
Hotline: 1-888-818-4856
Email: admin@workbookpress.com

Ordering Information:
Quantity sales. Special discounts are available on quantity purchases by corporations, associations, and others. For details, contact the publisher at the address above.

ISBN-13:   978-1-957618-42-5 (Paperback Version)
              978-1-957618-43-2 (Digital Version)

REV. DATE: 02.01.2022

In dedication to all the military officers around the world, particularly the ones I have counseled.

For my high school best friend

Veteran Air Force Sergeant Marica R. Lawrie

and

my new girl friends
Elaine Augelo, Brooklyn, New York State
Joanna Jacques, Brooklyn, New York State

In memory of
Nancy Cook (1961-2015)

Note from the Author

After writing my first novel which will be published soon, I found myself creating more romance novels with a twist. Marine Moon is my third. Yes, there are 3 more. I have this energy creeping into my creativity with new concepts of romantic notions and mystery. I love creating each character and throwing conflicts at them with holistic solutions.

I hope this book offers each of you much pleasure as much as it gave me to create and write. I start thinking about the military officers around Planet Earth who served countries especially my uncle Warrant Officer Mohammed Ahmed Khan (1935-2020), his son Flight Sergeant Martin Khan and grandson Corporal Simon Khan. Three generations of British Royal Air Force Officers.

A huge thank you to Cam for the technical aspects and special effects.

Questions and comments welcome at rizefromanger@ yahoo.com

Thank you and enjoy!

Rea

1

The A MI-17 helicopter hovered above the makeshift United States military base in Afghanistan. In the far distance, a British AH-64 Apache helicopter seemed to ponder as it stood still in midair. The parked A MI-17 engine kicked into life. A Marine on the ground partly lifted the girl into the arms of another Marine officer into the helicopter and guided her into the empty seat. He proceeded to buckled her in and gave her a helmet with earphones.

He saluted the Marine on the ground and gave the pilot instructions that they are ready for takeoff. The Air Force pilot waited for instructions from the British AH-64 Apache helicopter that stood in mid-air before he raised the machine to join the other A MI-17 helicopter. Dust and smoke blew in the far distance as well as near, clouding the vision of officers and civilians alike in the air and on the ground. About twenty or so military officers were watching this take off, not oblivious to the fireworks from the war around them.

The smell of death pickled the air as the sound of guns exploded on the mountain terrain. An accurate vision on what clear precise action to take next sought through every soldier's thoughts because the only way out of this mess of firing squad that came from those distant mountains is up. Even up is not safe with the firing of missiles.

The girl in the chopper peeked from behind the opened doors of the A MI-17 and saw a marine looking at her with wonderment in his angry eyes. The era of this dawn is not over, so much less anger with both military officers and civilians. The chopper was climbing slowly to a higher peak as the girl achieved euphoria. The sun was setting over the horizon bathing them in a glorious burst of flaming light.

One Marine, however, watched the chopper rise and disappeared over the mountain in the heat of the night. With the wind rippling through her hair and the sun reflected in her eyes, the chopper had slowly ascended. The marine looked on and felt the sun behind looking on too. The sun sank, unveiling the moon. The moon's light chose that particular moment to come out from behind a cloud and illuminated the tangled wildness of her black hair that crept out from the helmet. She smiled at him, he was sure of it. His heart slammed against his ribs and feelings he did not know existed poured out from him. His temperature raised a few knots and he wondered what was behind her smile. He stood his full length of six feet and let out a breath he realized he held when she walked past him bunker down on his knees looking through an MK46 machine gun. The moon dust silver on this early hour as he made a decision. He wanted to live, he wanted out of the Military and he was going to marry *HER, that girl in the chopper!*

As the helicopter became a speck of dust, the officer on the group returned to the task they were assigned to as if the visit was not important. For each of the officers and civilians, life for them is a battlefield. With the choice of staying alive and the decision on marriage twirling in his thoughts, he turned and walked the short path to his bunker for some much-needed sleep. He knew now that he has a renewed purpose for living and a huge smile tugged at his lips.

Life in Afghanistan was not what he nor millions of other officers including those officers in other countries signed up for when they decided to join the military agencies. Who would believe that there is corruption in the military, that it is the most effective organized crime unit in the United States of America? The things he saw, and the things he saw other officers did, do not add up to fighting for freedom. Whose fucking freedom are we talking about here, certainly not Americans? They were all free before these wars, now they are trapped in a hell of a revenge war. Revenge for what is everyone's guess. Yes, they all had freedom before the wars in Afghanistan and Iraq.

The illegal trade of heroin the United States Air Force smuggled into the country makes him a believer that it wasn't the war on terror more greed. The physical abuse that these innocent Afghans and Iraqis have to endure is beyond anyone's comprehension. He can't believe that his people are so cruel. The lies and deceit told about both wars are insane and inhumane. The man who started his is no different than Hitler. Politic sucks.

The American news spoke of half-truths, making the United States look like a powerful leader when it's all about one man's stupidity of ignorance. People around the world now think and believed that all Americans are not only greedy; they are also bullies. It is disgusting to know that the people of the United States are native or maybe they just do not care about what is happening here.

Oh, hell! Let's not forget the hundreds of military officers from the other countries who joined forces with his military that died for this stupid greed. These innocent deaths as well as Afghans and Iraqis who died in the name of good old America greed!

The realization of these facts finally took a toll on the Marine. He suddenly buckled over and bring forth all of what was bothering him in the form of expulsion. He has been nauseous for weeks and could not fathom the obstacle that obstructed his stomach into knots of squeamish sensations. He felt dizzy. The marine stood up straight as officers asked whether he required assistance. He shook his head communicating "no." They all respected his space as they too have been there. He loved his country nonetheless this war is all fucked up! What a mess!

As the officers quietly give the Marine space, he continued to his bunker for his much-required sleep. He cannot remember when last he had more than twenty minutes of solid sleep. Hell, he needed more than sleep, he needed a woman to hold him, to cuddle with, and a good long hot shower, well maybe not in that order. He wanted to see the girl in the chopper again; he wanted to feel not just need to feel again!

The Marine bunked down for what he assumed is his regular haunted twenty minutes. He closed his eyes and took a deep breath and let it out slowly. He saw her face and her bright smile. He blinked his eyes to stop the images from disappearing. His fingers itched to make the images real, to capture them on paper, to imprison them in his heart, and to store them away so they cannot leave him.

He pulled his length into a sitting position and took out his pad with a pencil from under the mattress. On the opened page he started to draw. The trapped images in his brain flowed through him into his fingers to the tip of his pencil onto the paper. He could not get them out fast enough and soon filled three sheets with her smiling face. He did not feel contented; he needed to draw more, of her. After he'd capture every image on the next twenty pages, he felt free, only then did he dare to rest and sleep.

The marine felt his emotions sinking ship and she was the only lifeline left. The song by the group "The Who" came flooded through and the Marine found himself whispering,

"Somebody save me
Let your warm hands break right through
Somebody save me
I don't care how you do it
Just stay with me
Stay…….come on
I have been waiting for you
Just stay with me
I made the whole world shine for you."

He accepted that he needed help and he knows she would understand this suppression, this numbness of feelings in him. She can assist him in discovering different approaches to discovering these emotions that are hidden somewhere deep in him. His tongue ran over his lips and the last image he saw was hers, her light brown eyes, her short black hair, and her thin fragile body. He softly whispered her name. He fell for the first time in uncountable years of solid eight hours of undisturbed sleep.

Four days later, a group of ten officers commanded by the Marine was on an exploration mission along the dirt road that led to a village with strange usual activities. A Swedish Air Force officer reported it a few hours ago on his journey home. He could not elaborate because he was flying too high avoiding missile attacks. The Marine and his officers were dispatched to investigate because they were the only unit available until new batches of officers were fetched in to do these types of investigation. It was not the work his unit of Marines usually do; they are more beach recon and overseeing construction due to his engineering degree.

This is more search and rescue, search and rescue ID-improvised explosive device roadside bombs before the ID search for him and rescue him from living. Being a first lieutenant and as experience, as he is he was ordered to do this investigation on the usual activities. Everyone was overtired due to the uprising four days ago and the gun battle that followed. He was deployed to return home when the gun battle broke out and he could not leave due to transportation. The other marines who were with the girl in the chopper were scheduled before him. Lucky devils? He had to be the one staying behind.

All is still; too quiet. The Marine looked up towards the sky and then the surroundings in front and around him. This is trouble, too seriously quiet. He can feel the blood leaving his face and surged into the large skeletal muscles in his legs, allowing him a fast escape. He wanted to flee and not fight. His face bleach with fear as blood shunted away from his nostril, creating feelings of blood running cool. His body froze for a moment allowing time to gauge and making it possible whether hiding is a good reaction or running. This is fear.

He can smell trouble. He can feel it in his stomach. His instinct is riding high. He has been in intelligence and operations for too long not to know what is coming to them. He can hear his heart rate and breathing rise as well as those of the other officers awaiting his orders. Through his communication apparatus to his men, "High alert, slow," he commanded. The circuits in his brain's emotional centers triggered a flood of hormones putting his body on general alert, making him edgy and ready for action. His attention fixated on the threat at hand and he knew the faster he can evaluate what response to make, the merrier.

If only he knew what, where, and when disaster would strike, he would be flying high, well not high, be happy. He took his binoculars, spying on the landscape all around him. He saw nothing. He told his troops again to move forward slowly, very slowly as he peeked through his binoculars again. The Marine stepped a few feet to the side from the Humvee and was about to take another step when a smoky smell hauled him back for a moment. He sniffed the air and listened. He was oblivious to the sting of the sun burning into him. Fog oozed out from the cracks from the earth and misted the roadside, sitting low around them. His eyes taunt the view ahead and around him. His expression was obscured. Fog in a midday sun; this is not right? The Marine turned to look at his troops. This is not fog or mist. It's smoke.

"Something is going to happen, stop." He ordered his troops still standing a few feet away however facing them. "Anyone sees anything?" The Marine said in desperation.

All replies came back negative. He stepped forward slowly to the right a few feet away from his troops scanning the silhouette of the rugged mountain terrain all around him. He knew that any calmness which occurred before the eye of silence is imperative

"Something is going to blow, Lieutenant." The Marine second in command Lieutenant Hill said into his First Lieutenant's ear through his communication device.

"I can feel it." The First Lieutenant replied as he stepped a few feet forward in front of a huge rock about fifty yards away. He peeked through his binoculars again, scanning the ridge for any signs of life. He saw nothing. He can still smell the air filled with death. Death of the past and death of the coming, his death!

The sound reached him before the blast shook the vehicle that some of his men were in and send the others who were standing outside the vehicle and him who was some distance away, flying in the air. The binoculars flew out of his hand into the air and landed on an officer's helmet. They were landing everywhere. The missile rocket hit its target, the Humvee at the same time a roadside bomb exploded.

The Marine landed a few feet behind the rock. He lay there watching bits and pieces of men, metal, and truck raining down on him. "Fuck you, Bush." He whispered angrily. He tried to get up and found out he just could not move. He laid there watching the bits and pieces of human flesh falling on the dirt road. No one should ever have to see want he just witness; his men were blown to bits. He laid his head down and stared up at the sun until the last bit of debris fell a few inches from him.

Heavy black smoke poured from the burning wreckage at the site that sparked a fireball and littered the dirt road with shrapnel. He sucked in his breath trying to gain control. A bone clicked as he clenched his jaw in a rage then regret flashed through him as his guilt gnawed at him. Why was he not dead? Make no doubt about it; this bombing was planned down to the last minute. There are IDs planted along the road and the missile rocket came from the hills in the distance; fancy both being American made. How ironic? Where did the activities come from? No doubt, the unusual gestalt of conflicts arrived from a trap to hunt and kill.

The Marine turned his head to the right and saw barren land and then to the left and saw the rock. He has to get there somehow. He has to get there and hide before the terrorists come checking for survivors. The lieutenant's disposition was extremely low on his list of concerns at the moment. How is he going to do that? He still cannot move. He knew if he wanted to live, he had to have the courage to drag his body there. The rock is a good cover.

Why is it sunny one minute and dark the next? Is that the sun or the moon shining? Those were the Marine's last thoughts before his world went blank. The moon hung high while its filtered rays pierced through him delivering the curly light on the unconscious marine. He was knocked unconscious for a long time after the brutal incident. For how long he does not know. He guessed, judging from the position of the sun he has been in and out of unconsciousness a few times over a period of about two or three hours.

He glanced at his watch; he did not know the time because his watch had stopped at three-thirty in the afternoon. It was broken from the impact after he was tossed into the air and landed on the ground. Since there was no watch to measure time, time passed very slowly.

The song came to him, "Somebody save me......."

His thoughts drifted back to four days ago when he first laid eyes on the lady that disappeared in the A MI-17. Her name sailed through the airwaves across the seas and evaded his space. He heard she was the best in the business. Hundreds of officers knew about her. If he wanted to meet her he had to live, even if she cannot do anything for him, he had to meet her, no, he wanted to meet her. It gave him something to live for in these depressing moments of living hell he is facing, presently. It has been aching in his heart since he saw her as he sat in the front line in this horrible war against whom he does not know, he has lost the purpose of fighting in Afghanistan. All he knew was that he wanted to go home and hide from the world. Silence would be golden for him.

These were new emotions more of an emotional elevator for him to ponder on. He reveled in intense anger that he wallowed in. He looked around his surroundings, at the dead, and stroked it with a white-hot fury. To keep at bay the soul-wrenching pain and emptiness threatening to destroy his last effort of survival instinct, he pulled one of the drawings of the girl in the chopper he kept in his shirt pocket and looked at it with the moonlight. Another day will dawn and on that day I will meet you, never mind his future looked scant.

The light of the moon shone on him. He closed his eyes for a minute and then opened it looking at the moon. He figured if he kept looking at it he would not be unconscious again. His thoughts were hazy and surfaced with images of the haunted past mixed into the present moment. He couldn't focus on any one thought or image. He asks the moon, why? He thinks the moon answered him.

"Tonight is a Marine Moon, shining just for you."

"Marine Moon." The Marine whispered before he sank into unconsciousness again. He gained consciousness a few hours later. It was dark. He looked for the moon and could not find it. He blinked and saw it tucked behind a cloud to his left.

"Don't play with me. I am not in the mood for hide and seek."

He softly whispered to the moon. "Come on out and shine your light on me. Make me walk." The Marine looked up at the moon looking at him. He swore that the moon smiled and the light becomes brighter. He turned his head left and then right looking for enemies. He moved his fingers and leg trying to determine his injuries. He rolled over and his hand fell on something soft.

"Fuck. God damn it!" Upon realizing that it was a part of one of his men, the crux of his anger turned his eyes dark green with cold and finally frozen in rage. His voice and his gaze remained as cold as a glacial on a polar ice cap.

Thoughts that had lingered throughout his conscious moments had come unbidden, now made his blood turned to fire. A steady pressure pounded through him, with the blood of anger flowing from his hands, it was easier to grasp a weapon or strike the enemy. Heart rate increased sending a rush of hormones that generated adrenaline pushing a pulse of energy strong enough for vigorous actions. Unclenching his fist, his heart beat faster, he could tell the battle that waged inside him.

His shock body lay limbed and numbed to all pain. He let the bit of body part go and slowly pulled his body into a sitting position. He listened to the silence of the night and waited for a long time. He tried to move his legs and felt immense pain; he couldn't move them. He looked around assessing the damage and saw nothing neither breathing nor standing. A tight smug expression covered his face as he pulled his body with his arms behind the rock. He felt the pain ushered through him, however, he was in no position to care. He could not radio in and get help even if he could move. Everyone and everything was in bits and pieces all around him.

He knew that he will have to wait it out until someone from the military base dispatch more soldiers to search and rescue this unit. He didn't report in upon his designed hour. What is taking them so long? His subconscious recognition of the superstition number of six, six, six, passed his rational thoughts and send a chill down his spine. He killed the thought as soon as it came through to him as the devil. Dark shadows lengthening over him as he pondered from hallucination to delusion.

Since sleep was not part of the equation, however, desperate he wanted to sleep, he was not seduced by the moment. Determine to savor this moment where fantasy and reality collided, he began to think of her. He's a man with the courage to spin fantasies until somebody saved him. Victory is his emotional haven as he tried to engrave her images; he could feel it fading with each moment passed. This is not just a joke….she is real. He pulled the drawing from his pocket and looked at it with trembling fingers for a long time until he ran out of fantasies and his thought went blank.

Sitting in the predawn light in this milieu, a dozen different expressions fought the territory of his face as the Marine tried to get a hold of his shocking experience. The shock was overwhelming as a windmill in a tornado. The blow of the incident now falls freely and shackled vivid horrible traumatic images that swept across his closed eyes in a boomerang toss. He kept his eyes open so that neither images nor other illusions can cascade in his thoughts. From this singular action, no more confusion was created, for a short time.

Lurking in the back of his unconsciousness, deep in the trek of his interior thoughts, other past traumatic images become loose and begin to run amok. For a brief few minutes, he had relieved. Then more images of past and present forged their path through and rocked him into reality. He realized that the suppression of thoughts no longer worked. It only bought out the quarry of more intensifying deep-rooted thoughts, more of making life in the present moment hell on earth.

He struggled against the aghast of deadly images that kept popping up regardless of whether he closed or opened his eyes. He was unconscious for most of the night and now fumbled to survive, one minute at a time, moment by moment. This Marine enthusiasm for this type of adventure overrode all other influences of pleasure. Inspiration infused on countless other times, however, it's dead today, when he needed it the most.

Lying on the edge of time, his desire to create a fantasy to ease the burden of pain seemed to be all he has presently. What he thinks is slowly joining his dead feelings. The smog of shallowness enveloped him making decisions difficult. He lost focus and tried to think of the lady from the A MI-17. He lost it, he couldn't retrieve it; even the image of the one lady that had kept him going. He no longer knew what is real or what is an illusion; he once again drifted into the path of pain.

Where is my moon? Where is my Marine Moon? He glanced up into the sky only to see crows picking the meat off the bones of his men. He could not stop them as bits and pieces were everywhere. He looked up searching for the sun and could not move his head or his hands. How long was he unconscious this time around? Besides, he knew if he leaves this rock that was shedding him from the sun's rays and hiding him from the people who blew his men to bits and pieces, he would be dead too. Someone had to be alive to tell his officers' stories and to see their family. This is his job. It was his unit.

First Lieutenant Christian Andres Vincelette lost all his men to war. On what? "Fuck, oh, hell fuck." He whispered to the midday sun. Andres is the Spanish for Andrew meaning man warrior. He does not feel much of a warrior right now. He turned to see if there were any movements and saw nothing. Why is headquarters taking this long to send rescue? Then he heard voices and his instinct kicked in for he knew that this is no rescuer. He held his breath as the voices came closer and closer; he realized that the language is not English. This was the enemy! He heard shots from a semi-automatic going off and singing. God damn it, they are singing and dancing over his men. Who are they, locals taking revenge or terrorists? This is a triumph for them!

Lieutenant Vincelette waited for a long time. He listened to the silence as the singing died down. He knew the shooters were there, looking at their handy work and seeing whether they can retrieve anything useful from the wreckage. Ever so often, the reflection of the sun bounced off the barrel of their guns and reflected in the space between him and them. He breathed slowly and carefully. One movement and he would be dead. He knew a search party is on the way, what's taking them so fucking long?

It was a little over an hour; he heard a cloud of noise that poured steadily, becoming louder. It cascaded and flooded the air adding more noise to the already pounding sound in his ear. The noise laps at this neck adding more confusion between reality and illusion. What is it? Dare he thinks of what he wished it to be, rescued? He knew he had some broken ribs and maybe his legs are too. He felt pain all over his body which was not his concern; his concern was surviving until rescue came.

Then he heard it again and knew what it was, what he

was dying to hear for so long, the sound of an A MI-17, no, more than one. There are two; three of them based on the noise of the engine. He heard voices again and shouting. He somehow knew the terrorists who were singing and dancing over his men are now running for their lives. He couldn't care to look and see which direction they were running. All he wanted was to go home, out of this hellhole!

The first light of dawn had not yet invaded the concrete structure of the military hospital when First Lieutenant Christian Andres Vincelette opened his eyes, two weeks later. The room was flooded and releasing the awful sounds of pain and suffering. The window across his bed showed dawn chasing the darkness away as a ray of sunlight slowly crept into the room. He knew this place very well as he was here over the years, visiting his friends or recovering from some injuries. He sat at the edge of the bed and stared at his shaking hands. He still had more recovery to do and a whole lot of healing. He is alive!

The rescue team had to maneuver heavy missiles before they found him. No signals were coming from his unit, therefore the search was challenging, fighting off the missiles and gunfight that targeted them. The captain of the rescue unit saw the flack of black crows and knew it was the sight of the wounded and dead.

He was in a stable place despite the crisis in his life. The thought of dying created a rise in adrenaline and cortisol in the bloodstream sending his body into overdrive. His internal war blurted out the truth and nearly tore it from his lips; he remained silent. His eyes flashed with anger, darting from side to side daring his thoughts not to remember that dreadful day; for a second it obliged, suddenly the memory jumped out. He remembered that day where he lost all of his men. Then he felt guilt for being alive. He felt his heart and breathing rates rose to a high and blood flowed from his hands down to his toes preparing him to scream or strike. The energy of shame and guilt jumped immediately to the maximum.

Christian was first airlifted with some other injured officers to Incirlik Air Base Hospital in Adana, Turkey for a few weeks before flying into Landstuhl Regional Medical Center in Ramstein, Germany. This meant that he will be going to the Naval Medical Center in Washington, D.C until he is fully recovered. He is in heaven. First Lieutenant Christian Andres Vincelette smiled so wide that he couldn't stop himself even when the nurse came to see him. He wanted to jump up and kissed her. On second thoughts, he will save it for someone else. The nurse checked his vitals and left him to rest. He is out of danger; she thought well physical danger anyhow. The mental danger is a whole different ball game!

Nurse Marie Morning saw the spike on the monitor she managed by her station however she put the Lieutenant's smile to his waking up after two weeks and found out that he is all fixed up almost as good as new. Physical therapy would be on the list next for him, then off to the lady counselor to fix his brain or whatever is left of him. Christian gave the nurse no attention as his thoughts were directed to the lady in the A MI. How the men talked about her, he had never in his thirty-five years of living heard such talk from men about one woman. If he did not know who she was he would think that she is a whore, a very high-class hoe, a sex worker.

He knew that was not the case because the things that came out of the officers' mouths were sexy, not sexual. Everyone who saw her, including him, thinks that she is sexy and those who were fortunate to meet her knew she is sexy. Sexy in what she does for the officers and sexy mentally and physically. Mentally had to do with how many endless hours she freely gave to others. Physically sexy looking in the army uniform he saw her so long ago. Everyone called her "Doc" and no one in actuality knew her real name. He has to see her. What should he tell her about himself? How much is too much? He doesn't want to tell her what he had witnessed in Desert Storm, Sudan, Somalia, or Iraq much less Afghanistan.

He does not feel comfortable telling anyone of the daily torture he felt and endure every time he closed his eyes. Hell, on a good day he doesn't even have to close his eyes, the gruesome images just popped up. Blinking makes them go away and then these bloody forsaken images have to show up again in his sleep. How dare they? He wanted her to notice him. He wanted to date her and make love to her. He wanted to wake up in the morning and see her next to him, just lying there. How can he stand out from the others? How can he make her notice him?

Christian felt the tiredness of his body and then it hit him that the nurse had injected something into his saline drip. He was too happy smiling to ask her what it was; his thoughts were on a different timeline. Oh, boy, he looked up at the ceiling and saw the moon shining so bright at him.

"Marine Moon." He whispered.

His wide smile returned and the lids of his eyes slowly closed as the physical elements of earth no longer were in his vision. Christian was in a different place in a different time zone where the sun joined with the moon, the moon is inside the sun, and the moon glowed a little brighter at this moment-an eclipse of his cold heart with her warm ones.

Two bodies highlighted by the moon's glow lay on the beach wet from the incoming tide. They were locked in each other's arms, uncaring of the passage of time. She quivered at his nearness and turned to look at him. Their eyes met, held, and stay connected. This was his solar eclipse.

"Marine Moon." He said as the sound was lost on his lips. He once again sank into unconsciousness, this time it was deliberate.

Doctor Zuri Anana Curruni looked at the long line of officers sitting in the waiting room and out the door into the passage leading to the outside onto the road. She smiled, not looking at any of them as she entered her office. She knew all their eyes followed her. Her assistant, Rae Jean looked at her with a wary smile. She put some new folders on her desk.

"Twenty new officers for you." Rae Jean informed her.

"Anana means happiness and with that, I am exhausted, however, very happy," Zuri told her assistant.

"I take it you see the long line and there is more joining them." Rae Jean peeked through the blinds behind her desk.

"This last session of three-hour counseling, the seats were full and twenty officers were standing in the auditorium. This is the aftermath of that session!" Zuri took several long deep breaths. She did not sign up for these long hours of counseling military officers when they returned from wars. She does it anyway. The line for individual counseling gets longer with each group counseling.

She had counseled a few military officers as a favor for her brother Anil whose girlfriend had returned from Iraq. Before she could wink, she was counseling all branches of the military. Word flew fast about her new techniques of relieving traumatic images and pain, what they call Post Traumatic Stress Disorder, hence PTSD. Now, here she is with Rae Jean after three years. The knock on the door brought her into reality. She moved behind her desk as Rae Jean told the intruder to enter. Two pairs of eyes were on the short stout sergeant who came into the room with more files hold in her left arm, a huge stack of them.

"I need an update on the suicides and here are some more for you." Sergeant MacAuther told her as she handed Rae Jean the folders.

"You always want status reports. You want me to close these cases quicker than I can. All you ever seem interested in is how close I am to solving their conflicts. How come you never asked how I solve it?" Zuri vexingly told her.

"Be happy, my beautiful loves. I know you are overworked and underpaid, never mmm, let me take that back...not paid, voluntarily do this from the goodness of your heart, nevertheless, I know you can perform miracles, coz I've seen it. You are it. You're all we have. Thank you, my beautiful ladies." Sergeant MacAuther bowed as low as she can and backed out of the room with a salute closing the door behind her. She looked at the long line and told the officers in the hall who occupied the chairs.

"Pass the word around the doc is tired and need some tender loving care. Be gentle with her, boys." The officers nodded silently.

Back in the office, Rae Jean moved from behind the chair she was standing and walking towards Zuri, smilingly she told her. "The sergeant has a crush on you. You know she is gay. So when is the first date? You look like you could do with some sweet loving touching."

The look Zuri gave her as she sat in her chair was one of "oh please." A happy grin reached her brown eyes as she commented on the remark. "Yes, I do require some TLC. I want it from a nice-looking hunk of a hunk and not a female. Thank you. I have nothing as you know against gays. Now, kindly get me some latte. Get out, will you?" Rae Jean laughing left and closed the door behind her. She stood in the Hall looking at the officers who await Doctor Zuri's attention.

"Alright Officers, folders please?" The officers extended

their folders to where Rae Jean read the last few lines and put a star next to where the doctor has to sign. This also means that after the visit with Doctor Zuri, they are free to move on with living life. When Rae Jean makes no star that means there are more visits to be made, more counseling is required.

"Here you go madam, two lattes." Officer Reading informed Rae Jean as he waited for her to finish writing so he can hand her the lattes. She smiled at Officer Reading, thank him, and collect the first ten folders from the officers, walking into the office. She handed the folders to Zuri who was mourning over a suicide victim report. She had seen him in the ward after his first attempt and then after his initial twenty four hour suicide watch.

The officers knew the drill. The first one followed Rae Jean holding the two lattes that were handed to him from Officer Reading. He stood awaiting Rae Jean to take the lattes from him before he sat in the chair and waiting for Doctor Zuri's attention. Zuri read the first folder that Sargent MacAuther bought in and realized that his wounds were far too deep and he had already given up. He had shot a child in Afghanistan thinking that the young boy was strapped with explosives. He was not; the officer was devastated and could not live with himself, he had excessive guilt. He didn't give her the opportunity to counsel him. She read two more folders and put them aside.

Rae Jean waited until she closed the last folder and handed her the first ten officer's folders. "It will be a long-ass day, Doc. I think it will be an easy one as most of these officers are in good shape. Here is your coffee."

Zuri opened the first folder that Rae Jean had left on her right. She read her last insertion and smiled at the officer now sitting in a chair in front of her. She asked him some questions, wrote some notes, and marked closed. She closed the folder. Rae Jean will stamp closed on the front of the folder, post two copies of completion for his chart and the other for his commanding officer. Rae Jean will notify someone who will come and collect the box of closed files for storage.

"You are clean, free to go." Officer McKenzie.

"Oh, thank you doc. I feel so much better than I ever did in my life. I can sleep for hours with no images and nightmares. I am grateful for everything. Thank you so much." The young soldier said in a raw southern brawl.

The last of the one hundred officers left the building. Zuri had closed as many as fifty cases with a clean bill of health. They have to complete the final journey and receive a report from the military psychiatrist, psychologist, or psychotherapist for final clearance before returning to duty.

She admitted another sixty officers and knows more will be admitted tomorrow, another good long happy day for her and Rae Jean. They worked tiring long hours, however, it is extremely rewarding. She has the best assistant in the world as they share the same values in counseling. They work fabulously together. Rae Jean's wicked sense of humor made the long tiring days short and less stressful.

The military did not give her an office because there was no one to spare. They give her a room and installed a restroom for personal use after word reached that her therapy worked faster and effectively with very few relapses. Zuri refused the money they offered her because she just couldn't accept any for her service. The officers did not sign up to fight in two useless wars and this is the least she could do for them. Besides, she did not need the money because her books and lectures around the world made her a very rich counselor. The World Health Organization validated her work and even given her numerous awards, sending her books on the bestselling list for a very long time. The demand for her counseling is more than she can do. She had started to train others in her field when the military situation fell in her lap.

Ah, she thought as she rubbed her eyes looking at the files Sergeant MacAuther left. Free time to do what she wanted was gone a long time ago. Seeing her family and dining with friends seem to be long forgotten. Not forgetting her snorkeling and diving exhibitions around the world is also history. When last did she had fun? Fun for her is watching the sunrise and the sunset, and the days falling into nights. Oh, what she would do with a soak in a sauna, manicure, pedicure, facial, the works of giving herself some good old fashioned TLC. She needed it for her body and she also needed some nurturing from a hunk of a male. Fancy her ever meeting one!

Her last relationship was some five years ago when the World Health Organization validated her techniques for healing. Logan Ahmed Morrison could not manage the competition as he puts it and asked her back for his ring. Competition! Would you believe the dork? He is a psychiatrist and she's a counselor, so what competition? Who was competing? She was not so that left him competing with her for what, money or status or love? In some small manner, the line of attack was justified by her having more money than he does and that shattered his ego. Men were supposed to be more in command in a relationship, not the women. He accused her of being controlling. Six years of dating turned out the best in him until the validation and money came to his knowledge.

It had taken her years to be accepted for her work as a counselor. Her two doctorates in several countries assisted in her endeavorment. It was hard work and sacrifices made to arrive at the present career destination. It took several more years to market herself as the product of her techniques in removing pain from the suffering. When she completed marketing her techniques, she was confident that she would be working for the highest bidder in her field. She didn't have the opportunity because here she is, working for no money. How dare he? She is not being paid; instead, she is a volunteer worker with no pay. This means the lowest paying job ever!

How stupid was he to think there was competition. She was relieved that he broke up with her. She was planning on doing it, however, she didn't possess the courage to do it. When Logan came forward she was so happy that she wanted to jump up and dance and kiss him and dance again with joy. She was ever so over him. The minute he stepped through the door, she flew into Turkey and took belly-dancing classes. A wide smile tugged at her light red lips.

Where is the hunk who would understand her and love her no matter what she possesses, after all, it is what she contained in her heart that matters the most. She would give it all up just to find that one special someone who she can lay in bed just cuddling. Rae Jean made a sound from her throat and bought her out from her daydreaming. Trust the girl to keep her on her toes. She smiled and nodded her exhausted head.

"In ten." She informed her assistant.

Ten meaning ten minutes were exactly that, however, it was well as after ten in the heat of the night that Rae Jean and Zuri left the white-painted building they worked from in the military compound. Nights like these, they do not even say goodnight as Rae Jean drove Zuri to their building. Before they can blink an eye they were fast asleep starting the same ritual all over again at seven in the morning, seven days a week. It had been like this for six weeks straight. They both are badly in need of some fun and excitement in their lives.

The next afternoon as Zuri walked from her office, the sun dipped into the horizon, way beneath the depths of the ocean. Night slowly drifted in and soon a new day dawned, a day that brought new meanings to life, in a world where peace seemed so distant. A new day where officers hope would deliver them from the wrath of violence into the warmth of peace.

Little do Zuri and Rae Jean knew what the late August wind is about to blow in their direction.

2

As the moon greeted Planet Earth, the exotic beauty that lies beyond the clouds was slowly knitting together in the sky, enhancing the natural formation that lay within its atmosphere. Darkness had fallen on Zuri during her walk from the office to her living quarters, wrapping around the military compound in a velvety blanket of vague beauty for a short few minutes before the light of the moon shone its light.

"Savor the beauty of the moment; tapped into the well of joy," Zuri whispered in the moonlight night. She walked out from her sleeping quarters into the spread of darkness right into the path of the moonlight. Sleep could not invade her on this late August night. She was preoccupied looking at the moon when she cannoned into someone. This someone she soon realized is male with a solid muscular chest. She stopped with hands in her jacket pockets trying to analyze the current situation. His hands were also buried deep in his jacket. They stood close with breath held.

Would she have any brain damage, you think? Zuri questioned. His chest is so muscular, oh; she moistened upon smelling his scent. Her head rises from her five feet five inches to look at who bumped into her, his six feet. The moon reflexed a touch of anger in her eyes. She moistened her lips and look down. What a hunk? She let out her breath. Her awareness of the hunk grew as the brightening of the sky with the dawn.

This hunk's face flashes with anger and she too trembled softly with anger. His eyes seemed cold and empty, nonetheless, they were neither; they were burning with an out of range control. She knew the target of his anger. Her head quickly rose again and the look she gave him was full of love and compassion. He was burning with anger and welcomed the brisk summer air to cool his emotions. He had felt as if a freight train ran over him. He didn't bargain in bumping into anyone. A wall of fatigue slammed into his head; he saw it in her profile. A muscle leaped in his jaw and his stomach growled against his spine. Doubt sliced into him sharp and hot when he realized that she was his dream. A flash of pain clouded his features and the hunk pulled thoughts together very quickly. He saw her face in the glow of the moon; her brown eyes reflexed the pale moonlight and he thought he saw tears in them.

She had come forth as the dawn and as gorgeous as the moon yet resplendent as the sun. In his heart her love and compassion was moonshine. He sensed the attraction between them as a gossamer thread stretching around him, tying him to her gentleness, her softness. They were caught in a web and no matter who pulled and brushed, they would not be rid of the invisible strands that bound them together. At this very moment without her knowing, a tear that was simmering before the impact broke, stemmed, and rolled down his left cheek. Gazes collided and locked into each other as brown eyes held green ones; they stayed connected. Moments of mixed emotions held them anchored to each other and speechless. Nothing happened for what seemed hours; reality caved into their space, time no longer stood still. What Zuri saw left her in disbelief and shock. She shuddered.

The cool wind of the night's breeze had dried the tears on her twitching cheeks. Different shades of bruises cupped under his eyes and around his face. A two-day growth of hair covered his chin and mouth rolling down this neck. The struggle of pain in his frown etched his forehead and the depth of his eyes. She saw right through this heart into his soul. She knew that he couldn't see her feelings because his pain had covered anything that is connected to emotions. The night had robbed the green color from his gaze; it's deep almost black and dead. She saw anger banked in the iris of his eyes. Shaking her head, she trembled with fear for him as he shook with rage. Her gaze flitted from his straight nose to his mouth; she felt warm and shaking internally with sensations of euphoria. No male ever had that effect on her!

The moonlight added a catalyst to their profile that is no different from a firecracker, lighting internally with the love and compassion she sends him. Electrifying sensations rocked from her to him and from him to her simultaneously. Her eyes reflected the same desires as his as the captivating sensations intensified. A frisson raced along her spine; his hand now out of his pockets caressed her shoulders and raise the level of fire burning inside her heart. His touch melted away her anger. She was aware of his muscular hands on her shoulders sending a surge of warmth through her entire body, laying to rest in her heart. His fingertip slid across her bottom lip opening it slightly. She laughed shakily even as nerves lifted goosebumps into her skin. A muscle twitches along his jaw and she drew in invigorating breaths. He sucked in her refreshing breaths, ignoring the piercing pain in his ribs. She was a slave to his wounded spirit.

Christian could not believe how fortunate he was to bump into Zuri so suddenly. He was aroused and knew with relief that he no longer was impotent. All the fantasy flew out the window of how he was going to make her fall in love with him. He knew they were meant to be together and in time, they will. His entire body became alive and he felt feelings for the first time since long before the tragedy in Afghanistan. The shadows fused with their feelings, heightened the electrifying passion between them. Immense waves of intensified magnetic energy of hunger to be loved radiated off from one into the other, transfixed in the cool air. It initiated a surge of awakening to what was once suppressed emotions now began to burn the same as a wildfire in their hearts.

Unconsciously, his lips took hers in a warm kiss of surrender, and automatically Zuri responded. A deep ragged cry rocked its way through him and she felt him shuddered. She shivered. The atmosphere of the moonlight had reached out to embrace them more than any music, images, and life itself. She pushed against his chest gasping for air. Her knees buckled and she held onto his jacket for support. His hands tightened their hold and his body relaxed. She let go of his jacket and stepped back from him. He allowed one hand to drop and kept the other anchored on her waist, just in case she needed it. Unknown to him it gave her strength and courage; she stepped back and let his hand dropped.

"Marine Moon," Christian whispered to her and looked up at the moon shining its light upon them. Zuri turned to look at the moon and then back at her encounter and found a space. He had disappeared into the night. His sleepy tousled look was sexy beyond all others. She looked at the Moon for a second time wondering what about it? Is he blaming the moon for what took place with them? She hoped not and besides what is Marine Moon? What does it mean?

The breeze scented the air with his masculine smell. It lingered in the night's air. She inhaled deeply and breathes every fragment as if her life depends upon it. The scent comforted her and left an imprint in her nostrils. Her awareness of him was the same as the brightening of the sky of dawn. She hadn't the strength to withhold any emotions right now. She turned to the path that led to her quarters for what she hoped was a good night's sleep.

Dawn was breaking the darkness, lightening the sky, and giving dainty to a new beautiful day. It was also giving way to the morning dew and fog that has settled in the early morning. It would be another four months more before this military base faced winter.

Christian stared out the window opposite him into the pastel greyness of the first sight of dawn that added traces of pallid to the white spaces outside. It was raining lightly. He blinked and rubbed his eyes with his fingers because for a split second he thought he saw the doctor stirring with a shaft of dawn's light from the building door across from his quarters. He lost himself as he remembered the sound of her breathing as he waits for dawn to decorate its first strides of color across the ceiling of the sky.

The Marine once depleted penis currently on a constant high rise. He had felt depressed for many years of his life, he cannot remember the excitement he experienced after meeting the doctor. Nothing had ever lightened his eastern sky with any sort of delight in years; he can feel the feelings burrowed into the bed sheet that covered his naked body, breaking forth as this dawn spring forth. He couldn't manage to forestall both dawn and his truth. He had given up all hope on everything, until last night when he came completely alive. He didn't expect the encounter of the doctor nor did he expected the electrifying sensations that few between them. He doesn't regret any of it nor does he know what to do about the intensifying feelings. All he knows is that he welcomed the feelings and accompanying sensations, all of it. It felt great to be alive. He couldn't sleep last night; he was hoping away the images of his past by taking a midnight walk. Rage presently seemed to be the fullest expression of his essence. He knew it's more dangerous to dwell on the past, nonetheless somewhere along with his agony it became a ghost that constantly haunts him.

Christian knew referring to his past and thinking

about his future created delusion, however, it constantly flashes with images making illusionary appearances when he least expected it. Nights were the worse where there are missing sequences in the images. Since neither the past nor the future can prove that they are separate from the present, he becomes confused and cannot live in the present. His brain had frozen in the past, inducing painful memories and the mere thought of facing it alone drove him crazy.

This is his conflict of interest; more times than he dared to count, he had mistaken traumatic images and illusions for reality. He knew that he will never be over his past as long as he gave it permission to wrap around his future. Looking back strictly into his past, he acknowledged there's no reason to either invent or invest in the future. His entire past now shadowed his future, what's the point? This is why the doctor is here, to help them sort through the images and illusions from reality. What was it that Doctor Yuri Anana Curruni wrote in one of her books, "Wishing to know your past or future you have to willingly look at all of it with your present behavior." He had bought all ten of her books and read them during his long months of recovery. He took notes, lots of notes, maybe too many notes. He was intrigued.

He had listened to her three-hour lecture on traumatic and abuse experiences coupled with Post Traumatic Stress, Syndrome, and Disorder. She made a valid point on most people who are victims of traumatic and abusive experiences. They filtered life through the slaughter of perceptions that carried various illusions confusing the already out-of-sequence images of past and present conflicts making the future distorted. This slaughter of perceptions directed his days and haunted his nights along with millions of officers and civilians. Adrenaline changes things, while fear altered perception, she mentioned in one of her books.

Christian reflected on the time the soldiers found him. He heard them and fell into unconsciousness; he didn't know anything. They flew him into Incirlik Air Base Hospital in Turkey and operated on his broken legs, mended his broken ribs along with five different vertebral in the middle of his spinal cord. His legs were the worse because the doctors had to install 10 pieces of a titanium rod into each leg. He hoped that this rising sea of desire is not asking for a Band-Aid to mend his truly cracked body and heart. He felt as if he was a patchwork quilt with so many implants stuck all over his body. He lost count of who did what and wherein his body including why over the twelve years spent in the military.

Everyone, even his family was so impressed with his external recovery, they never bothered looking internally. Just as well, because he wouldn't share his tormented thoughts and mental agony with anyone. He thought that's what happens internally showed on the externally and what happens externally has an impressive internally. He didn't know the differences, he had learned them from Doctor Zuri's books. Guess no one ever bother to look inside his personal package to see his truth. The military experience had made him what he is today and helped him cement the layers of emotional bricks together for a solid strong foundation of delusions, illusions, and profound pain. His strong foundation had taken a crack and is breaking into pieces rapidly. Little do others know that throughout his physical therapy months of recovery, all he ever thought of was Doctor Yuri Anana Curruni. She gave him his yin and yang, a reason to live and hope for the future.

He had signed up for twenty years in the military, however, due to his injuries he will be honorary discharged within a month or two depending on his emotional recovery after therapy receives from the "Doc." He planned to take his savings and build a log cabin in the woods somewhere and live there with his distorted images and illusions. With his disability check, he can survive without ever having to work for the rest of his life. Counseling was a choice the military is offering to all active or inactive officers. He hadn't any plans of ever receiving any counseling until he saw Zuri so long ago. He doesn't think there was much of a future for him until he laid his eyes on the doctor all those months in Afghanistan.

Well, not exactly, he realized that his future was dark and clouded with rage, only after he had looked into her eyes this morning, he had hoped his future is light and filled with color and beauty. The doctor was also made with the same ingredients as he did; the ingredients of integrity, trust, and passion. No, not trust; take that ingredient out of his recipe because he trusted no one not even himself, not anymore. Although he had hijacked her biography through Googling Wikipedia, he still knew very little of her personal life. Her professional career was spread over thousands of websites, however, nothing of her true personal essence. Any husband or two, children or family? It seems that Zuri is a private person and a sad smile touch Christain's lips, he likes privacy.

This was serendipity for them, cannoning into each other. He was as shocked as she was and preoccupied with painful images and illusions from his past. Why was she out so late? Does she have images and illusions as he does? After a thought or two about the matter, he let it go because he knew if she did she would be on the receiving end of therapy as he and thousands of officers are from her. All the fantasies of their first meeting went out the window. He understood that he has to stop projecting images of them into the future. It doesn't work that way and placing those expectations are only going to lead to despair and disaster. He has been avoiding going to see her for counseling due to his deflated penis. He wanted to have sex again and knows he can, with the right girl.

Christian understood putting it off is what he yearned for and wished that sex with a special someone would happen. The very things in life he had pushed aside are very things he carved for this moment. He carved to see her again, however, he knew that he had to work through his rage. It constantly burned inside of him and kept taking him into his blurred painful past. Bumping into her with tears flowing onto his cheeks was devastating yet it was nourishing for him. He can feel! He can feel! He had permitted his grief and anger to be expressed through tears; he didn't expect anyone least of all "the Doc" to be a witness to them.

This wasn't what he had fantasized; he realized during his fantasies, he was emotionally dead. No wonder those fantasies were such an enormous disappointment that only bring him heartaches. He is going to have to let nature takes its course in the development of a relationship between the Doc" and him. He knows there would be a relationship between Zuri and him. He felt it in his heart; his instinct told him besides two people cannot experience such wonderful emotions and let them dissolved into nothing. The energy of this magnitude and intensity doesn't dissolve, it grows. He can do this. He has patience, for both of them.

He hadn't planned on distracting her with the Marine Moon bit much less on kissing her. It just happened. Disappearing had taken every ounce of his energy and then some to walk away from her. The kiss had made him come alive with emotions that he had not experienced since before he joined the military service at eighteen. Emotions he heard from some of the other officers, he had never thought he would experience. The best of all is that he knew she felt the same as he does because he felt it in the kiss. What a kiss?

The kiss is taking his sex drive into overdrive while giving his heart sheer pleasure. Together they become a wildfire of awakening that has nectar flowing directly into his core. His adrenalin is up among other things; his once depleted penis that was paralyzed with fear is up and tingling the minute he had cannoned into her, scenting her aroma. He is a stallion in heat of a mere!

The Marine smiled and stared into the darkness that was now being lifted from the eastern horizon. He watched as the sun broke this darkness into dawn. He narrowed his eyes against the sun as he glanced down at her dressed in the typical military outfit, walking slowly to her office. She didn't look to him as if she's a high-calorie goody, rather exotic. Today is the day he as an appointment to see her for therapy, hoping she would do what she does best, what she did for the thousands of officers, he hopes she can do the same for him. "Doc" as she is known, is earlier than usual, guess she couldn't sleep either. She suddenly stopped, looked around, she scented him as he scented her. Instinct flying high for both of them it had shot through warning them of each other's presence. This is how it's going to be moving forward. They would know when the other is in the vicinity. Would they express it? It's one thing to know; it's a whole different matter to express what they know!

Last night before serendipity showed her face, he had fallen hopelessly in despair and unexpectedly bumping into her, he felt hopeful for the first time in years. He left the roof of his quarters and ran down the stairs to his bed. He needed to rest before he sees her later in the evening. He wanted to be the last one there so he can walk her home, conveniently.

Zuri walked to the office she uses for therapy and gave in to a yawn that peppered her into exhaustion. She had dozed off for a few minutes after bumping into the hunk. At four-thirty she had finally given up on sleep and taken a long hot bath and a strong cup of coffee; she yearned for a cup of latte. She is exhausted, overworked, and desperately for a long vacation. A week off in a nice Caribbean island would do her the world of good. Yes, that is what she will do, request two weeks off and take off for Barbados. Doctors Ty and Sian Wiltshire in London own a beach cottage there in the far corner of St. James. She'll send them an email asking whether it's possible for her to stay there in December. With a plan that pleased her, she quickened her steps making a mental note to send the email before reading any files. She stopped dead in her tracks and looked all around her. She scented him. She knew he's somewhere looking at her, so where?

A microscopic patch of warm sensations bowed at her spinal cord, giving her knots in her stomach and her back sat up straight. Zuri felt her emotions doing somersaults in her stomach and felt the heavy beating of her heart. Her skin turned hot and her cheek red. Darn it, all she had to do was sensed him and her body goes up in flames. She wondered about him. The kiss, she guessed was a spur of the moment thing that happened between two people standing in the moonlight. Oh, who is she fooling? It was fantastic and she enjoyed every second of it. She couldn't function after his lips touched hers. She felt deeply touched, oh, more than touched, and responded more than she imagined. He knew that she's attracted to him as he is to her. They both felt there's something special there. She shuddered at the thought.

He looked familiar because she felt that she met him before, not in counseling. She had never counseled him because she can see the rage in his eyes with emotional debris that stood in the path of his recovery which would tamper with any effort of rehabilitation. Ah, she is ready for him because she was confident that her techniques would eliminate all DNA of rage from every cell in his body. She smiled as she opened the outer door that led into a long narrow hall to another door that took her straight into her office. She gladly relieved her trembling legs off from her weight. She was not heavy, nonetheless, she felt heavy, no, too excited and happy. She leaned back in her chair and spent several minutes in deep meditation. From now on she has to be objective, especially when meeting him. Oh, yes she knew he knows who she is and she is clueless as to him, well not so clueless, personally yes, not professionally.

In her meditation, she surrendered all emotions that she felt towards him. She did one for when he does visit her, she is one hundred percent professional. By the time she was through, she was in an excellent frame of thought to produce an effective outcome with the incoming traffic of officers entering her office in two hours. She sent the email to see whether the beach house was available. Then she read other emails from various colleagues, clients, and friends. She was so absorbed with her emails that she didn't notice the door opened and Rae Jean, her assistant entered. She jumped as she spoke.

"I see you didn't sleep. I did with a nice looking officer. We're sneaking around. I have been seeing him for a few months now. Last night was heaven. I am so in love." She concluded.

"Oh, Rae I am so happy for you! This is so wonderful, can I borrow him,
    you think?"

Rae Jean gave out a loud laugh and dance over to her desk. She leaned
    forward and slowly whispered, "Over my dead body, Doc. Go find your own."

"So tell me who is he?" Zuri wanted to know.

"You counseled him a few months back and he had asked me out. I told him it is against policy for me to date a client. He waited until he had a clean bill of health and asked me out again. He is Air Force, Captain Ernest Rawlins. He's a rather handsome black hunk and his parents are from Antigua."

"Girlfriend, skin colors don't matter cos at de end of de dey, how well ya fit together is wa counts." Zuri echoed to her in a heavy unknown accent with no origin.

Rae Jean seriously looked at her boss and said with the saddest eyes, delivering the following. "Doc, you will find someone soon. I can feel it in me bones."

"Thank you," Zuri murmured to her just as the reply she was waiting for in connection with the beach house popped up. She acknowledged with a "thank you" and sent another to the man in charge of her at this military base letting him know that she is taking two weeks off in December and January.

Zuri was on top of her game as she and Rae Jean went through the schedule for the coming weeks and the day ahead. It would be another long few days before a few scattered hours here and there they can claim and relax for a short time. It doesn't bother them, They are used to the schedule and appreciate whatever time they have because they happily enjoyed every minute of what they do.

They had a two-hour break, Zuri hurried home with the Burrito that Rae Jean gave her for lunch. She ate her sandwich with coffee and read the mail that awaited her attention. She was enjoying a hot shower when she heard the fire alarm going off. Fear rose in her throat and sending terrifying emotions through her body. She turned the shower off and pulled slacks and a shirt from the closet putting them on shoving her feet into a pair of white snickers standing at the door and ran out her quarters buttoning her shirt.

She looked around to see where everyone was gathering and ran to the officers standing in rows. She pulled her five feet five inches next to an officer who was standing in the last line, still buttoning her shirt. She was breathing heavily and felt the fabric of her clothing soaking through from her wet skin. Her short black hair was dripping wet upon her shoulders. Eyes widen, lips sealed as she remembered that she had no bra or underwear on either. Oh, Bloody Hell, what a disaster!

She had been in fire drills before, nonetheless she and Rae Jean were always on duty and never caught off in an uncomfortable compromising situation. The drill sergeant pulled his six feet in front of her. She looked up and was furious. The drill sergeant didn't recognize her and was unconcerned about her emotions yell in her face. "Have a problem, officer?

"It's Captain, sir and there's a problem." Looking at him full in the face and giving him eye contact. The drill sergeant lifted an eyebrow as he was shocked to hear a reply from a Captain of all people.

"What problem, Captain, you should go see the 'Doc," replied the drill Sergeant Madcaft in an amusing tone.

"I don't appreciate a fire drill while on my break and furthermore, while I was in de showah."
"Oh, is that so, Captain? What is your name?"

"Which one, sir?"

The sergeant now angry at this smart ass cadet and was thinking exactly how he will make him repent from his wise answers. "Both, all of them." He ordered her.

"Captain Curruni." Zuri breathed out still giving him eye contact and sweetly smiles, "Doctor Zuri Anana Curruni, sir, at your service, sir. Maybe you should go visit the "Doc." With that anger burning inside you; it looks like you are about to be a dangerous fugitive." She gave him a soldier's salute and watch as his smile disappeared as fast as it had appeared. The sergeant realized that he is caught between a rock and a mountain asked, "who gives you the title of Captain?" He just had to know now that he knew who she is and cannot punish her. He found the whole incident amusing; it would be a good story to share with the boys during their poker game tonight.

"I did, sir," came Zuri's reply.

"Why?" He wanted to know thinking that this better be good.

"Because everyone I counseled is a Lieutenant and down the rank, to an officer so I figure I am Captain as I am Captain of my ship, the only ship presently working seven days a week for the last two years, sir. I bloody deserve it. Any objections?" Zuri let out her breath.

"No objections, Captain." The drill sergeant replied with a shake of his head. Then as an afterthought, he said, "Doctor" saluted and nodded at her. He then yelled, "Dismissed."

Zuri let out a deep breath, look up at the officer next to her, and saw a wicked grin coming off his face. Her lips parted as she looked deep into green sad eyes. Her instinct shook her into alert as her lips formed the words. "Do I know you? Have we met?"

"No." Came the deep replied from the red hair and green-eyed officer.

"I have seen ..." Zuri was cut short when Sergeant Wendy Philips came forward and apologized to her about the drill.

"Sorry doc, if I had known you were on break I wouldn't have pulled the drill. The Sarge never met you so excuse him. He did recognize your name. I appreciate everything you have done for us here and next time I will check. I am truly sorry."

"It's alright. No harm's done." She smiled at Sergeant Philips, reassuring her that there is no anger attached. As Sergeant Wendy Philips saluted her and walked towards the drill Sergeant Madcaft. Zuri turned to the officer that she was standing next to, only to discover that he had disappeared. Darn it, he is good at disappearing. He's going to have to stop this if he wants a relationship with her. He better show up, otherwise, it would be worse than a disaster. Oh, this is so silly of her. The vacation to Barbados is what she needed to live in reality.

As she walked away, she sensed his scent in the air. She became aware that he's the one she cannoned into last night. Where did she know him from? There's no way she ever remembers everyone she counseled for any length of time. Mmmmm, how does she know him? He stirred emotions in her that she had put to rest for years. Oh, well the memory will come of where she saw him. She entered her quarters and change into her usual military uniform. These were given to her so that the officers would feel at home during her counseling. It worked like a charm.

She has uniforms for every division of the military, sailors, soldiers, navy seals, air force, and marine. Now, she wore the Marine uniform because Marines are the officers of the afternoon. Rae Jean usually tells her what to wear and when, otherwise on rare occasions she wears a dark blue or white t-shirt with either jeans, khaki slacks, or shirt. She returned to work and was so occupied that no more thoughts were given to "her Officer Hunk" of last night and at the fire drill. It was late, close to nine when the last Marine entered her office. She was standing with her back to the door, looking at his file and reading the form filled out on her questions.

Everyone has to fill out a definition sheet on certain words and answered questions concerning pain and emotions. After she had given a three hours counseling class on pain and suffering, the officers can sign up for personal counseling. As she was turning to greet him she sensed his presence before his outline appeared through the door. Her lips parted as his masculine scent of tainted fuchsia reached her before he did. She held her breath; her face gave way in recognition of the officer from last night, the fire drill from the chopper in Afghanistan was the same one standing now in her office, shaved and in Marine uniform. No wonder she could not recognize him, he was unshaven and out of uniform last night and at the fire drill, however, his scent was the connection and the uniform. He is wearing the Marine uniform the day she was accenting into the sky from the chopper looking down at him on the battlefield. Karma is a wonderful thing. Oh, boy serendipity. She just loved serendipity!

Zuri turned the pages in the folder and looked at his photograph staring at her. He was in his uniform, of course, the photo told her nothing she hadn't hazard a guess, he was mentally, verbally, emotionally, and physically dead. They all were, nothing new? She can do this and put her emotions on hold. She is objective, she convinced herself. She shifted through the stacks of paper on the desk searching for the notes she made earlier. Finding them she pushed her chair backward, still looking at the notes, pulled her body onto her feet, and walked to the front of the desk, and laid her backside to rest there.

Rocking back on her heels, she turned and looked at him without smiling. She blushed and Rae Jean witnessed the whole exchange, smiled sweetly. The doctor just found her lover; her body language gave her away; he is attracted to her as she is to him. Whoa, a moment here, this is the romance she has been praying for Zuri. The tender loving care she required to nurturing her essence. Rae Jean stood still and silent as she watched both of them looking at each other. The officer with red hair and green eyes filled with rage is standing in front of her and looking down at her boss.

Zuri's conscious thoughts didn't recognize his face, however, her subconscious did and pushed through to the surface of the present moment. He was the one secret producing in the corner of her thoughts ever since she left Afghanistan. He was the only one standing there watching her being lifted off in the A MI-17. She looked down to see him looking at her and the same sensations she felt then stirred in her again when they bumped into each other that night and again earlier today at the fire drill. No wonder he felt familiar. She could barely contain herself. She flushed some more; she still couldn't find her voice.

Christian sensed her attraction the moment she flushed. It became a gossamer thread stretching around him touching his heart and binding him to her soft sensuous nature. He found himself being caught in a web and don't know how he can pull out and at the same time brushed at the chemistry between them. He couldn't get rid of the visible filament; not that he wanted to because he loved the texture it proved in his body. His rustic emotional response came alive with the gesture of arousal. If only she knew how often his emotions of his enemy, the horrifying images skirmishes with him even in this room.

The room grew hot as bodies felt slick with moisture. The fantasy was becoming a little too real for him and too hot to manage. The chemistry evoked his emotions and he wanted to kiss her instead. He smiled and the smile not only showed his teeth; it reached the warmth in his green eyes. He saw a flicker of warmth returned as his smile touched her warm brown eyes.

Rae Jean knew she better do something, otherwise, they would be on the floor in a few minutes. This isn't good for a military base operation, well, only for her as she remembered her sexual escapade a few nights ago over at the pantry in the kitchen with her lover. She gave out a loud giggle. Two pairs of eyes, one brown, and one green turned to look at her.

"Doc, I'll be leaving in a few. Can you close up, since the Lieutenant is your last one?" It's not unusual for the last officer to walk her home when Rae Jean had to leave. It had become standard practice and the last officer knew his duties. This was why Christian waited because he was hoping to walk her to her quarters.

"Oh, mmm what? oh....... mmm yes, of course. Be off and have fun tonight." Zuri gave her a wink and looked at the hunk in front of her.

"Have a seat, please." She nodded towards the chair next to hers and opened his folder as she sat opposite him. Neither one of them heard the door closed behind Rae Jean, who started to dance in the hall as she left the building.

The officer, who was managing the video feed in the Hall, choked and swallowed hard. He felt his erection as the brown hair doc's assistant did her sexy gig. He looked around hoping the other officers didn't notice. He lifted himself off his chair and told them that he is going to the restroom. He sexually released himself and gave his shoulder a nice path as he returned to this chair.

Back in the office, Zuri was all composed. She was reading his file and the forms he filled out upon signing up for her classes, counseling, and therapy. She was lost and absorbed with the hallmark of his traumatic experience. She was trying to figure out what to do for him, the quickest and shortest therapy session. She pulled herself on her feet and walked around her office. The pen that she was holding touched her parted lips; she was hitting it back and forth, back and forth against the opened folder she held in her right hand. She was trying to tame her rage and be objective. Normally, she doesn't feel her client's pain, however, she felt his and she wanted to hold him. She looked at him completely engrossed in assessing him. There was nothing sexual in her stare.

Christian witches nervously in the chair, anger banked in his eyes as moisture pooled at the corner of his still dead eyes while clammy sweat on his pasty forehead. He composed himself when he saw her staring at him. He knew that not all his traumatic experiences were in his file, well only what he wanted her to know. He was curious about how she can cure him without knowing his history. All that was written in the pages in his file to her were his name, address, cellular phone number, rank, where he serviced, and her questions on excessive anger and addiction.

Zuri would be able to pull him through these emotional traumatic experiences all she had to do was stay objective. She turned to sit in her chair in front of him and swung around to face him. "Okay, this will be painless. This is strictly confidential, including what you say to me. I am going to remove the energy of all your traumatic and abusive experiences that created the pain in your thoughts, emotions, and body cells.

"Do you want your pain to be removed, so you can go on living your life without unexpected traumatic images popping up, so you can sleep at night without fear?" Zuri gave him her professional look, the look with warm caring eyes, warmth voice that spell was strictly professional, and a frown that says "it's your choice."

"Yes." He whispered softly. The fierce exhilaration that surged through him at her words swept away his control. The constant sound echoed softly throughout the quiet room and penetrate through his subconsciousness. A soft voice commanding him out of the shadowland he visited all too often into a bright reality.

"Do you understand the terms of our agreement?

"Yes."

"Oh, good. This is the beginning. You have to do more investing in yourself and build a strong foundation after the release of these painful images. I advise you not to drink any alcohol or eat any heavy dinner. This will avoid addictions, however, you can work out. You have to come back tomorrow for more instructions. You got this!" She finished, giving him full eye contact. There was neither anger nor any overtones in her voice.

"Yes." He said grimly. He knew that this was one

hundred percent Doctor

Zuri. Last night along with the fire drill meeting didn't exist between them. His nervousness disappeared and so were all sexual sensations, well except for one.

"Good, relax." She glanced and wrote in the file. She looked at her client and said, "Relax." She said firmly and sternly as she watched him struggled to release mental agony into trust. She never had this conflict before with any of the thousands of officers she counseled. She had to give him time to relax due to their sexual attraction and the three experiences they had shared.

"Not good enough. Move your body into a more relaxed stance." Christian moved his full length and put his hands over his manhood. He didn't want her to see what type of stance he had. He is trying to keep himself under control and due to this stance situation of his; it is keeping him from relaxing. There were months he couldn't have an erection and now that he can, it seemed that his penis has a mind of its own. There's a constant stance similar to being a teenager once again.

He looked at her; she was looking into his file. He cannot imagine what was so interesting in his file for her to keep looming in it so much. He guessed that she is giving him time to relax. He moved his left hand to rest on the side of his face as if his face needed to be held; he left his other hand laying limp over where his manhood lay. His spinal cord swings into relax mode and he shifted once more to push his weight towards her. She sensed him more relaxed and looked up.

"Close your eyes." She ordered him.

"What?" Christian asked.

"Please, sir, close your eyes," Zuri instructed in a more commanding voice, however firm and at the same time soft.

Christian looked at her and fear flickered in his cold green eyes. He was speechless and stared at her. He has no desire to see what is behind his closed eyes or give up all of his control. He already knew what is there for he had seen the images a thousand times. What the fuck is she trying to? He refused to close them or give her control. He continued to stare at Zuri and her voice became firmer.

"Close your eyes and relax, Lieutenant. For this technique to work you have to want it, to relax, eyes close, and only listen to my voice." Her stern voice instructed him.

Well, since she put it like that, I can work with it, why didn't she say that in the first place. Listen to her voice here I come, he thinks. Christian found his eyes were closed faster than the speed of light upon hearing her used his title. Hell, she is good. Using his title and giving him those commands. Stay focus and wipe the faint smile from your lips, you old fool he warned himself.

He was so involved in his thoughts that he was unaware that she was watching him. The next thing she did had them flew open slightly. She had kicked one of his boots with hers, she looked straight at him and softly, nonetheless firmly stated, 'Reelaax Lieutenant."

Zuri saw Christian's body suddenly relaxed, she lowered her voice to a whisper, enough for him to listen and follow. His response upon her kicking his boot told her he didn't feel threatened, he felt safe. This is good. He trusted her as a therapist. He doesn't know her intimately to trust her, well the kiss; oh, he does trust me because she didn't report his misconduct. Her heart missed a beat and she had to take three long breaths to stabilize her voice and become professional again. Christian heard her breaths and realized that this is difficult for her, more difficult than anyone else. He relaxed more because the sooner they get through with the program, the sooner it would be over and he can be there for her. He knew there may or may not be together as he had fantasized. He had given him up when he realized that fantasizes and reality are different combinations as oil on the water are; they don't work.

He waited. He will wait for her. Zuri's emotions are under control, she went through the ritual of removing his negative energy. He had layers of them, how much she wouldn't know until tomorrow. Christian body became tense as she touched the core of his conflicts of interest upon losing his men in Afghanistan. He had closed his thoughts off from all persistent voice of logic. With the ritual of detaching his pain from the traumatic experiences, he opened his eyes and quickly closed them again, listening to her explanation of his emotions.

"Denial, blame, and guilt are destructive forces that affect emotions violently whenever you permit them to live in you. They will eat at your thinking and feelings obstructing your views of life. You are still in denial. Your subconscious has erected barriers against the harsh reality of what happened to you and your men. Your feelings have built a protective defense mechanism to help you manage until you mentally, verbally, emotionally, and physically heal. The withdrawal created the opportunity to mourn the loss. Do it. That is an order. The frustration you are experiencing and the rage within are normal for someone who experienced what you did. Healing is here, take it. As the energy of healing takes place, plan new beginnings. Don't allow the consequences of past experiences to jeopardize your future and make you vulnerable." She let out a breath and paused for a few minutes looking at the officer's response. Receiving none she continued.

"Lieutenant, it's time you quit feeling guilty for that you are alive instead of the others. You had no control over the war and as situations arise, you managed with the information provided. Let it all go.' Zuri concluded the session with a smile and very serious brown eyes.

As she finished the last sentence, just before she permitted him to open his eyes, she glanced where his hand was folded over his anatomy. She was used to the male officers having an erection. It meant that they are excited about the release of pain and nothing else, however, with this officer she was overjoyed, a huge smile began to form and quickly died, back to professional stance. She is out of zinc with him or maybe too much in zinc with him. She will have to transfer him to another clinician. This is too close for comfort for her. She felt her sexuality as she becomes aware of him as a male, a male to mate. This counseling session took all of her energy from her because it was personal. As she told him to open his eyes, she lifted herself out from her chair and walked the few feet to her desk. She put the folders down and turned to lean against the chair.

Christian rose to his full length of six feet and stood there looking at her. He's tired, too exhausted, and lightheaded. He can't feel his feet touching the ground. He looked down at them and saw he has his stance, feet apart as a military officer. He turned to look at her with confused eyes.

"This is how you will feel for a few days, light very light." She smiled at him as warmth touched her eyes. "Take it easy, soldier."

The Marine walked towards her and found his hands going for her shoulders, pulling her to stand in front of him. A strong finger reached out and traced the contours of her lips into her chin down her collarbone. The finger returned to her chin and pushed it up gently toward her face. Her eyes flew open wider as she dreamily gazed into his warm sexy light green eyes. Before she could let out her breath, he leaned down and brushed his lips on her parted ones. Her eyes were closed, she ran her tongue over her lips. Christian saw this as he backed out the office door and smiled. When he kissed her he had nothing to lose. He had made her his whole universe and this moment is eternal because he didn't have any plans and was not going anywhere. Just kissing her was overwhelming for the rest of his life.

Zuri stayed there a minute more enjoying it all. Her body drank in every sensation as her life depended on it. Her life depended on it! It's her oxygen. She opened her eyes and looked at the door. She knew he was gone and continued to stay there for another minute enjoying the experience. "I hope he would quit disappearing on me like that, it sure as hell doesn't work anymore." She told the door he just walked through. She let out a long-held breath and headed to the door in her office that led to the restroom. She had her private restroom and was glad of the comfort of splashing cold water on her face to compose herself before leaving for the night. Good thing he isn't walking her home, he would be in her bed!

She walked out to her desk to pick up her purse. With a twist seductive smile on her lips, she glanced into the mirror hovering over on the wall next to her desk, gave herself a wink, and left the room. She turned and walked out of her office, taking her thoughts and his scent with her.

Doctor Zuri felt curling sensations of warmth the same as quicksilver shooting fiery feelings that squirreled all around her body deepening in her stomach. Her heart picked up speed and at the very time, it sank deeper sending quivering desires throughout her body. Her legs were jelly and as her heart pounded at a frantic rate she ran the few yards to her quarters across the street from her office. Let her see what she can do for him before she became carried away in this destructive affair of the heart. It will be destructive for him if she couldn't do her job. She wanted him back on his feet all in one whole piece. It will take all the energy out of her; she's in love with him, she knew that; more than ever she can do it, for him; not for them!

3

Christian saluted his commanding officer and waited to be acknowledged.

"At ease, what can I do for you, Lieutenant?" Captain Anwar Morrison asked.

"Doctor Zuri is going to Iraq and Afghanistan and I am volunteering my services to protect her, sir."

"Why?"

"Sir, I am very grateful for what she's doing for me. It's the least I can do to repay her for her service. I have been seeing another clinician. Doc Zuri ...". He was interrupted before he could finish.

"How's it going?"

"Yes sir, I am still in counseling and soon to be released. I have an appointment with the Doc this afternoon."

"What time, soldier?"

"Twenty hundred hours, sir."

"The last one, huh, you're always the last one Lieutenant, huh?

"Yes, sir.

"Let me think about it, dismiss." He gave Christian a salute who automatically returned the same, turned, and headed for the door.

Captain Anwar Morrison rather sent a soldier who is capable to fight and who can protect Doctor Zuri. He was given orders to find an officer to protect her; he was thinking about who he should send when the Lieutenant came forward. The good Lieutenant can defend her if needed, however, due to his injuries he cannot fight in a war zone. The military doesn't have enough men alive to save the mess in both wars. God help the USA.

Christian let out his breath and turned toward the direction of the mess hall. Since that afternoon of the fire drill, where he saw Doctor Zuri all wet with nothing under, again in her office attending counseling as well each day with the other clinician Doctor Melson, he has been sleeping for a long length of time and eating healthy. To avoid adding weight he had increased his daily workout from three hours to five, which included swimming and running. The workout hadn't stopped his sexual cravings for her; the sexual appetite has increased with intensity electrifying passion so massive that his skin had glowed with warmth and have a light pink color. He's a man in love. He had never felt healthier in all of his life and wondered why Zuri sent him to Doctor Melson, conflict of interest he guessed. A thin smile tugged on his lips.

The next day when he returned to Doctor Zuri's office, she briefly assessed him by asking him some questions. She was warm, however, extremely professional. He saw her every day for the last two weeks as she walked home. Whenever he had to visit her, he was the last one to leave. He had fashioned it this way because he can kiss her at the end of the day. He had seen the surprise on her face the second time he kissed her and left without walking her home. Her eyebrow lifted with a visual sweep that permitted light to strike the retina, giving her information on the unforeseen occurrence. She was trying to figure how to feel, what to do, and to formulate a plan of action when he exited the room. It felt good; he knew she enjoyed it as much as he did because she responded. This is the last time he will be dismissed from counseling. The Lieutenant was emotionally healing from his traumatic experiences; he's a free man.

Rae Jean, her assistant along with some other volunteers took over for the rest of the counseling giving instructions on building self-esteem, character, how to look and manage differences, difficulties, and challenges in life. There were endless documentaries on behaviors, the brain, thoughts, communication, emotions, and all that concerns people who have experienced traumatic and abusive experiences. It was a compact and complete program coupled with two weeks of intense counseling every day. Christian didn't see Zuri in those weeks, only watched her from the roof of his building. It was known that the last officer would walk her home unless she and Rae Jean worked late. Although he never had the opportunity, he watched her walked to and from her quarters every day. He heard the other officers spoke of her with laughter. Sadness and anger is now a distant cousin and no longer taken over their life; they all have much to laugh about since the pain has diminished. His sexual appetite is no longer in hibernation.

He watched how everyone light up whenever Zuri visited with the chef in the mess hall. He kept a low profile, however, he's always aware of where she is and what she's doing. Damn it. He sounds the same as an obsessive-compulsive man, he's not; only a man so in love. In a few minutes, he'll be seeing her for the final appointment then off for clearance with the military psychiatrist. He would be given with others an honorable discharge. He's no longer on any prescription drugs and has no emotion or physical pain or mental agony. How blazer is that?

Zuri opened the folder and saw Christian in his officer's uniform looking up at her. She smiled and whispered, "Last day huh soldier? I don't want your anger, I want your love."

"Say something doc?" Rae Jean asked with a wink.

"No, just get out of here, will ya?"

"Oh sure, doc whatever you say. Just don't do anything on the new carpet?"

"The carpet is not new. You know who I am talking about, don't you Rae?"

"Yes, me thinks you should slip him your number."

"You know I can't do that. It's unethical."

"May I reminded you that you didn't counsel him. You were not his counselor. You removed his pain and referred him to Melson. Do you want to see him is the question?" Rae Jean had to ask.

"Yes, I do so very much. It takes all my energy just to stay professional. I am so bloody glad he's the last one." Zuri replied with a frown and sadness in her eyes.

"I bet. I'll let him in." Zuri hardly heard her as her eyes return to the file in front of her. She was thinking and writing in the space left for final words; she didn't hear Christian entered; she scented him.

Christian had completed all of his challenges. Time to close his case; he can move on with courting Zuri. He fell in love with her and the thing is, he sensed that she returned his feelings; he wasn't so sure. He wanted her to say it to him. She has no way of conveying her feelings to him unless he creates opportunities for them to be together.

Zuri realized even if she did see him she wouldn't know how to do so because she is drained from overwork. On many occasions, she walked away with thoughts of kissing and making passionate love to him. The idea found its way in somehow and her breathing quickened at the fickleness of her thoughts. When his lips brushed her mouth the very first time she was shocked. The second time she gasped in surprise. The pleasure was exotic and jolted her pulse into overdrive. She couldn't catch her breath, she couldn't slow her heart rate from its fast and furious pace. Urges stirred and edged treacherously close to her heart and the vague ill-defined emotion that poet called love spurn forward unexpectedly. There's nothing left in her to give him in a relationship. She has to let him go and believe that one day when she's finished here they can be together. She hoped that it wouldn't be too late.

Her breath catching, it sent a spasm of alarm throughout her quivering body. Her heart pumped faster teetering on the brink of the emotion of true love. She looked into his light green eyes and felt the love sank right into her heart. A spark of flared passion ignited between them. He grasped involuntary, always surprised at the euphoria reaction it gave him. Every time he looked at her he felt the tug of warmth pouring in abundance from his heart.

Christian absorbed his stance and the door to his heart flew opened and she drowned in his eyes. No matter what he did the effect ripped through them as though it were a soft breeze across a pond. His eyes send fission of passion through her heart to her hot pulsating zones. She had the urge to touch him; he came alive under her interest. They looked at each other for more than a minute before Zuri's body was pulled by the intense heat of electrifying energy between them from her chair. Hearts tingle and eyes mate. She was mid-air from her chair to meet him when the door flew open. She looked to see Captain Clyde Walker entered, gave Christian a salute and a "Lieutenant" acknowledgment.

Zuri stood her full length, walked around, and lay her backside to rest on the front of her desk; she accepted Captain Clyde's hands.

"Doctor Zuri, how are you?" His left hand came to rest upon the hand he held.

"I am fine, thank you, sir."

"Martha sends her love and says you should come soon to dinner again.

She beats me up every day on how I overworked you. I don't hear the end of it."

"Oh! How sweet of her. Do tell her I am off when I get back from de wars zones and could do with some TLC."

"I'll do that and let her call you. You're leaving in three weeks, correct?"

"Correct."

"I've your agenda here. Can you go to Afghanistan too? I have some officers in really bad shape and they can do with a morale boost?"

"How can I turn that down? Of course, Captain." Zuri replied with a wary smile tugged between her lips.

"Oh, good that's my girl. Take him over there for protection.' Captain Walker moved his head in the direction of Christian. "He knows the drill. Thank you for all you do. We're very grateful. We don't have any other that volunteer and work as hard as you, Zuri. Thanks again." He released her hand and walked over to Christian. "Lieutenant, take good, extra care of her, do you understand? As if your life depends on it." He ordered Christian with a salute.

Christian saluted the Captain and shouted, "Yes sir." This was what he had promised himself, to protect her and be there for her, forever. He's halfway there. This felt so good. He was so controlled of his sexuality before he entered her office and with this wonderful news, he's on a high rise, again for the hundredth time.....more who cares; he lost count. This is the best prescription drug ever!

Zuri knew he was different from all the males she counseled. She felt it, nonetheless, she didn't have the time for romance. This is forbidden love; she can't sleep with her client. Well, in fact he wasn't technically; he was in a somewhat small tiny way, somewhat. She did the initial intake and assessment; oh, yes he removed his pain with a technique she invented and referred him out to Melson who in reality did the work. She's reviewing the progress, a sort of double-checking to be sure that Christian can be released.

This procedure is typical of all clinicians; they usually check each other caseload before release, technically he's not her client. Guilt forth itself forward, shame surface and pledge itself forward; she tucked them far away before she broke down in tears. She can't see him for the life of her; Guilt will not control her.

Oh, fuck it all……she deserves some fun and she'll have to work through her guilt. Zuri saw a deep meditation session line up in her already hectic schedule, tonight before she goes to sleep. She had to fly to the two war zones. Christian had volunteered to go with the squad to protect her. He's Zuri's secret hero. Rae Jean had told her this little piece of information two days ago. How she knew is anyone's best guess. Christian had requested to protect her on her trip. She was happy beyond life itself. She had meditated that it worked; it did and her heart missed a beat.

The door closed, the two were looking at each other. Zuri bent her head and let out a deep breath. She was leaning on her desk, rather than sitting on the edge of it. She doesn't trust her legs. She picked up the folder and hand it to him. As Christian moved in to collect it, she said. "Clean bill of health. Good luck soldier, see you in three weeks." Christian took the folder and gave her the widest happiest warmest smile. It reached his beautiful green eyes and dip deep into her heart. What he saw there shocked him. The love was hidden so deep he blinked and looked again. He pulled her into his arms and held her there.

"I'll wait for you no matter how long it takes." He whispered in her ear, quickly brushed his lips in a light feathery kiss, released her, and left the room. His voice was filled with sensual promises that electrified her senses. Zuri felt his arousal and went bozanko. Brown eyes followed him as he walked to the door and left the room. She tried to process what just took place. It was too much for her. She reached over her desk and pulled her handbag from the opened draw in her desk, rise to her full length, and put one foot forward; she sank onto the carpet.

It was well twenty minutes later, she pulled her body off the carpet, walked, and locked the door. She needed a long hot bath and a huge glass of wine. Oh, yes, no wine, meditation first then wine, she thought. She had to work through her guilt. A very light feathery shiver danced in her heart and along her spine into her stomach. An image appeared not of Christian in uniform, of her leaning against him wearing nothing at all. As soon as she entered her quarters she let out a long-held breath and flung herself upon her bed. She was asleep dreaming of them together.

The fighter helicopter touched down on Iraqi soil at midnight. The moon was fat and heavy with rain. It was engorged and red as it smoothly sailed close over the back of a distant horizon. The ever-changing light rode in a filament. A hundred or so wide-awake officers greeted them. Zuri went to work right away as she talked with them in groups. No time for individual conferences. It was about three o'clock in the morning when Christian gave her some black coffee and a cheese sandwich. She took it without looking at him as the next hundred or so officers entered the tent that was provided for her to work in. Two days later they left Iraq for Afghanistan. She was sleeping on Christian's shoulders as they sat waiting for the A MI-17 to lift off. Christian glanced at her and his heart missed a beat. She hadn't slept much since they left Balad Air Base. He was the only one assigned to protect her. The other officers were pulled off at the last minute for some other duties unknown to them.

Dawn was upon them as the chopper lifted off headed for Afghanistan. Golden light spilled across water and hand painting everything in sight with a promise of peace. Zuri had been going on sandwiches and very little sleep. This is his life. He can do it. He can stay awake for three days. She's holding up pretty well for someone who isn't trained for this type of work. Although they were in a battle zone, the joy felt had shown in both of them through biological changes in their body language. The increased activities in the brain center inhibited troublesome feelings not express that projected externally. The brain fostered increase energy, quieting the feelings that generated worrisome thoughts that require expressing. The shift in their biological changes as well as physiology offers the body a general rest from difficulties of not being able to express feelings to each other. The readiness and enthusiasm for other tasks became manageable as striving for a quiet time together become challenging. Frustration surfaced for Zuri, tiredness took control. Officers noticed the sexual chemistry between the Zuri and Christian and the difficulties they are trying to hide. They kept silent and wished they would one day work out their feelings for each other.

Christian smiled at the sight of her and felt he became sexually aroused. This was such a wonderful feeling. She looked so sexy sleeping on his shoulders. What he wouldn't do to put his arms around her and pulled her closer to him. He can't, he has to leave it as it is because he can get a neat warning for sexual harassment. The table had turned; he is the one who has to be professional. Instead, he leaned over and kissed her soft mouth and watched as her mouth curved into a dreamy smile. He echoed it unconsciously attaching it to his heart. He was still smiling when the Air Force pilot came aboard. The officer noticed his smile and envied him. He would be smiling too if he had a sexy lady sleeping on his arm. Lucky bastard, some men have all the luck in the world.

Zuri opened her eyes the minute the engine roared to life and lifted her head as the chopper took to the air. She glanced at Christian, he gave her a warm smile that made her blush. She touched his cheeks; he turned his lips into the palm of her hand and kissed it. She wanted to reach out and shared his warmth; she knew that she couldn't, she smiled and leaned her head upon his shoulders again looking out into the blue sky as the chopper ascended.

They landed in heavy artillery; things were flying all over the place. In the heat of this battle, Christian grabbed some gear from the ground of the chopper and jumped out. He put his hand on Zuri's head pushing it down gently so she wouldn't bump it on the ridge of the chopper, he lifted her out. He pushed her against the chopper as he put a bulletproof vest on her body and a helmet on her head, pulling her into a sitting position. His hand held hers very firmly, however, it was warm with comfort.

Christian pulled his gun off of his shoulder and positioned himself into place ready for action. He kept one eye on the target and another on her. This was their position for a good half an hour before a soldier confronted them to follow him. The officer's body language spelled disgust. A response indicated a void by the senses as his eyes squinted, he turned his face away from the war curling his lips and wrinkling his nose suggesting primeval. The same reaction is used against tasting poisonous food or the aroma of noxious odors. Zuri read into his behavior and the emotions he held in check broke loose.

"Watch up and be careful of how you walk." The soldier's voice was the jury of an icy tone; falling from suppression can be seen in his icily glittering glaze as he looked at her. He gave a weary sigh as his shoulders stiffened. The concern showed in her tone as she gave him a smile; she continued in thoughtful silence as compassion poured out from her. "Thank you," she touched his hand. Zuri was between Christian and the soldier as they approached the bunker, then a missile from the enemy flew into the air and collided with a US counterattack one. Debris hit the soldier on his head, sending him crashing to the ground. Christian pulled Zuri into him and hit the ground a few inches from the officer. He reached out to check the soldier's pulse and finding none, pulled Zuri on her feet and ran with her to a tent for safety. A cold glint came into his eyes. She watched his reactions to her mention, "Is he dead?"

Christian captured her gaze for a moment. She learned nothing from his stoic expression and a spidery touch of sorrow drained her spirit. She was unable to put her conflicting emotions into words as heavy waves of movement shook her. Her face flushed and her breathing uneven; the remnants of her emotion and evening meal had enough. Zuri's body objected to the maneuvering and violently expulsed the remains of sandwich dinner from her stomach upon the arrival at the tent. Christian shouldered his weapon and put an arm around her as she leaned over in agony. He pulled her up and held his weapon in his hand ready to protect her with his life. He waited until she was finished and pulled her into the tent. He shouldered his weapon as his two strong hands gently fell upon her shoulders with pressure insidious easing her backward until her body touched his front. He held her in this position for a moment as the back of her head came to rest upon his chest.

"Breathe." He ordered her. Sharpness entered his tone. "Breathe." He heard her breathing became soft. "I am here, you are not alone. I love you." He told her with retainable ardor and with endeavoring whispered in her ear; he turned her around and gathered her against him. She buried her face into his shoulders for her sanctuary. A soldier entered the tent and Christian looked up and recognized him. They exchanged looks of silent communication only they understood. The soldier nodded and stated, "I will stand guard Lieutenant, sir."

"Thank you, Officer Riley."

After another half an hour, things quit blowing up. In

the next moment, this horrible battleground went dead silent. Officer Riley looked out and said, "All silent for now. Best you keep the doc here for a bit longer. The less she sees the better." His loose sprawl tightened with the next sentence. "I am going to her as soon as my shift is over so keep her safe for me, you hear, sir?" Christian nodded. "You can lie with her on the operating table for a bit. I am going to check out the condition and be right back." Officer Riley's hands reached above his head and pulled down the covers over the tent. He glanced at Christian who nodded and left.

Christian saw the sadness while Zuri heard it in his voice. The drop in energy accompanied by a sunken posture with deep breathing made it easier to access thoughtful processes, providing there's no suppression of emotions. She shared sadness with him. She has to pull herself together regardless of how she felt in Christian's arms this moment. She pulled sadness out from memory and ran it through in her thoughts. Sadness is supposed to help with adjusting to a significant loss or death. It's normal for her not to want to go and counsel anyone because she just saw death right in her face. The energy in her body dropped and she has no desire for any type of activity even a pleasurable one. From experience, depression is next and that would slow her body metabolism. No sir, this is out of the question. A little more of Christian holding her and she would have the strength to move forward with what she was supposed to do here, what she came to do.

Christian understood the officer, as he wasn't so long ago stood in his place, hoping to see the doctor one day. He lifted Zuri's lifeless body upon the table and lay with her on their sides holding her close to him. He knew she was awake. He let her rest for a bit longer and then he raised himself on his shoulder and pulled her hair behind her ear. He kissed her ear and whispered very softly, "You will be pull through this for the men. I am going to hold you like this till you are ready to stand. I will be with you forever. I am going to protect you till I die." He felt her muscles tightened; he pulled her closer and kissed her ear again.

"I'm not planning on dying today, Zuri. Not now that I found you. It would be a long ass time." He softly whispered in her ear. He felt her relaxed and then it was only then that he rested his head next to hers on the table. It took Zuri a good thirty minutes before she stirred. She pressed small kisses against his neck; kisses that meant to heal him, to take away the pain she felt trembling inside him from his past time here. Understanding her comforting him, he let her finished, after all, he loved being kissed by her. She raised herself with her arm and looked around the tent. She looked at Christian with loving warmth eyes.

Upon hearing movement in the tent, Officer Riley entered. Zuri felt the rustling of the fabric door opened and smiled at the officer who had stood guard at the entrance. Christian had also risen and nodded at the officer. Neither of them had heard him entered the tent. Officer Riley came forward and extended his hand to Zuri. She placed a hand in his and looked at him, smiling brightly.

"You are here for all of us. Who's there for you? You shouldn't have seen that soldier died. It's our life here. This is why we come to you. This is a nasty war, we fightin' doc. His name was Officer Allan Farmswoth, doc." At Zuri understanding, she nodded that he meant the dead soldier, he let go of her hand and left the tent. Zuri turned to Christian and saw a drip of red trickled down from his cheek into his shirt collar and continued with several wicked drops into the fabric of his uniform. She touched it and looked into his eyes. She saw passion burning in his light green eyes. Her eyes sheltered for so long, suddenly shone on the same frequency with the energy of passion. Christian lowered his mouth and touched his lips to her tender ones, giving comfort. Before she could respond, he lifted his lips and tasted her on the area of her neck, soothing it with his mouth in exotic light touches, no other healing could ever do. Zuri reached out and touched his cheek with her hand then her lips.

He lifted her a few inches as his tongue caressed the sensitive area in the hollow of her throat below her chin. His strong fingers traced the contours of her collarbones feathering downwards over her breast, feeling her swollen nipples as a blind man would, his fingers supple inquiringly over her body. Everywhere his fingers touched, he left sensations so exquisite that it set her on fire with hunger so sear that it flooded her body with spiraling warmth of love. The long lonely tiring years were washed away in this beautiful splendor of their lovemaking, for both of them.

The voice of Officer Riley pulled them apart, "Lieutenant? It's safe." He lifted the hood over its roof and let the light shone into the tent.

"Lead the way, Officer Riley," Christian said as he took Zuri's hand and pulled her with him. His weapon was held by his other hand as his eyes dart in and out of every visible corner he could see in the heat of the moment. Zuri was sandwich between them and was careful not to look too much on the ground. She doesn't want to see death so close again, not when she has to counsel a group of officers in a few minutes.

It was some twenty-four hours later that the chopper lifted off in the dim light of dawn as it peeked through the door before Christian charismatic pulled it shut. Zuri saw the muscles flexed in his arm and a smile touched her lips. He's so sexy and warm. She can lie in his arms for hours, no forever. She looked at Christian wondering if there were any horrible memories of past and present. As reading her thoughts, he shook his head in a "no." She smiled at him and looked away. There were other officers with them, therefore professionalism is required.

They were headed into the US military base in Germany then home to West Virginia. A long hot shower, a glass of wine sounded good and maybe a smooch from Christian would make her rejuvenate her energy. Her luck she would be cast away in talking to a group of officers. This thought made her feel guilty; after all, it was what she does best. Thinking selfishly during the war isn't healthy. Christian is with her and the love shared would be expressed in time. On second thought, this is healthy for her. It nourished her essence and she desperately required many hours of nurturing. With her thoughts rationalized, her body came alive just touching him. He looked down at the hand resting on his thighs and gave her one hell of a sexy smile. He was thinking exactly as she was, only if they could be together for a bit, he would show her his love.

Little did they know that when the chopper laid them down in Germany; they had four hours to themselves before the plane was ready again to fly them and others to West Virginia military base. It was a shocking surprise when they were left alone after being escorted to their rooms and added surprise when they found out that they had adjoining rooms. Christian and Zuri showered and changed. She couldn't believe their luck as she stepped into the shower and let the warm water ran down her tired body. She took her time and washed away all the week's misery from her body. With the huge white towel wrapped around her, she looked at the only mid-length dress she carried in case of an official dinner she had to attend. She unzipped and pulled it over her head.

She entered Christian's room as he was stepping out of the bathroom. Coming from him she felt hot as the lightning of summer's breeze. A steady rhythm of water dripped into the white tiled floor. He had a towel hanging low around his hip as he stood at the door leading from the bathroom. Upon seeing her he ran the few steps and lifted her off the ground, his towel fell. Their bodies touched as feathers dancing in the wind. With her arms around his neck, she bent and kissed him for a long passionate kiss. Zuri poured all of her love into that kiss. Christian welcomed it and received everything she was willing to give him. He was giving her the same amount of passion he had locked away for her all those lonely months.

It wasn't until he had unzipped the back of her dress and it fell to the floor, he realized that his towel fell off from him, not that he cared. He picked her up and she folded her ankles together in a knot over his backside. She ran her lips over her upper lips. Eyes send forth beautiful energy of feelings darting between them, he entered her. She tilted her head back; he kissed her neck under her chin, down to her cleavage. She released a sweet melody as she received all of him. He sank deep into her as their lips touched with an adorably kiss. His lips nudged hers as she sank her teeth into his lower lip with a gentle love bite.

Christian's hips rocked against hers as he gave her more of him, pushing into her hips, his hand cupped her backside firmly, keeping her anchored into him. He pushed her away from him a little, lifting her to him, giving himself deep access into her. They begin to pick up a rhythm, their rhythm, as he bent his legs and his whole weight went downwards till her spine touched the fiber of the carpet. His body covered hers as he desperately wanted in his heart, down to the pit of his manhood. It was red hot with burning sensations of passion. She moved closer and arched into him; he made a sensuous sound-sound of pleasure coming from deep within him and pressed his hands against her breasts. She let him touch her. Their kisses became more intensifying, more all-consuming as they sank deeper into the carpet.

The attraction that had first drawn them together

that night so many months ago and the passion that continued to flare between them during the weeks that followed exploded between them. She didn't know he possessed passion nor did she know he could unleash the same passion from within her. They held onto each other lost in the forest of emotions of true love. He held his chest off of her while she adjusted her legs and fixed them into his, anchoring them together. Brown eyes met green eyes, welcoming the sweet pleasure pouring from each other. His palms brushed the brown upright peaks of her nipples, making her blood burned in her core. Her body trembled and arched against him instinctively and he pushed all he can into her.

Zuri contracted her muscles and he pushed soothingly again and again into her. Her hands above her head folded in his boldly without shyness; he anchored her with his soft green eyes that spelled love. His body drew taut sensations from her as they danced down his spinal cord. She yelled out his name and stirred more sensations deep from within him. She contracted her pelvic once more for her finale; what was also to be his as well, a ride to ecstasy. He pushed his manhood up and out, she let go in a high-pitched melody that had him arching himself against her again and again, bucking fervently as he emptied himself into her accessible lady's well. They laid together for a good half an hour until their heart cooled to a normal beat. The silence between them was soft and beautiful as they captured the long-awaited anticipation neither had guessed would be so soon. The basket in the aftermath of their lovemaking, each not knowing when the next opportunity would arise.

Christian lifted his body to his feet, raise her to his waist, and took her towards the bed. They fell into it and he rolled onto his back, pulling her on top of him. She climbed aboard his heated engine as he hardened all he can, pulling her inside of him. Tongues mated as he cupped her backside and tensed his muscles against her constant contracting her pelvis. He let her explore him for a minute or two then he took charge. He sat up and took her nipple one after the other in his mouth. His hand stroke her back and she arched against his mouth filling him, completely. His mouth sorted hers as his palms molded the perfect curve on her nipple's sweet hardness. He removed his tongue from inside her mouth and rolled it against each nipple again and again.

Zuri whispered his name ever so softly; he felt every fiber of his core being lifted into a catalyst chemical reaction that produced a shortage of oxygen. A tightening of muscles and a high-octane explosion in his blood surfaced, he sought his release just as she collapsed with hers on him. As heart rates slowed, Christian said to the top of her head. "We have to shower and get to the mess hall soon. You better look as if you woke up from a nap, otherwise, we're in a lot of trouble."

"I know. I know," she whispered against his neck. That's so silly, not to bother, I have this under control. Did you say showah?" A smile tugged at her lips and warmth surfaced in her brown eyes as she lifted her head and looked at her lover. With that said, Zuri picked her body off from him and ran into his shower. She turned it on to hot and felt a hand around her waist.

"I wanted to touch and kiss you ever since I first saw you." He ran his fingers down her middle and into her feminine core. She arched her body against his hand and leaned her head against his shoulders. The hot liquid of the shower poured upon the very spot. Sensations rippled through heated sensuous bodies that neither had ever experienced. She exploded into his hand and her body went limp. She pulled away from the spell of the hot water and leaned against the walls of the shower. He waited a very short minute, held out his hand, and reached for hers, pulling her gently into the heart of the shower and against him. Hot water ran over them. He cupped her backside and pulled her gently into him, gluing their bodies together in a surge of comfort.

He whispered in her ear, "I love you." His tongue slipped in and out tracing her shell of her ear as his teeth nibbled her lobe. He entered her very slowly watching her facial expression as she took all of him into her essence. Her eyes filled with love, yet to be expressed. Her lips rocked back against him.

"Zuri." He softly whispered her name.

Another infinitely, tender feeling gently guided and knitted hearts together, beckoning them to yield to this delightful moment. He held her tightly against his body as they picked up speed and he released himself into her. She came again and slid to the floor as the heat of the water poured over her molten body. In the glorious warmth of their heavenly bodies, the grief and loneliness felt for so long slowly melted into the background. The scent of their lovemaking tingled at the nostrils. Christian turned the water off, bent and picked her up, pulling a clean towel off the shelf, sat her on the bed that they made love in, and dried her; he then proceeds to blow-drying her hair. He collected her clothing from the floor and carefully dressed her.

Zuri lifted her shoulders, bent and kissed his chest as he pulled her dress over her head, she whispered, "thank you." He lifted her to her feet, kissed her on her lips, "you are welcome anytime, my love." She smiled at his face and left the room. She went into hers and apply a light touch of foundation on her face, followed by brown eyeliner, no mascara, and a light touch of pink lipstick grace her smiling lips. She stepped into the hallway looking for the mess hall.

Upon arriving, she didn't know how in heaven's name Christian was there before her, dressed in a clean uniform. He spotted her the minute she was made visible through the opened door. He deliberately turned his back as she entered. She would recognize that back anywhere and smiled. A young officer seeing her smile stood up and came to her. Business as usual, except for now she wasn't exhausted, she was joyful.

As dawn broke into new days, November flew into December, the days become colder. Zuri had seen Christian on the roof of his quarters watching her leave for work early in the morning and returning at night. She knew he was there as they both had a secret smile tucked on their lips. They had not been together again as it was impossible for them due to various elements of protocol and time. Christian had the time, however, Zuri's time was stretched. They knew this from the beginning nor have they discussed how they can be together. It was too risky. Christian was due for his horary discharged in two days. They both will have to wait silently for an opportunity to knock again to be together. The anticipation is worth the wait.

Zuri had dinner at Captain Clyde Walker and his wife Malory one afternoon. She and Rae Jean managed a few early evening here and there for drinks and dinner. Most of the time was spent with work and the long hours continued for stretches of weeks. The December wind was colder than usual, as though it were trying to keep spring at bay. In two weeks, Zuri would be in Barbados for a long-deserved break. Sitting in front of her was Christian and she was about to ask him to join her. Christian was there to ask her to join him in a cabin in the woods he was going to rent for Christmas. He knew she had two weeks off and he would be free, retire from the military. As usual, he was the last one in for the night.

No one suspected of their love affair and if Rae Jean guessed she didn't say a word. It was accepted for him to come in to check on her from time to time, due to what she went through in Afghanistan. It's customary for officers to visit during her free time. His visit is nothing unusual. Captain Anwar Morrison knew of her experience, therefore completely approved of someone check on her besides Rae Jean and Lieutenant Vincelette, might as well be with someone she shared a traumatic experience with; can't have the doc having PTSD!

Zuri was looking at him, lips parted from behind her desk when Rae Jean walked in with a short Chinese male, saying, "this gentleman demanded to see you. Said he knows you pretty well." Zuri leaned to her right side to look behind Rae Jean to see who wants to see her, which of her brothers. She rose and walked to the side of her desk next to Christian's chair; she opened her mouth and then closed it again. Zuri grasped and ran to greet the man. She threw herself into his arms.

"Oh my god, how lovely to see you, my handsome young man."

"It's always a pleasure to have sexy ladies throwing themselves at me. How are you, my love?" He pulled himself away, hold her by her shoulders, looking at her. He swung her around to face him again. "Too thin, I say. It's the food, isn't it?"

Zuri ignored him and asked instead, "what are you doing here, Pong Jung?"

"I am here on business, my love. I had to come to see you."

"Oh, I am so glad you did. I was heading to Barbados in a few days for a long two wonderful weeks of desperately needed hols."

"Have it all arranged, huh?" Pong Jung asked.

"Well, yes kind of. I wanted him, Christian to come and I didn't know how to get it done." Zuri concluded.

Upon this information, Pong Jung turned to Christian and introduced himself. He sensed the intimacy between his goddaughter and his young man. He was happy for her; she needed a strong man with a gentle hand and warm heart after that one, who he cannot remember. It doesn't matter. He looked at Rae Jean and Christian and said, "I am the long lost odd family member of the Curruni's family. Zuri's godfather." He informed their puzzled faces. "I can make magic happened." He turned to Zuri and said, "Leave it to me. I'll make it happened. Give me the dates of your visit to Barbados. I'll send the plane for you both and deliver you back here."

Zuri threw her arms around Pong Jung's neck and kissed both his cheeks. "Thank you so very much." She expressed in Mandarin.

"You are welcome, my sweet little princess. I have to leave you. I'll be seeing your family next week. I'll tell them that you're fat and happy." He kissed both her cheeks and gave her a tight hug. He turned to Christian and said, "take good care of her, man" and bowed to Rae Jean. Pong Jung turned at the door and smiled at Zuri. As soon as the door was closed, Zuri turned to Christian and asked, "any objections."

"None whatsoever." He rose on his feet, move forward, and quickly brushed her lips with his, and turned toward the door.

"Christian, let me give you my cell."

"I have it."

"Okay, give me yours so I can call you as soon as I hear from Pong Jung."

"You have it in his file." Rae Jean happily informed them.

"No, I don't. It has gone to storage. Besides if I did it's unethical for me to take it and use it for personal gain. You have to get it for me." Rae Jean gave him a pad and pen and he wrote his cellular phone number on it without a name tore it off and handed it to her. She took it and pulled his shirt collar to her and gave him a long deep hungry kiss. He returned it with an intensity and urgency that spoke of his unconditional love for her. He turned, smiled at Rae Jean, and walked through the door into the Hall. Zuri sank into the chair that was emptied by Christian. She was exhausted at the same time filled with the energy of excessive passion to make love to her lover. She was weak in the knees and was trembling internally.

Rae Jean looked at her, "oh my, you naughty girl. You want to tell me about it."

"No. You haven't told me anything about you and the mystery man in your life. Why should I tell you about mine?"

"Christian is not a mystery, anymore. I know your secret."

"Well, my personal life is not up for discussion, well until you spill about yours." Zuri wickedly told her.

"My goodness, that's pure blackmail, doc."
"Ha, of course, it is."

"I don't believe you would do such a thing!" Rae Jean tried to be shocked and was nowhere near it.

"Wait a minute; I never give Christian my cell number. How did he......." Her voice trailed off and she sat up straight in the chair looking at Rae Jean.

"I have to go now. I got a date, bye."

"Rae Jean!" Zuri yelled after the closed door.

Christian pulled out his wallet and looked for the piece of paper he had stuck deep in the folds of a pocket. He looked at it and silently read. *Call me sometime. I need you. I want you desperately.* It was given to him by Rae Jean. He knew Zuri didn't know about it nor was it in her handwriting. He had seen her handwriting during the group counseling session, besides she was not the type to pass him her phone number through an assistant. He breathed in and assessed his feelings when he saw Zuri hugging Pong Jung. He didn't feel any jealousy and for the heck of it, he couldn't phantom a guess why he didn't feel any emotions. He pondered for a moment and realized that his moment with Zuri was more than he had anticipated; he's grateful for whatever time they have together. She hadn't told him that she loved him and that doesn't bother him. What is going on here? Why doesn't he have emotions for either one of the experiences? He knew he wasn't emotionally shut down, he felt alive every day. He still can taste Zuri and seemed forever to have an erection around her. Doggone it, he felt so alive!

Life has a funny way of turning things around for him. He was going to ask her to spend the two weeks with him and she was thinking the same, except in Barbados. Well, that's about settled it for them both. It does justify them thinking of the other and only of the other. They meant something to each other, therefore this is real. Nothing matter except the coming two weeks spending with the love of her life. He was too excited about going with her to Barbados. Spending two whole weeks with Zuri and having the freedom to say what he wanted without constantly looking over his shoulders. They would have the freedom to be themselves. Two whole weeks!

He wondered how Pong Jung is going to fix it with his Captain without anyone suspecting anything intimacy between him and Zuri. Christian realized he didn't care and turned onto the path that led to the gym. He better be in top shape for his two weeks of pure loving!

Christian was summoned to the Captain's office an hour before the ceremony for his honorary discharge. After the salute and at ease was issued, Captain Anwar Morrison told the Lieutenant that he was to accompany Doctor Zuri to Barbados. Christian's heart was rejoicing, however, his eyes hid its dance and his face was serious. His training came in handy just about now.

"Any questions?" His Captain asked.

"Yes, sir."

"What is it, Lieutenant?"

"Why?"

"She needs someone to look after her. What she witnessed and went through made her fragile. She's vulnerable and a vital asset presently to all of us here. She's here for millions of you officers and no one's there for her. You were there with her in Iraq and Afghanistan. Now, you'll be there for her as she rests and recuperates. You're to see that she gets ample rest and that she eats healthy. She needs to add some pounds onto her bones. Is that understood, Lieutenant?"

"Yes, sir?"

"Any more questions."

"No, sir."

"Dismissed." The Captain didn't get any explanation as to why this particular officer had to accompany the doc for her rest. It came from the big boss and he had to comply. He doesn't care who took care of her besides thinking about it the Lieutenant is perfect because they shared a devastating experience together. Seeing the light of the issue he gave his approval. What he did know was that it had to do with Yung's Engineering and the contracts the military has with his company. He doesn't care except he does agree that Doctor Zuri does need someone to take care of her. He was sorry she had to be a witness to war. He wouldn't wish that on anyone much less her. She's the hardest effective volunteer worker he ever set eyes on and the sexiest!

4

Winter had made an early visit this year. It would be a very long time before the sun's ray announced that it will soon be over and slip into spring. It doesn't mean a thing to the two sole occupants on the private plane that took off from The Ronald Reagan Washington National Airport in Virginia on a cold day before Christmas heading towards the Caribbean island of Barbados.

Zuri and Christian sat opposite each other, sipping the rum and coke that the hostage had made for them. They enjoyed the view of the lakes tucked in neatly among the rolling green and patches of white hills. Hunters, not of man nature have prowled through the thick terrain before winter, piercing the core of different landscapes of various animals making the place their home and tripping over things on the floor of those rolling white patches. Many lost their lives as they venture out looking for food or a mate to keep them warm.

Thunder roared in the distance, way down a little below the plane. The ocean moved as a restless beast, constantly prowling through the debris of trash and other objects that occupied its waters. Beneath, deep on the ocean's floor, volcanoes all around the world roared to life, kicking steam up and killing all life forms in their path. Regardless of the season, life moved ahead and evolution is vivid.

Zuri leaned back in her seat and closed her eyes, imagining the shape of Barbados growing from a mist dark shape into a tantalizing paradise of palms and jungle, wild jungle. No jungle there, only flowers, green hills, and warmth. She inhaled deeply and a smile tugged at her lips chasing away her wild imagination. The silence was with the lovers since Christian collected her from her quarters. Rae Jean drove and chatted with them to the airport. Zuri was silent, she desperately needed silence. Christian understood that and logged lazily in the back seat looking out the window of the car. Zuri couldn't help herself and kept glancing over her shoulders at him. When she first thought of her two weeks of bliss, she hadn't included him. Karma is fabulous!

Zuri eyes flew open when she felt Christian next to her, she turned to acknowledge him with a smile that was felt throughout her body. He felt the pounding thunder of vibration that ran through her and responded with intensity to match her feelings. She surrendered before he ardently kissed her. Without taking his eyes from her face, he shifted her hand until his mouth found her palm. Using his tongue and lips, he explored the taste, making a circular motion in the delicate hollow in the center of her hand. He moved and used his tongue to explore her lips, to taste the sweetness including the spot on her collarbone. The sensations made her as moistened as a mist and drunk with hunger. He wanted passion from her; he will get it eventually, however, not here!

Zuri allowed him to seduce her; her time will arrive when they are alone in the beach house. She had planned to do everything possible with him before the two weeks are up, even a little bit of belly dancing. She stroked a finger over his cheek to the corner of his mouth, giving his lips a tantalizing teasing love bite. His hand discovered the tip of a nipple on her right breast while her hand gently squeezes the swollen bulk in his jeans. Sensations upon sensations swept through bodies as a swell of emotions so intensified that they both wondered how they ever managed to bury them for so long. Whenever his mouth covered hers, every part of her body responded with a zap of a thousand volts of smooth electrifying awareness, taking her into ecstasy.

They were caught in a fast-running stream of strong sensations that carried them toward a heated waterfall. They are riding the turbulent waters of true love and knew there was no way they ever wanted to avoid the devastating plunge. They would gladly take it. The journey felt as if the floodgates of the sky opened and dumped the ocean's worth of water on them. Christian knew he had opened the gate of true love, however, Zuri was the flood.

For the rest of the journey, they had a dialogue of smiles, light kisses, holding hands, and feathery touches. The hostess served them dinner and poured wine. She knew to leave them alone. The silence was the desert for the next few hours that etched with private thoughts. Every so often they squeezed the other hand and reached over for a kiss; a kiss that spoke of what they felt and the undying love. In the midst of one such thought, Zuri fell asleep.

Christian moved the armrest that separated them. He asked the hostess for a pillow and blanket. He put the pillow on his lap and gently pulled her to lie on it. The hostess removed her shoes upon his instruction and he covered her. His thoughts of making love to her for two weeks occupied him until the hostage appeared and whispered to him that they were half an hour away from landing in Barbados. He waited until the lights of their destination glowed in front of them before he woke her up with a gentle touch and a light kiss. Zuri rise from his lap. "We are here?" a little dazed from being awoken.

Zuri glanced through the window and saw the shape of the island lilted and grew larger from a misty to a bright shape into a tantalizing paradise of palm trees and beach. She felt the energy of exhaustion from years of overworked lifted off from her shoulders. She was thrilled to be here with her lover. She turned and smiled at him, brushing her lips across his and squeezing his hand.

The journey to the beach house ran past midnight as Zuri stopped at various shops to purchase food and clothes for her and Christian. She refused to accept money when offered by Christian; she explained it as her gift to him being here, a place she loves. She had planned it; they can be alone tomorrow. The housekeeper is off on weekends.

In the beach house, the lights and the air conditioning were turned on. Zuri put the food away while Christian took their cases into the master bedroom and opened them. He hung their clothes in the closet and store personal things in the drawers. He had taken a deep breath after touching her silk and lace lingerie and several other personal things. He didn't look at any of them because he rather waits until they are on her beautiful body. He'll see them soon enough, those images of her clad in her lingerie are welcome anytime. He drank in her sweet feminine fragrance of a rose.

He found her in the kitchen opening a bottle of wine; he took over the task from her. Zuri moved behind him and put her arms around him. She leaned her head on his back for a few moments before she began to kiss him there, while her hands wildly explored his precious package that stood erect, just for her. Christian let her have free reign. He loved it and doesn't want anything in the world more than slow lovemaking. He savored the sensations that her touch evoked in him. He was about to pour the wine in two glasses and decided to let it air for a while. He knew by the way he was being seduced neither of them would have time to drink it anyway, at least for a while.

Yuri's hand had covered the distance of giving a slow tantalizing stroke in his jeans. He let her have her fun for a bit longer and then suddenly turned around, pulling her top and bra off; he greedily took her nipple. Splaying one hand against her back he twined the other into the curtain of her hair and with the other hand encircled her waist, pulling her against him; his lips captured her mouth. He ran his tongue down her to her stomach. He lowered himself to his knees, pulling whatever else clothes she had on, off. He looked up at her, seeing what he wanted to see, her lips opened with a smiling face that lit up her eyes, his entire body lost control.

Christian rose and took the other nipple in his mouth as he slipped his jeans and underwear off. Zuri finished undressing him when she pulled his t-shirt off. They stood there for a split second before he cupped her neck and moved in to kiss her. She gave his lips an alluring bite, at the same time he rolled her over so her back was to his chest and molded her body against him. He entered her quickly, gave her a few thrusts, and then pulled out. He rolled her over again and lifted her breast to his mouth, brushing the nipple with his tongue.

With his hands on either side of her waist, he moved his head freely over each breast and without any warning down the center of her body between her thighs. Zuri let out a sound of pure sweet music, wounding strands of his hair around her fingers. He splayed his hands over her backside and tilted her middle up against his face. She began to arch the lips of her sexuality as it became swollen with warmth. He enjoyed her for a few minutes.

"Oh, Christian." She whispered his name. He kissed her navel and the soft skin beneath it. The little puffs of warmth he breathes became intensified stirring her skin into a deepening surge of magnetic energy that sends electrifying sensations through her core. He kissed his way back to her side of her neck. As soon as she moved her hand to his wait to hold and caress his manhood, he turned her over and entered her again. This time he stayed there as she bends over to accommodate him. He took a love bite from the back of her neck and held it between his teeth. He gave a few more thrusts and then pulled out, turning her over and kissed her full on the lips pulling her sweetness to his urgent care, her pelvis to his penis.

Christian placed his arm around her hips, quickly turned her around, and pulled her closer until erected sweet-savory was firmly pressed against her soft firm backside. He lifted her slightly and entered her core with one hard thrust. Zuri let out her triumphed music as he let go all of him into her.

In a very short time, as soon as he caught his breath, Christian picked her up with both arms and made his journey to the bedroom. She landed on her back on the bed. The juncture of her thighs formed a cradle at the back of his neck, lowering head as his tongue danced in and out from her core essence. His hand clasped her waist With one swift motion his hand clasped her waist; the other hand tugged her backside closer to his manhood. They were both sexually charged as he kissed his way to her mouth.

The lovers touched and played with each other for a very long time. They nourished the other with kisses and laughter as they learn every inch, every curve, and every sexual core of the other body. They teased and kissed, laughter filling the air with the music of true love. As he slowly entered her, he pressed his open palm against her mound; then a finger slowly and softly played with her centerpiece. The inner walls of her body contracted around his manhood. The stroke of her inner muscles was the magic fist that massaged him, milking him of semen. He nuzzled her neck beneath her ear; she was lost in the sound of his breathing, She joined him in a huge double pleasure as Christen watched her as he lay empty.

"Welcome to Barbados." He told her as she opened her eyes to look at him after her double pleasure. Her laughter filled the early morning with more foreplay. Wrapped in each other's arms, they waited together for dawn to paint its first strides of pink across the sky. They watched through the sliding doors of the master room that overlooked the beach.

"So, you love me because I'm high fiber?" Zuri asked Christian as they sat outside on the patio having a very early breakfast of toast and marmalade an hour later. The sun was up, however not the inhabitants of the island. Six o'clock on a Sunday morning was too early. It's a lazy day for the islanders.

"One of the many reasons." Christian grinned at her as he took a bite from the banana.

"In the summer, I'm honey-colored and in the winter I am caramel color, you're welcome to trot off to my side of town for a taste anytime."

"I think I've already had, my love."

"Well that's true," suddenly her face became semi-serious. "Christian, what were you in the Marine as?"

"Marine scout sniper."

"Anything else you want to tell me."

"No, I joined the Marines at eighteen and been in wars it seems all of the time," chuckling darkly.

"Tell me something." He asked as he leaned his elbows on the table.

"What, my love?" A frown appeared and disappeared as quickly.

"How come you never asked us what we saw out there?" "Oh I don't have to, my love, everything is energy. You turned mental and physical pain into energy and guide people to let it go. Plus I don't want to know. Do you think the military would want a volunteer counselor hearing all its secrets from officers?" Reading his thoughts, Zuri continued, "I did sign a life confidentially contract, however, I don't think I can hear what every one of you have to say and continue to do what I do. I would go crazy."

"Point taken. I take it you don't know any details of what I endured in my life except what I wrote." Christian had to ask.

"Yes."

"What do you know about the guilt I carried?"

"The way you answered the questions I asked on the questionnaire you had to fill out before I counseled you. I had an advantage. The night we bumped into each other. I saw what was in your core, all your fears, guilt, and rage. You saw my tears and I saw yours."

"I didn't then nor do I feel ashamed of what popped up. Why's that?

"It's because we feel comfortable with each other and we do want this to work. I am beyond the joy of meeting and being with you. I couldn't wait for you to finish with the Military. I kept hoping to develop a relationship with you, though I had to admit it looked hopeless." Christian threw his head back and laughed. "I knew it was hopeless and was settled just watching and seeing you whenever possible."

"Is that why you were on the roof every morning and night as I walked to and from the office?" Zuri asked in surprise.

"Yes. I didn't know you knew."

"Of course I do. I can scent you anywhere."

"A horse to his mere," Christian whispered and looked deeper into her soft brown eyes. He was amused.

It was Zuri who turned to laugh; her face because serious. "You can tell me about your experience when you feel comfortable doing so otherwise, I wouldn't ask." Christian was speechless and didn't know how to respond. For one thing, he has no attachment to that fateful day and it seems a very long time ago, Right now his thoughts drew a blank.

"No, I don't. Christian, I would never ask you. I will

wait until you feel comfortable to tell me."

"Thank you." He touched her hand that lay on a chair next to him and gave it a squeeze. He moved his hand behind her neck and pulled her halfway, planting a warm kiss of thank you on her sensuous lips.

A few moments later, Zuri picked up where she left off, in the conversation. This was their moment to secure their relationship. Getting to know each other will come later. These moments in time together are the uttermost essence, to build off from in moments of difficulties.

"Christian let's spend these precious days talking about you and me, no family, only us and what we want for ourselves separately and together."

"Yes, I agree. I want us to be secure with each other, no matter what happens nothing can ever come between us. I want us to be forever. I want to have babies with you." He concluded.

Zuri belted out a loud laugh, jumped out of her seat, and landed in Christian lap. She gave him a long adoring kiss and looked him in his eyes. "I feel the same way and want the same things. Christian, my wonderful lover I never want them with anyone else." Christian was the one giving the adorable kiss. This kiss spelled out his passion of love for her.

"I am so exhausted from all the counseling I have completed. I have very little to offer you. Sometimes, I am lost for words to express the simplest of things. I get restless, I am overworked. I refuse to stop at this time. Do you understand?

"Yes, I do and I don't want you to, either. I would never ask you to and I don't even want to think what would happen to the officers who have no one to turn to in the time of need."

"Oh, thank you, my wonderful lover." She planted a longer teasing kiss on his lips, which was returned just as teasingly.

After they broke for some well-needed air, Zuri said, " I hope what I am about to tell you wouldn't make you feel less of a man. Christian, I have lots of money, and I mean lots and lots of money."

"I figured you did and no, it doesn't make me feel less of a man. I am glad you mentioned it. I'm going to look for a job when we return and with my disability check I am sure we can manage somehow."

"What are you thinking, I mean for a job?"

"I have a degree in computer engineering and a minor in architecture. I look for something in those fields."

"You see, we are going to have some challenges ahead of us."

"I know."

"We're not on the same page, my love. We are talking about two different things." Zuri informed him

"Carry on."

"Well, I know that you were honorary discharged, we can freely see each other without anyone telling us anything, or is there any conflict of interest? she asked. Upon receiving a nod of approval she let out a breath and completed her thoughts. "We don't have to announce that we are a couple. We can get an apartment outside the base, a small cozy apartment." Zuri expressed. "Are you sure they wouldn't tell us anything? You know with you being Captain and me being a lower rank," Christian laughter filled the air with a teasing glint. "Very funny. I was so mad that morning of the drill. If the military does it again, I will leave. Besides, they aren't paying me. I am a volunteer counselor."

"What?" Christian couldn't believe what he was hearing.

"Even if they permit me to charge I couldn't do it. I have enough money. My brother, Adnan and Pong Jung invested my money from the sale of my books. I have more than enough. I don't have to charge for counseling.

I was doing it for free around the world before the military asked me to join them." She recalled.

"If you ever want me to sign any paper of keeping your money I would do it."

"Thank you for saying it, Christian. That would never be an issue with me because you see my love, I trust you unconditionally with my money and my life." Christian was about to say something and she put her finger on his lips with a quiet "shhh." Her lips joined her finger and replaced it with a kiss that stated no argument. The kiss sealed the trust.

"We have more important things to talk about that would or might create conflicts in our new budding relationship."

"What could that be, my princess. We are 100% sexually compatible."

"Oh, we will never be a conflict in making love. We have it down to perfection. I'm sure. Keeping, building, and maintaining the relationship will be a challenge?" Zuri was looking at him, becoming serious.

Christian saw the seriousness in her eyes. "What can be so damaging?" He wondered and completed his thoughts with words.

"We both cannot possibly work and have a healthy relationship. I cannot give you something I don't have. When I'm finished in a day's counseling I can't come home to you and give you anything, sometimes I don't have any energy left to make love to you. I'm that exhausted." She signed.

"I see. What would be best for us? Zuri, I'm willing to do anything and everything I possibly can to keep us together. I want you to know that."

"Yes, please. I can't leave, not now, not until there are enough people to do what I am doing. I've about 20 officers presently being trained and about another 25 civilians that I was personally training before I joined the military. I'm going to have to figure how to do this, together." Her left-hand pointing at him and back to her. She continued, "The sooner I get help, the sooner I'll have time to contribute and nourish our relationship." She added with a shrug and sadness in her voice.

"What's the answers or rather what do you require of me?"

"I was wondering if you can hold off working and in that way, you can hold the relationship together while I do what I have to do."

"I can do that. I don't have to work and the break would do me wonders. I can develop myself and see what other attributes I have deep inside of me." He gave her a warm amused yet serious smile with a wink.

"You read my books? When did you do that?" Zuri has inquiring thoughts.

"During those long months of recovery." He leaned over and kissed her. "Those were some very good ones and thanks for writing them. It helped a lot of us during those long difficult mmm challenging times. The other officers and I had something to talk about as we try to figure out what you mean and understand what you wrote."

"Did you, I mean did you understand it?"

"I did. I did read a few paragraphs a few times over and over again. And sometimes, I let it be and returned to it. Other times, as I recovered I got your meaning. It made all of us think about ourselves and our lives in a very serious manner. The question was what did we invest in and what do we want to invest in others, other things?"

"Oh, good that was what I wanted."

"Really?" Christian showed surprised.

"Yes, I wanted people to think differently and not traditionally. I hope you are not a traditionist, cause, my love I am not. Oh, no sir."

"I love Christmas." Christian expressed.

Zuri laughed, "Maybe you will be very lucky this year

since you are spending it here with me locked up in a beach house." She kissed him seductively. "If you want me to sign those books, I will."

"You already have in more ways than one." He planted a seductively teasing kiss on the ridge of where the shoulder meets the neck.

"Christian," Zuri became serious again. "We have to go into details about how we want to build, maintain, and keep our relationship strong. You are going to have to carry the bulk of it for both of us most of the time. To top that, you are going to have to maintain the apartment, cook dinner, laundry, and just about everything else."

Christian laughed. "Isn't that what I was trained for, I am a Marine. I can do it all." He puffed out his shoulders and grinned down into her serious soft brown eyes.

Seeing she is still not convinced, he gently touched his lips to hers and said, 'piece of cake. I'll do it. After what I lived through." He said without any pain surfacing. "Everything else would be easy and not even a challenge."

"Oh, thank you so much. You will..."

"Sshhh no more talking." He lifted her off from him, rose, and picked her up to him, her legs around his hips, and headed inside the house.

On the brink of dawn, shadows of light evaded the blue colored room through the draperies onto the kitchen. Christian stood washing dishes by the light of the window. Zuri was in bed sleeping from another bout of making love. The last dish was washed and put to dry in the dish rack. No dishwasher here. He brewed a fresh pot of coffee and sat outside where they did not so long ago. He touched his heart and felt the love for living life and the lady who he loved. What more can he ask for in this second chance he was given?

Four days later, they were watching a limbo dance while having dinner in a nearby restaurant. It was their first outing since they arrived. Zuri was enjoying breadfruit and flying fish stew as Christian watched her. He had ordered fish and chips as they talked about the food they enjoyed and what he can cook. Zuri is a vegetarian while he was not; he's all meat and potatoes guy, well, more at stake than chicken or fish. Zuri doesn't care what he chooses to eat. On those days she can have vegetables and salad or soup.

"I have recipes for everything I eat so you can use the book."

"How do you like your clothes, madam?" He asked smiling.

"Silk are hand washed while cotton is machine wash and all ironed."

"I am de masta of de iron."

"Oh, good coz I is horrible wit it." Laugher poured out of them.

"Can you explain sex and trauma to me?"

"Of course, I can," Zuri said seductively and took a sip of her wine. "Traumatic and abuse people don't know the difference between pain and pleasure. They want to have sex directly after they have survived life-threatening experiences. Their external picture of males and females' physical change differs during their transitional age, the teenage years.

"The illusions and fantasies are mixed up; they become the same. They think it's reality, it's not. Pain and pleasure mixed with sexual experiences become a habit of entertaining themselves. They craved more of the same so they seek more, often going off to inflict pain on anyone and anything then they jerked off, women do the same. Neither of them experiencing an orgasm. The sex is meaningless. They craved more no sooner than they ejaculated.

"Lust captures their thoughts and makes them slaves so they forever chasing lust and never finding love. They chase the pain through pleasure developing sexual additions. When they cannot get the pleasure they inflict pain." She lay her knife and fork on the placemats and took a sip of her wine. When males and females think they are in love they are infatuated. Their thoughts are filled with fantasies of illusionary desires and deceptions. When they come into contact with their lovers the desires are never satisfied and they go chasing the desires as their thoughts conjure another image with another lover.

"They chase one illusion after another creating many different fetishes and sexual addictions, always with the understanding of installing pain and pleasure. They don't know the difference between desires and passion." She took another sip of her wine and continued. During sex, the release of endorphins is increased in the euphoria producing chemical phenylethylamine (PEA) in the bloodstream. Sex, in turn, is the ultimate release of emotions and orgasm. Orgasms are the ultimate release of energy and the unequivocally affirming of true love. Love is a powerful motivator that makes lovers victims and curses them to do crazy things that they don't normally do. Love differs from true love and they don't know that either. True love is the foundation of living life." She took a sip of wine and looked at Christian.

"I love it when you talk dirty to me."

"Oh you naughty boy, you are so going to pay for that."

"I am counting on it." He grinned at her.

"Christian, why do you want to know?"

"I always want to know about pain and pleasure? I know too many people addicted to it and didn't know what it was until I read about it in your books. I also experienced it?"

"Every human person has or will experience pain and pleasure because they are together in the same pod in the frontal lobe of the brain. It's part of the makeup of our software. This is where we have evolved at this present time. Was your recovery a long one?"

"Oh, yes, too long. I'm still recovering from the physical aspect of it. I have many implants I've lost count of and forgotten where they are in my body. I was a mess, I pulled through in a short time, ten months because I used you as my motivator."

"Well, darling you can use me anytime. I've no problem with that, whatsoever!" She leaned over and pulled on his t-shirt, planting a promising kiss on his lips.

"Mmm, ready to go. I would like to continue this in private." He pulled his wallet and paid the bill, pulled Zuri's chair out, and took her hand. All was forgotten about the limbo show. They took the path on the beach leading to the house. Zuri said. "As soon as we find a flat, I will ask Pong Jung to ship my things from New York. I put them in storage and only have necessity with me. Rae Jean......."

"Sorry is that his real name, Pong Jung?" He asked.

"Hell, no. I couldn't pronounce his name as a little girl so I called him that. Our family goes years way back as far as I can remember. His grandfather and mine became friends when they met somewhere in India." she answered candidly. It's time to bring some things out in the open.

She continued from where she left off before being interrupted. "Rae Jean was the first officer I ever counsel. I bumped into her in the coffee shop buying Lattes. I saw her in so much pain and asked her if she wanted me to remove it. She soon got me the other officers; she automatically became my assistant. She was in Desert Storm. Were you there?"

"Yep, there, Iraq and Afghanistan."

"I saw the marks on your body. That's an awful lot, I say."

"Some were from childhood playing cops and robbers and other games. Is that what you were doing this morning, kissing them, my scars?" He smiled down at her and gave her a light kiss. He had woken up to her kissing him all over his body. It was a magnificent feeling.

"Yes." She gingerly admitted.

"I am going to find some more scars to put on my body, you will never finish." He stated.

"Funny honey. You don't need scars for me to kiss you. I love kissing you everywhere. You know Christian, let's always be by ourselves at this time of year."

"What without Christmas? I love Christmas and all those gifts!" He excitedly expressed.

"I don't care for Christmas as I don't celebrate it. I love New Year's." She informed him.

"Okay, I guess I can give up Christmas, it has been years since I spend it with my family. My parents always post my gifts wherever I am stationed. I want my birthday spent with them. I love gifts!" The little boy in him came out. Zuri loves it.

"Guess I can work with it. What about religion? I am spiritual and don't go to churches." "Good, cause I can't stand the place. It's a ripoff, too communalized for me. I never got anything going to them. I don't really care for any particular religion." He concluded.

"Do you talk to your family often?" They had arrived in front of the beach house. Zuri had let go of his hand. She stood at the water's edge as her feet started to play with the surf that rolled in for the high tide. They both had their shoes off before walking on the beach.

"I talk to my parents once a week. They lived in Maine with my two brothers, an older and younger one plus an older sister. My brothers and sister usually email often. They took turns staying with me during my recovery. My parents are retired, they were there all the time."

"I haven't seen any of my family in two years. I have seven brothers and two sisters. It's a mess when we get together, in a good way."

"Ten of you. How did your parents manage?" He wanted to know.

"Grandparents, godparents, and nannies helped. My parents were contracted engineers and traveled the world over. Each one of us was born in a different country. I was born in China. My mother designed bridges and my dad built them. We traveled with either one of the grandparents and a few nannies. The country that contracted them usually pays for it all. They are still working somewhere in Asia."

"Like me, you have traveled."

"Yes. Christian, I want one place to settle in. I want to settle there with you." In one-foot length, she left the water edge and molded her body to him. He took her in his arms and he agreed, "I would like that too. Maybe we can find a place in the wilderness, a few acres somewhere, and build a house."

"Oh, away from people. I like that very much. I think I just want you all to myself."

"Oh, good. I'll start looking for an apartment than a car. I can take you to and from work. I think I know where I want to live. I'll show it to you as soon as I check it out. If no one bought it then we can. I stumbled on it on one of my Boy Scout days a long time ago."

"Sweetheart, what would you like to do with your life?" Zuri asked him.

"A long rest and spend some time with me. Later on, I would like some land with a boot camp."

"Boot camp?" Zuri asked in surprise moving away from him and looking into his eyes.

"The officers have a difficult time adjusting to civilian life after what they experienced in the wars. Many of us just want to go live in the woods away from people. If there was a kinda boot camp for them to visit, rent, camped out, and stay fit, it would make them feel at home."

"Really?" She raised an eyebrow.

"Yes, we can have our weapons with us, go fishing, climbing, and other things we did in boot camp. We feel safe, somehow. I would feel at home more out in nature than in some house." He said softly.

"Then boot camp it is, on one condition well two. One, we have a five-bedroom log cabin and it's near a town."

"Why?" Christian asked.

"Well, for the log cabin it goes with the woods. One bedroom for us, one for an office, one for our parents, one for our son, and the next for our daughter. The town must have a school for our children and an airstrip so Pong Jung can visit." She answered quickly and in one breath.

"That sounds wonderful. Pong Jung?" Christian asked with a question and a frown after the last bit of information was processed.

"He's my godfather and he has to visit me most of the time, at least every month. He has been visiting me at the office. He had been in my life more than my father!"

"No kidding."

"Yep, I talk to him every day of my life, except these past few days. I told him about you, my parents don't know, yet. Pong Jung knows and he likes you."

"Oh goody. I was afraid I had to go learn karate and fight for you." Christian teased undaunted and jokingly. Loud laughter rang out in the moonlight air from Zuri.

"Christian." She studied him for a minute.

"Huh?"

"I want to spend the rest of my life with you. I don't believe in marriage. I will marry you if you want to.

"You do cover things rather quickly." Then he remembered that she's not a traditionalist, he continued. "It'll take a bit for me to get used to you not being a traditionalist."

"I want us to be secure with each other because once we return I wouldn't have the time to say anything to you.

I want to say it all here, this minute. I don't and can't live with insecurities between us. It would kill me. I want to know that this is what you want, we can build our lives with these goals."

"I agree. Time is so precious and I don't want any assumptions between us either. I want integrity in our relationship."

"Ha, you read my book on relationships." She was flushed and blushed.

He took hold of her hands and pulled her close to him. "Yes, my sweet love. I want it too. Are you going to write one on sex, you think?

"No, I am not experienced enough to do so." She bit into his lower lip.

"Mmmmm I can sure fix that, right here and right now." His hands pulled her dress up and two fingers slipped into her. He pulled out as fast as he was in and started to walk towards the path that led to the beach house. Zuri didn't reply only laughed. She went in front of him and stopped him from walking. She tiptoed and pulled his neck, her lips touched his. She whispered on his lips.

"How about a dip in that gorgeous waters. Let me make love to you in there."

"Sound like a wonderful plan." Christian laughed. "We can swim in the nude, can't we?" He began to undress her. The altered top dress was over her head before she could breathe another breath. His t-shirt and shorts joined her dress on the beach, next went the underpants. They looked at each other for a minute. The breeze lifted a lock of Zuri's dark hair, Christian touched it. He reached for her hand as they venture into the warm waters for a swim. The moon was hiding behind some clouds and a pale luminescence was reflected from the brilliance of the ocean. The high tide of the quarter moon was on the verge of cresting; the two lovers swam out to sea and back to the beach; they took up a post on the sand. Christian pulled her down on the sand and moved her legs so he can be between them. He entered her and she received him. He was incredibly compact, while she was wet and snug. His green eyes locked with her brown ones; he pushed deeper, she clamped her lower lips on his whispering his name in his ear. He was fully seated inside her; she contracted her pelvis muscles. He grimaced with pleasure and pushed more firmly while contracting his pelvic muscles. She caught the contraction and returned it in kind. He pressed his forehead against hers while a handheld her waist still and the other was under her backside anchoring her down for what is ahead. She couldn't move even if she tried. Her legs were fastened between his, sealing him tight to her. They were one.

Christian began to move back and forth. Zuri raised her hips and he pushed her up with his hand on her backside, to meet his smooth driving force. They combined the rhythm together to have a smooth melody. The breathing picked up speed as these lovers moved to the same beat creating a pattern together. He waited until she was about to climax and came with her. He sank all of his fingers into her hair and held her between his hands, kissing her mouth as passionately. The coupling made her orgasm long and intense, more than what he can ever endure. He allowed himself to climax with her as he buried his face into her neck and drew a patch of her skin against his teeth.

It was a long time before any one of them moved. The ocean surf cascaded on their body and the moonlight shone brighter as their love was celebrated. They sank deeper into the sand with the ebb and flow of two or three inches of foam insinuating itself about them. He pulled her in his arms as he rolled onto his back. The sand felt sexy as the water tingle his feet and Zuri's head rested on his shoulders. He glanced up at the Moon hovering over him and whispered ever so softly.

"Marine Moon."

Zuri gaining control of herself opened her eyes and looked at the moon. It was bright with beautiful silver light shining down on them. This moon was rising silvering in the midnight air. All around them silver shadows melted in the blue haze of the landscape in the moonlight. Every muscle in her body stretched taut from their lovemaking; she enjoyed the dizzying as well as the ecstasy that invaded her senses. This was the most spectacular romantic moment of her life.

"The moon helped me through my dark days." He told her as if reading her thoughts. Sensing her moment, Christian turned, kissed her lips, and pulled her closer to him. The union invisibly nourished by their love created a pattern of a steady flow of emotions. It froze the moment and changed the endless beauty of their unfolding love for each other. This particular moment frozen was the definition of a moment adding essence to their life. Unknowing to both of them, a seed was planted in the middle of this high moon, which will sprout and flower throughout the summer into fall.

5

The sound of a roster welcoming dawn stirred Zuri out of sleep. She rolled over and kissed Christian. She settled her chin on his chest waiting for him to open his eyes. She smiled at him as he looked at her. He lifted his head and kissed her.

"Good morning, love. I love opening my eyes and seeing you. What's for breakfast?"

"Mmmm let me think?" She replied and turned over and her head rested on his chest.

"Christian's hand reached over and squeezed a nipple. "Any ideas, yet?" Zuri jumped up and off the bed. "You are going to have to catch me first."

Christian gamed, lazily looked at her as she left the room. The nightgown she wore was creased, nonetheless, it looked sensual on her.

It was rare that Zuri fixed breakfast. The few times she was domesticated with breakfast, dinner, or supper she was amazing. They give the cook-off and they would cook together and talk about life. She had eggs, toast, and baked beans with coffee ready when he joined her out on the patio fifteen minutes later. He had shorts on and was shirtless. He pulled out a chair and sat in it.

"Christian, I'm going to be extremely busy the minute I get back. I don't know how much time I'll have to see you. I called Pong Jung and asked him to ship my things. He owns a shipping company, which reminded me I have a car in storage, we don't need one. It's a jag jeep, a gift from my wonderful brothers for something or the other."

Christian noticed her anxiety and nervousness. He'll

wait until she informed him of her various relationships. This is new territory for him; he watched her intensely. He poured coffee and added three teaspoons of sugar.

"I'm going to change things around a bit, at least I can work from nine in the morning to seven at night. It'll take about two weeks to get things moved around. Plus I am going to have Sundays off for a few weeks before I take Saturdays off."

"Good, that should give me time to find us an apartment. I think there's an apartment complex not far from the base. I hope they have one free."

"Okay. I think we should stay in that motel down the street until we find a place. I don't want to spend any time away from you."

"That's not a safe place for you to stay."

"I have you. Who would want to mess with a Marine?" She grinned at him and shoved a fork of eggs into her mouth.

"I guess I better find an apartment real fast?" He was serious as ever. The mere thought of Zuri arriving at that motel before he does make him

shiver with anxiety for her safety.

"We can stay at the hotel until you find a place."

"Now you're talking. I feel relieved. Let's do it."

"It's expensive you know. I can afford it." "Zuri, my love. Your comfort and safety mean more to me than my ego or pride. It's your money, you should enjoy it without feeling that you have to take my feelings into consideration."

"Oh. Huh?"

"Listen, love, I'm secure with my veteran disability check. I'll chip in whenever needed, you should never have to feel insecure or guilty for spending any of your money. You work as hard as I did. Stop thinking of money where we are concerned. Will you?"

"Okay."

"I have to go and visit the family of the men from my unit that were killed. I'll plan it for the weekends in about three weeks. Can you come with me?

"Will do. I'll work the time out. You should relax and trust what we have between us." She assured him. "I'm a bit anxious of not being able to spend time with you and feel guilty for not helping in building a strong relationship. I'm not in a place to even have one, Christian. Thank you for asking me to come. I love it here and spending all these days with you. It's heaven."

"Trust me to pull us through the next two weeks and beyond, Zuri."

"Yes, I will, my love; it's a new day dawn."

"No." He corrected her. "A new era dawned."

Oh, hell, this is going to be horrible. Christian was walking back and forth in the new apartment. A few of the officers were going to be here in a few minutes to help him offload the container of Zuri's things that were shipped from New York. He had called Pong Jung himself and had chatted for a few minutes. Pong Jung made him feel comfortable.

They have been back for two days and immediately found this one-bedroom apartment after spending a few days at the hotel. At least, he and Zuri had the nights together before he dropped her off for work. He guessed everyone knew that he and Zuri were a couple or at least together.

Ah, this is a whole different matter that is looking at him in his face. What does he do? He has to bring himself under control. Their life was flooded out of control when the second in command of the military visited him. He must have heard the gossip.

Colonel Fitzgerald of the Commandant of the Marine Corps and one of his assistants came and told him to move to another state and leave Doctor Zuri alone. The Colonel more or less threatened him that if he doesn't do as he is ordered, there will be consequences. How can the Colonel do this when he was honorary discharge? His life was hell until he met Zuri. He deserves to be happy; they deserve to be happy. How can he tell Zuri? The Colonel's firm angry tone came into view and his words stuck out as a ton of bricks hitting him on the head.

"Doctor Zuri is an asset to the military and you're not, you're a washed-up soldier. I ordered you to end your relationship with her. The military needs her to get the job done and you're a distraction. Think of all the officers including you that she has helped. You don't want her to stop now for a little fucking. Leave her alone and move." He didn't wait for any comment or answer from Christian, he turned on his heels and walk through the door.

There was a knock on the door and five officers walked in. The look on Christian's face reinforced what the officers were thinking. They tapped him on his shoulders, giving him comfort as they walked into the apartment. They had all waited in their cars upon seeing the Colonel's vehicle outside. The Colonel was rude and cruel. They knew this from past experiences with the Colonel. Basically, everyone knew about the Doc and Christian. Even if they were envious of Christian it wasn't enough to generate anger. They were happy for both of them. At least, Doctor Zuri has someone to take care of her.

"Do you want us to leave and come back later?" Officer Rojas asked.

"No." Christian shook his head. The off-color on his face was slowly returning to its slight tan color. "I'll manage thanks."

"Tell her." Patrick, a drinking buddy from his training days instructed him.

"Don't let that mother fucking prick come between you and your happiness." Andy another high school friend who joined the military academy with him verbalized angrily.

"Yep man, tell her." Phillip, the oldest sailor advised, fondly slapping him on his back.

"Don't give up your chance of happiness, man." Carlos from the air force and his high school mate informed him.

"Listen, we all deserve to be happy. The prick is not, he had to come here and project his anger on you, the fucker." Ty who is a sailor and Carlos' life partner finished the conversation off.

Christian had made his decision. He took bottles of beer from the refrigerator, handing one to each of them. "I appreciate the talk, let's have some fun."

"Here's to that and cheers." The bottle touched each other and the offloading began. The car took up most of the space and the few boxes were neatly stacked in the dining room with the fragile ones resting on top of the non-fragile boxes. For someone with lots of money, she sure has little. Guess, living light is Zuri's motto and having fun. A smile touched Christian's lips, his eyes soften and the anger was gone.

By the time Zuri came home at four, the officers were leaving. They all said, "Hi Doc," giving her a salute as they passed her on her way in from the door that led to the apartment. She gave them each a smile and stood looking at them as they drove off. She had taken an early day because of the offloading. She had one foot in the door when she spotted Christian heading in her direction. "Oh, I was just coming to get you. How did you get here?"

"Rae Jean gave me a lift. What were all those officers doing here? I don't want the officers I am counseling, come to my home. It's not professional, Christian. I don't even want them to see how I live or what I have." Her soft brown eyes questioned him and demanded an answer. He pulled her into the apartment and held her at her waist with both hands. She felt his tension and relaxed against his body. She didn't mean to create any tautness between them.

"They were helping me offload the container. They are old friends I grew up with, childhood friends. I've known them all my life. I didn't see any conflict. Ah, I see your point, I understand and it wouldn't happen again. I'm sorry I've messed up."

"It's alright." Zuri breathed in and out a few times as he pulled her into him and she molded her body to his, showing him how love and caring can be even in a time of exhaustion and misunderstanding.

Christian held her until he felt her body relaxed, however, he was not and Zuri felt his rigidity. She was not fooled for there was something else that he's withholding from her. She felt a slight hesitation. He was experiencing shock, she felt it in his embracement with her. She pushed him away and quickly glanced up at him. He saw the shaft of raw pain in her eyes.

"Oh, you're angry. You're not telling me everything. Spill it out, Lieutenant Christian Andres Vincelette. Spill it out this very minute, all of it, and don't you dare deny any of it. No, let me rephrase. Don't you dare deny me any of it?" Zuri's voice was a bit above its norm.

Zuri's anger blazed hot and fast, quickly burning out. She tried to hang on to her anger and failed miserably. He had the urge to kiss the angry words from her lips, nevertheless, he inhaled deeply and let his breath out.

Christian gaze narrowed in a mocking glint and his mouth tightened. She saw that dangerous angry twinkle come into his eyes as it flickered from light to dark green. The muscles in his jaw twitched. Christian walked away from her and moved behind some boxes and stood looking at her.

Zuri watched him and waited until he was in an emotional place to tell him what made her angry. She knew that anger is for both of them at the same time it is an acid that changed the composition of love and broke the barrier in a solid foundation in relationships. Secrets are another. Whenever anger or hidden secrets become a part of something there is no knowledge of what they will eat into or whom. She gave him his space and time to converse with her.

He turned his back and belted out what Fitzgerald told him. Christian's guilt called to her, however, his anger return chasing all guilt away. It turned to intense rage not because of Fitzgerald, because of what was written on her face. He didn't want to see her in his raw unfiltered pain. He shifted his gaze to her eyes and saw the different play of emotions danced in them, brown eyes turned black. Her silence was her technique of processing what was said and what she is feeling and what she is going to do. The emotions swelled and ebbed just as those waves he saw in Barbados washing over the rock onto the beach, in high tide. Beneath Zuri's angry front, she was nice on the explosion. He didn't expect any of it. He was mildly incorrect in what she was feeling. Her emotions were the waves tumbling through a very stormy ocean slamming into the rocks on the beach. She was beyond anger; she was furious.

"Why are you feeling guilty?" She asked him.

"I don't want to take you away from what you are doing for the officers. I would never do that and for a second I thought that I was. I don't anymore. I am angry because you shouldn't be going through this after your day. No one should go through this."

"Exactly my point, Christian. No one should be abuse like this especially from someone with authority." Zuri's anger simmered as hot as a sauna. Fitzgerald visited pushed her feeling into intensified anger. She turned to Christian, "hold me, please."

It was well into the next morning, sleeping on their unmade bed that Zuri wakened to the smell of coffee. She had fallen asleep for a good ten hours. As if sensing her, Christian bought a cup of the grub to her as she added his pillow to her, pulling herself up in a sitting position.

He kissed her and handed her the coffee as soon as she sat up. "What are you going to do about Fitzgerald? Please don't tell me you don't know." He pleaded with her.

Zuri grinned at him for knowing her. "I wouldn't. Let me do it first and then tell you later."

"Okay." He knew something needed to be done since he no longer works for the military and she does, volunteer or not, she's the one in a position to manage this unpleasant business.

The first thing Zuri did as soon as Christian dropped her off and left was turned around and walked to the head of the military office to see Fitzgerald's supervisor, the top of the military officers, the man who bought her to this base, the General himself. She started to remember what Christian told her and her temper rose again; this time it was in a splendid wave of intensity within a fine selection of words that expressed her rage. The words scalded her tongue and she refused to hold them in check any longer. She blinked at all the wild imagination she can concur when an ignorant old jackass of a fool messes with her life.

Zuri was manufacturing all sort of outcome as she flew past the secretary. She left the door opened and the secretary, Anna Peterson lured in the background. The General looked up from the papers he was reading. Upon seeing who it was that dare to burst into his office unannounced, he relaxed the second he recognized her. Doctor Zuri would not be here if it was not an emergency. The rage sizzled on her face and ran through her body was similar to water on a hot skillet. He treaded calmly and told his secretary, "It's alright Anna. Close the door."

The minute the door was closed. Zuri stormed to his desk. "That ignorant jackass of a fool Fitzgerald told Christian that he needed to leave me alone and stop seeing me. I am here to tell you that the jackass needs to retire. Send him into retirement or I'll be out of here. Call it blackmail or whatever the fuck you want. No one messes with my personal or professional life. The next time someone messes with my life I am taking this further and you'll be in retirement. No one fuck with me and any part of my life. Do you understand? You have one hour to fix it."

With that said she turned and walked out of his office and into hers. She flew past the officers who waited for her attention and gave them one of her best smiles. They can sense her energy, an angry one after all they read her books. They know the energy well because that's why they are here. They hoped she will cool down and be effective for them. They don't need her anger or her being angry.

Rae Jean knew something was up when she was not on time. She had called Christian and found out that he had dropped Zuri off some half an hour ago. Christian didn't volunteer any more information nor did she ask. She sensed he knew what she was doing. She had sent one of the officers to get them two lattes and as Zuri entered the office she gave her one. She pushed Zuri toward her chair behind her desk.

"Breath deep doc. Breath."

Zuri was in a rage over the whole mess and told Rae Jean the episode again, while she took big gulps of her coffee. Her heart rate was back to normal; she was ready to work. She sipped on her latte and waited to hear Rae Jean's comment.

"He's a meddling son of a bitch. He has created more conflicts with his arrogant pompous ass than the two wars we are fighting. You think he'll retire."

"Oh, yes. It'll look really bad when the president finds out and the people of American that the volunteer counselor has walked out due to an old ignorant fool. Let's get started, shall we? I want to be home by six."

"Six. That's a first. I wouldn't know what to do with myself."

"Go give your lover a blow," Zuri told her.

"I did that last night!" Rae Jean informed her.

"Do it again, men never get tired of it. Not that I know anything of that sort of thing." Zuri winked and gave her a wicked smile. Rae Jean laughed with a salute, "Yes, ma'am."

The rest of the day was taken with therapy and counseling. As usual, the minutes flew quickly into hours, she was home by six. She waved to Rae Jean as she unlocked the door leading to the apartment. There were boxes everywhere with narrow paths leading in every direction. Christian was going to unpack her boxes, however so sweet?

Christian was sitting on a sofa in the middle of the living room, remote in hand, shirtless watching sports on the television. Boxes were all around him open and the only one on a pack and set up was the flat-screen television. A smile tugged on her lips. Men would always find the television, the remote, and sports. She had paid attention to her brothers and their friends. Zuri shivered upon seeing him. She touched his shoulders and he jumped to his feet in a defensive stance. He was shocked to see who it was because he didn't expect her home till seven tonight. He moved towards her and lifted her off her feet, kissing her until she was breathless. He looked at her trying to capture another breath and quickly kissed her with a huge grin on his face. "I didn't hear you come in."

"How can you? The noise is very loud." Upon this, he turned the sound off from the football game. Zuri wasn't finished. She took the remote control from him and turned the television off. "You know for a Marine who went through wars you aren't very alert."

"I guess not and I blame you. It's your counseling, my

love. How did it go? What did you do?" He had her in his arms again kissing her on her nose, her cheek, working his way down to the ridge of her neck where shoulder meet. A trail of the wet path was left where he had kissed; she relaxed and enjoyed the ride.

"Okay, that will do for now." She lovingly laughs searching for his eyes.

"More will come later, much more, I say," Christian told her connecting his eyes to hers. He turned and lifted her off the ground and sat with her on the sofa. She was next to him slightly turned. "You're home early. Tell me what you did about Fitzgerald?" She told him.

"I know how you got to the military and who asked you? I always wondered about that and was so grateful to the person. I guessed that's the end of Fitzgerald. There was a statement on his early retirement due to health reasons." Christian finished.

Zuri sat up straight, "Well, my love my anger does mean something. I am so glad that I didn't have to call Pong Jung." She took hold of his hand and pulled it towards her. "Let's go eat, I'm starving."

"You were angry Zuri, you were furious in rage. You would have called him, Pong Jung?" Christian was on his feet looking at her.

"Yes. Pong Jung can fix things for me. He knows these men. They play poker. I was, I am not angry anymore. I'm cool as a cucumber. No one mess with me and my lover." She smiled and ran her tongue over his top lip, letting it stay for a second, curling in the corners.

Christian felt his arousal and pulled her to her feet. He gave her another breathless kiss and his eyes were filled with laughter and love. "I am so turned on; on how you fight for me. Are you sure you want to eat now?" He molded her body to him and let her feel all of his sexiness.

Zuri felt it and inhaled every fragment of him, however, while she was busy doing that her stomach reminded her of her original plan with a massive growl. She ignored it and unbuttoned his jeans. Christian pulled his shirt off.

"I will have you instead, for dinner." She wickedly pointed out to him as she ran a finger from his lips to his manhood. "Then I will have dinner and you for dessert with whipped cream." She finished.

"Well, in that case, dinner it is." He kissed her and walked with her to the bed and gently flung her on it. Zuri was filled with laughter as Christian stripped her clothes from her body. He hurriedly flipped her on her stomach and laid his body on hers. His knee positioned her legs apart and he moved one hand under her shoulder and anchored there. Zuri arched her backside up a bit and Christian entered her in one quick smooth moment. She turned her face to the side to breathe. Christian moved her hair away from her face as he moved in and out of her. He reached for a pillow and put it on her back for support.

"Christian, Oh, Christian!"

"Zuri, I love you more than life itself." Upon this admission, she contracted her pelvis muscles and screamed out pleasure as Christian pushed deeper into her. He continued with this action until she climaxed and he followed in a split second. They remained in that position until their heart rate returned to normal. Christian whispered in her ears. "Some food and then I want my dessert."

"Oh, Christian."

Christian moved his body to her side and pulled her to him. He threw one leg on her thighs and kissed her till she pushed him away to catch her breath.

"Christian, you'll be the death of me. I'm getting too old for these long kisses." She teased him with a kiss on his neck.

"Oh, you're not that old. How old are you?" He asked.

"I am thirty. How old are you, Christian?"

"Don't you know?" He frowned questioningly at her. "It was in my assessment."

"I don't look at rank, age, or things like that. Those are there for formalities. I only look at the answers to my questions."

"Oh, I am thirty and soon to be one in four weeks. I would like to take you to my parents. Zuri, they are going to have a huge birthday party for me. It would be a terrific time to introduce you to them and get all those gifts."

Zuri laughed shaking her head. "This birthday and gifts make you look like a little boy. Tell Rae Jean the times you want me off and I will gladly accompany you." She rolled over him, off the bed, and pulled him up. "I need to eat, where are we going for dinner?"

"How about American?"

"Seriously, I just had that." She rolled on top of him and planted a kiss on his chest. He smacked her backside, kissing her neck at the same time. He gently pushed her to her feet, he stood up holding her hands as they walk the short distance into the shower. They were dressed and out the door in half an hour.

Christian was telling her about his family when he saw a familiar face at the bar. Zuri followed his gaze and frowned with a question. Before she asked Christian answered her, 'Ex-girlfriend. We broke up before I was shipped out to Afghanistan."

"Okay." Zuri continued to eat her shrimp and potatoes. If she was spiteful she would wrap jealousy around herself as a warm old blanket. She was not, however, the ex-girlfriend was very much those emotions.

"Zuri, were you in a relationship with we bumped into each other?"

"No, I was not. I couldn't find the time. Really, I don't have the time. I need to go to the bathroom. I have to go and have a checkup with the doctor, Christian. I have been feeling funny, nausea in the morning. I'm a bit now."

"Do you want me to come with you?" Christian was on his feet concerned.

"Hell, no! If I don't return in five minutes come and get me, better yet call the brigade." She told him and saw his face changed from concern to worry, stress crept in, she changed her words, "I am fine, a little virus. It's all the making love we do."

A sign of relief lifted his pale face and he pulled her chair out. She tiptoed and kissed him saying against his lips. "Have another drink, will you."

Christian watched her walk to the restroom and settled into his chair and ordered another beer as the Doc requested. This is another one of her prescriptions she can prescribe for him anytime. His eyes kept a visual on the restroom. He glanced at his watch and saw five minutes were up. Should he go and get her? He gave a sigh of relief as she appeared through the door of the restroom. Then he gulped at the girl from the bar blocked her path that led Zuri to him. One hand was on Zuri's arm; the girl had stopped her. Zuri looked at the hands-on her arm and immediately it dropped. She looked at Christian's ex-girlfriend with a matter of fact frowned. They exchanged words.

Zuri had a smile on her face, however, Christian couldn't see his ex-girlfriend, Susan's face. His eyes were connected to Zuri's as she approached their table. He couldn't read her feelings.

"Can you pay and let's leave, Christian."

"Yes, I sure can." He looked for the waitress and asked for the bill. He paid; they walked to the door, he took her hands into his and smile into her eyes. She looked up at him.

"What was all that about with Susan?" He asked questioningly.

"Oh, you mean your ex-girlfriend?"

"Yes."

"She wanted to know what I have that she doesn't. I told her class among other things and give a bloody good blow." Zuri laughingly told him.

"You didn't." Christian stopped, flushed, and looked at her.

"Yep, I sure like hell did."

Christian picked her off her feet turned her around laughing. They were standing in the parking lot next to the jeep.

"I am glad you are so happy." He let her stand on her feet as he guided her to the passenger seat and tucked her in. He slid into the driver's side and kick life into the engine. "Remind me not to worry about you when you meet any more of my exes."

"There are more? How many more?" Zuri's eyes opened wide and serious. All she could get from him was a wide grin.

Another day dawned, however, on this day Zuri found out that she was pregnant. It was late into January, the last day to be precise; two days ago she told Christian that she wasn't feeling so healthy. He made an appointment with the military doctor and took her to see him. She finally acknowledged the feelings and the strangeness accompanying them. Rae Jean also noticed a difference in her and put it down to the changes in her life; being in love and moving to a new place with Christian and working fewer hours. Christian called her about the appointment with the military doctor for Zuri and asked her to cancel all of her appointments for the afternoon. She needed more rest, otherwise, he was afraid she would collapse from exhaustion with work. She agreed with him.

Rae Jean added the time and date in her planner. "I made a date with Doctor Turks."

"Oh, thank you. I was going to do that. I guess you see a change in me, huh? I hope it's not a cold. I've been eating lots of food and can't seem to get up in the morning; when I do I am sick. Christian is looking at me with a frown of concern. I know he would say something soon."

"He was the one who called and made an appointment with the doctor for this afternoon. We decided you also need the afternoon off."

"Oh."

"I noticed you are a bit less alert. I figured it was all the blow you were giving, I'm going to the Hall and informed the officers about the cancelation."

"Very funny." Zuri blushed and smiled.

Two days later, late in the evening she and Christian were in the office of Doctor Turks when he told them the news.

"Congratulations, you're pregnant."

"Pregnant? How the hell did that happen?" Shocked was expressed on Zuri's face. She stared at the doctor with her mouth opened and next at Christian.

"I think I can explain how it happened, Zuri." Christian was shocked, happy, and overjoyed at the same time as he looked at her.

"Oh." Zuri blushed as understanding surfaced; she smiled at him. "Of course you can, you were bloody there." She was slightly recovered from the shock.

"I take it that you both are happy about the baby and want to keep him or her?" Doctor Turks asked them.

"Of course," they replied simultaneously.

"Good, you are five weeks pregnant. I am going to send you to Doctor Rene Anderson. She'll take good care of you. She's also a military doctor right here in this building, one floor up. This is her card. Call her and make an appointment as soon as possible."

"Thank you, doc." Christian rose on his feet and shook the doctor's hand over his desk. Zuri followed and did the same with a smile, slightly shock.

"No, Dr. Zuri I thank you for what you do. We'll take good care of you as you have done for all the officers here. Congratulations again." Doctor Turks concluded. Christian pocketed the card, pulled his cellular phone out as they left the office, and called Rae Jean. They were outside standing by the car as he opened the door and tuck Zuri in; she was processing the pregnancy.

"She is fine. Overworked with not much sleep. I am taking her home and put her to bed." He told her.

"Oh good. She needed it." Rae Jean informed him.

Rea Jean wanted to know if to cancel the next day so Zuri can have a nice long rest.

"Yes, that's sounds perfect, Rae Jean. Thank you.

"What was that, Christian?"

Christian occupied the driver's seat and looked at her. He drew in a breath when he saw her nipples taut through her dress.

"I told Rae Jean to cancel your afternoon appointments and we agreed tomorrow as well, any objections."

"None. I need the rest and any excuse to spend time with you."

"I think you need a massage and some heavy tender loving care. I know the right person for all of it." He grinned at her as he kicked the engine into life, green eyes twinkled devilishly. He put the car in reverse and drove them to the apartment.

The ride home was a quiet silent one. They both were processing the news and were thinking about the change ahead of them. Christian was thinking about a bigger place and trying to figure out how to make it work for Zuri, their baby, and her work. Zuri, on the other hand, was thinking about how she can divide her work with whom to have more time off. Who is qualified to take over some of her work. She must have dozed off. The next thing she knew was that she was lying on the bed with Christian holding her.

"Zuri, my love. You are exhausted. How about a warm bath?"

"Yes, I needed one desperately and a glass of wine, well, milk, warm please." She said dryly.

Christian pulled her closer and popped a kiss on her lips. "We're going to have to be knowledgeable about our pregnancy and the baby and everything. I am clueless."

"I am too, Christian. It's scary when it's something or someone …yippee when it's a new experience." Her voice trembled when she realized that she's carrying a life. Her hands automatically touched her stomach. Christian seeing this cover her hand with his for a few minutes.

"Why does it feel like that for us, scary?"

"Good point, love. We fell into each other's life so unexpectedly, we're still here together, having a baby." She replied good-naturedly.

This true love they found in each other is a relaxed state that increased blood flow to the lips and hands. It's accompanied by open emotional and physical behaviors. Deep breathing is the body response that facilitated and generated contentment, arousal, and cooperation between them. The tender feelings and sexual satisfaction experienced entailed parasympathetic arousal; a physiological opposite of the fight or flight state. It mobilized fear and anger with a parasympathetic pattern dubbed by relaxation and calm. He recalled the description from one of her books.

"I guess love counters all."

"Yes." Zuri was kneeling on the bed. She leaned into her lover and kissed him eagerly for a long time. As she pushed on his chest to move from him and off the bed, she turned and connected her eyes with his, "yes, Christian love, do counter all, including us." She blew him a kiss and walk into the bathroom.

Christian remained there for a while and brought himself under control. He was trembling with pleasure, as much as she was due to her looking at him with such deep profound love. Never mind she never told him she loved him, nonetheless, he is feeling her love this very minute.

Zuri was in the bathtub when Christian walked in and kissed her on his lips. Her eyes slowly opened and she lazily said, "what are you up to, sailor?" "Sailor, huh? Since when did I become one or are you trying to make me into one?" He wickedly grinned at her.

"I figured you might want come sail with me in this massive boat and you wanna take your anchor and anchored me down until I can't breathe." She lovingly smiled at him.

"I believe my sweet love, I have anchored you." Looking at her stomach, regardless it was covered with foam. "I do want to take your breath away."

"Oh, good cos I have you till .... mmmm for a long while." Zuri's eyes closed for a split second; then opened and connected them with his light green ones again. Christian leaned into her and kissed her lovingly for a few minutes. He pulled himself to his full length and walked to the door.

"I figured you should relax and rejuvenate your energy for when I get back. I'm going and get us food." On thinking this through, he added. "Food for three for today and then some for tomorrow. I don't want to do anything. I want to spend it in bed with you. I want to touch and kiss you all over."

Before she could reply he disappeared. Zuri leaned her head on the ridge of the tub and closed her eyes. She was exhausted and wanted the very same her lover wanted. She loved it when he takes charged the way he does. She loved the way he touched her and know exactly what she needed from him. Life had become much more, more meaningful since Christian came into her life. They are going to have a baby, a baby that expressed their union of true love. What more could she possibly want in her life to make it fruitful? There is nothing, nothing more beautiful than having Christian as her life partner and his child, their child.

Christian walked into the bathroom half an hour later and looked at Zuri, the mother of his child. He knew she would be asleep in the bathtub as she had done so many times before. Today, he stood and watched her; his love for her sweep over him. He pulled the plug out of the socket from the bathtub, took his clothes off, and left them on the floor. He turned the tap on and took a hot quick shower. He returned to the bathtub, turned the hose on warm, and washed Zuri off from the suds that stayed on her. He lifted her out from the bathtub. He was towel drying her hair as she sat on the edge of the bathtub. She sleepily opened one warmth mischievous soft brown eye and wickedly grinned at him.

Christian tried to keep his face in a serious stance; he knew that his eyes gave him away. He had read her eyes and knew she would be ready to have some long hours of hot lovemaking. He toweled his hair damp. He had let the water of their bodies dripped dry. The somewhat drying on the body without a towel had a sensuous fusion that gave more zest to arousal. It felt different from a towel dry skin.

Zuri was watching Christian with half-closed eyes as he toweled dried his hair. He was looking at her body when he became aware that she was no longer half asleep. He let the towel slid to the floor and melted soft brown and green eyes as one. He picked her up and took her to the bedroom and put her to sit on the dresser. She put out her hand to hold his erection, playing with it as her tongue ran over her upper lip and next to the lower one. Never once did they break eye contact.

Christen wanted her now! He wanted her mouth, her breast, and her warm core that make her constantly call out his name. He had to let it go and let her do what she does best, make love to him. Feeling the hardness of him quivered in her hands, she began to kiss him spontaneously everywhere she can blindly touch. Her hand was working in long slides up and down his erect shaft. She could feel the intensity of his sexuality vibrating into her; she returned it by planting kisses on his body. Christian was watching her as they become more intensified with the sexual sensations combined with their energy of love. Another minute He decided to give her another minute before taking charge and pushed himself into her warm zone of sexuality.

"Christian," Zuri whispered in surprise. She pulled him into her closer with her legs wrapped around his waist and leaned back with her hands supporting her body. Her head touched the wall behind her for support as Christian nuzzled her nipples and gave her a love bite on her neck. She let go of some wild unheard sound that came from deep within. She was lifted and carried somewhere. She was too breathless to be bothered. Wherever Christian go would be sexy for her. Her head was rested on his shoulder; he was still in her. She deliberately contracted her pelvis muscles.

Christian felt the contract and she kept it there. He was seated in the chair next to the window a few feet away from the dresser. She drew herself straight and settled her knees on either side of his hips still holding the contraction on his penis. She grinned wickedly at him. He kept the eyes connected as he gently smacked her on one of her backside cheeks. He watched as different emotions played havoc in her beautiful brown eyes. He smiled and pushed her off from him. Eyes still connected, he pulled her towards as she climbed abroad his manhood and he pushed her down quickly.

A new note left their lips as she straddled him and contracted; he pushed and contracted simultaneously.

The sensations they received intensified a notch higher. He pulled in a sharp breath when he saw what she was doing. She was strengthening the sensations so powerful that it will heighten his orgasm. He wrapped his hands around her waist to lift her up and down his erection. She settled in him absorbing his length into her warm zone. The insistent rhythm inside them began to make it impossible to move slowly then it picked up a high-pitched electrifying sensation that they both gasped out loud.

Christian's voice ripped out from him as he let go of his laser beams into her. "Oh, Zuri, Zuri my love."

Zuri released her contractions and let out her own sounds of exoticism as she reached into her world of ecstasy. She lifted her head and kissed Christian for a very long time. His hands caressed her body. Eyes attached sending messages of love as heart rate slowly returned to normal.

Christian heard Zuri's stomach growled, laughed as he broke eye contact and looked at her stomach.

"I guess I better feed you two." He helped her off from him. He bent and kiss her stomach. "I am going to enjoy watching you grow." He collected her robe and put it on her body.

"It would be interesting to experience the growth of a child. Oh, Christian, I'm beyond joy right now." She threw her body on the semi-clothed marine looking at her with tears in his eyes. He held her for somewhat a few minutes until he heard her stomach growled again.

"I feel our daughter is trying to tell us something." He held her hands and they walked to the kitchen.

"Daughter huh?" Zuri said puzzled as she took two plates and cutlery giving the plates to her lover and setting the table with placemats, napkins, and cutlery. Christian put some vegetables, rice, fish with gravy onto the places. They were having Chinese food.

"Yes, a daughter then I'm ordering a son. I think two children is enough?"

"Aye Aye, sir." Zuri kissed his back as she passed him talking two glasses from the cupboard opposite where he was standing. "Two beautiful children it is."

"Do you want more?"

"It doesn't matter to me. I never thought of having children, this is wonderful, and having you with me is exciting beyond what I had ever planned with my life. I am thrilled, overjoyed, and over the moon, the Marine Moon, that is." He breathed out.

"You are my Marine Moon." He pulled her into him and planted a long loving kiss on her lips. He let her go upon hearing the growling in her stomach.

As they eat, he told her they need a bigger apartment. "There's going to be lots of changes in our life. We're going to have to be patient with each other as we work through whatever occurs."

"Christian love I concur. I'm going to see if the military will permit me to bring in the four civilians I was training before I joined them. I am putting Rae Jean in charge of the group training, I have to find someone to overseas the whole program."

"You are going to have to rest a lot more. Maybe you should split your day into two. I can drop you off at nine in the morning, pick you up at elevenish, you can have a healthy lunch and a rest before you return to the afternoon shift. I can drop you off at two and pick you up at eight. You can have someone do the paperwork with the officers and the little other things that Rae Jean does. She can focus on the bigger group counseling. You are going to need another assistant and also Rae Jean."

"Oh, thank you. I was trying to figure it out, I am bloody mentally exhausted I can't even think."

"Oh good, you approved. If you tell me what you are looking for as an assistant, I can go find them for you."

"A male assistant. I want to have various people work for me. A black gay male assistant. Can you find him?" Christian looked shocked, frowned in wonderment as the information sank in. Upon receiving and understanding what she was asking him, he roared with laughter. "You want me to find a black gay male assistant?"

"Why, Christian, do you have a problem with that?"

"Huh, not the gay part just me looking for one."

"Oh, Oh, you think he would think me handsome sexy hunk wants his body?" Zuri seeing this picture roared with laughter.

"Ya think that's funny?"

"Christian, you asked how you can help, I told you what I want and now you have a problem with it." Zuri was still laughing as she pushed her plate away from her.

"Guess that would teach me not to offer my help so eagerly. How in the hell am I going to do this?"

They stood up and stacked the dishes into the sink. Zuri rinses them off and put them into the dishwasher. She turned to see where Christian was and saw he was sitting on the sofa deep in his thoughts. Christian held her hand as she sat next to him. He let go of his thoughts and expressed them to her. "I would do anything for you. I can't look for a black gay assistant for you, Zuri. I just can't do it. I don't have what it takes."

"Relax my love. I was playing with you. I have one that will work out."

Christian looked at her with his mouth slightly parted, realizing what she did. Zuri laughed and planted a kiss on his lips. Perfect!

6

The new day dawned too quickly for the lovers; they had much to talk about, however, very little was discussed about their pending plans for the future. Zuri curled body lay on the sofa with her head resting on a cushion that was on Christian's leg. He's drinking a beer and watching a football game, playing with strands of her hair

She had called Rae Jean and discussed hiring Cory Mattson for the assistant job. Rae Jean would do group counseling while Zuri will do individual counseling coupled with therapy. This would free up some time for her to rest and give birth to a healthy baby. She hadn't told Ray Jean about the pregnancy as she wanted to do it in person. She spoke with her two associates who were on standby upon approval from the military for permission to assist her in the coming months. She had emailed General Aaron Flynn and requested permission for her associates. She did mention to him about her pregnancy; Rae Jean faxed all the necessary documents for the approval of her associates to commence work as soon as possible.

The football game went into overtime. She had fallen asleep; she felt Christian lips on hers and heard on television. She turned over to have more access to his lips, he pulled her to him, she sat on the side of his leg. He was shirtless and the tan he acquired in Barbados is a very light one. His eyes were pearly light and shun bright. Christian had emotionally traveled a long distance from those haunted days of sorrow. Green and brown eyes mated as she looked at him.

"What mmm, how would you feel if we go and look at the land for our log cabin? I think we should start building it before our children are here, we have something to retire."

"Yes, yes, yes. Let's do it!" She enthusiastically expressed as she moved from beside him and sat in his lap. She was all ready to listen. He moved his hands across her breast gently crunching her nipples beneath his palm. He felt them stand erected on his touch and his manhood dance to his play. He moved her so she can sit on him, however, she sat on his knees. Zuri undid the button of his shorts and pulled his briefs down over his erection. While she stroked his manhood, his hands shoved both his shorts and briefs under his backside, his feet waggled them completely off. He parted her robe so she sat naked on him with her legs tucked at either side of him.

She found her spot and nestled there. She played with the few hairs on his chest moving slowly to his nipples. He watched her as her tongue moved over them slightly gauzing them with her teeth. Zuri took hold of his firm manhood and gently stroked it. Eyes contract was broken as Christian shivered. She let go before he pre-ejaculated. He gripped her backside and put her on top of him. He held her in place as she straddled him, sliding down smoothly. She sank on his length and leaned back to begin enjoying the ride. Christian face was level with her breasts and he began kissing them, barely touching them at first, then he lowered his neck and buried his face in the valley between her breasts. He kissed his way to a nipple and felt it harden then moving over the other one and took it fully into his mouth.

He raised his head and gave her a long loving kiss which she answered him as their tongues mated. He lowered his head and took her nipple again between his lips and nipped it with his teeth. Her head fell back upon her shoulders and her back arched way past his knees. She surrendered to the hot urgency of his caress as he tasted the other nipple then he pulled it deep into his mouth. He raised and kissed her possessively. He moved his head down again and kissed one breast and the next, building a rhythm changing angles from side to side teasing and tasting her completely.

She anticipated the movement of his mouth, each stroke, and pick up a steady rhythm. Her hand behind his head guided him as well as her sound of music to what pleased her. She closed her eyes as his mouth opened to take as much as he can of her breast then settled on a nipple drinking in her sexual scent tainted with rose. A hand squeezed the other as she watched him devouring her. The moment became intensify with sexual energy as their hips mated, adding more enjoyment to the finale. She felt her climax spiraling as sensations exploded into a burst of exquisite pleasure from Christian to her and back to him again. Zuri threw her head back, arched her spine, and rode his crest up and down, back and forth as she heard Christian's sound of music exploded into a heavenly delight in her neck.

The next day Christian drove Zuri to work and off to a park. Yesterday, all day they play with each other, talked about the upcoming addition and names associated with their child. He wanted to sort out his emotions and think things through. Massive changes are coming to him; he wanted to make sure he is secure with his choices and feelings. More now than any other time in his life he has a reason for living. Does he want a purpose? How does he feel about staying home and taking care of Zuri and their daughter? How does he feel that Zuri pays for most everything? Money is automatically transferred to their joined account so that there is never a shortage. He contributed to what he can and pays all the bills. Zuri never asked about any of it. How's the cabin going to work out for him knowing she'll be paying for it, most of it?

Christian sat for a long time thinking about nothing as he allowed his brain to sort those questions through before adding more to them. Logic prevailed and guided him to reality and truth. He knew that Zuri had given him a reason for living. She does the same for the other officers, that is something he will never stop her from doing. She had also allowed him into her life, he was the one who cared for her on those long tiring night. For him, that was a pleasure; he's not fighting, he's creating and giving pleasure. He understood as he briefly reflexed upon his past when he saw his squad all killed in a single blast from a missile and a field full of IDs, leaving him the only survivor. He witnessed and lived through hell for years in the military service. All that emotional suppression had taken a toll and he had paid dearly for it.

Then it hit him hard, there was no pain! The attachments to all his painful experiences were all gone and as he looked back now he realized that no, he felt that it was someone else and not him. This is what it must have felt to be a witness in your own life. He was reading some of Zuri's spirituality books while he was soul searching and found out that detachment from painful experience is the key to living life. Zuri had clear the energy of pain from him and told him he needed to invest in himself and discover his purpose. He didn't care that he was the one staying home and she works. No, he would care less. He would care for her, their daughter and son, and the house. He is overboard with joy as that is better than what he had endured in the military service. He has no regrets about his service to his country. He had learned hundreds of things being in the military and love being a Marine. The wars were what he does not like and what happened to his men.

Those experiences made him who he is and taught

him how to appreciate this present life. The question is how does he feel about the current upcoming change of events? He would welcome being a father and felt joy in his heart. He would be a darn good one as good as a partner he is with Zuri. The question that keeping surfacing and haunting him is what's his purpose in life? A wide smile tugged at Christian's lips and warmth poured from his heart into his eyes as he went down memory lane with Zuri and their love-making. No, he's a magnificent lover, a wonderful partner according to Zuri. The funny thing is he felt it. Another thought surfaced, Zuri never told him that she loves him! Tracing their time together, he was the one that kept telling her he loved her; never once had she mentioned it. How come he never realized this before? Oh! How does he feel about that? Christian checked into his emotion of true love and found that he felt loved by Zuri and that was the reason he never realized she never told him she loves him differently, through her behavior. Does it matter?

Yes, two things in his life mattered, his purpose and Zuri saying she loves him. With the decision made, Christian pulled himself off the bench, climbed into the jeep heading in the direction of the supermarket. He made another decision as he entered the supermarket and pulled a cart to do their shopping. He'll wait until Zuri is ready to tell him she loves him. He remembered the conversation in Barbados when she told him she cannot give him something she doesn't have in her. She does have love in her; he realized, however, voicing it was her conflict.

Grant you, she's forever exhausted. She has expressed her love to him every day, however, she does not have the words to deliver that message to him. He would think that Doctor Zuri Anana Curruni would, considering what she does for a living. Then again she gave so much to others and talk all day that maybe she cannot talk when she's home. This would explain the silence from her every day he picked her up from work. He stopped thinking of justification and agreed that he wanted Zuri to verbalize "I love you" to him. Christian remembered the times the silence worked. He would hold her in bed each night. Come to think of it, they rarely talk when she works, only when she is off and well-rested, which had been far and few times. They are still young in their relationship. It's back to one question, what's his purpose in life?

By the time Rae Jean dropped Zuri home, Christian was on the computer and telephone with a plan that served his purpose. Zuri found him as he blew her a kiss while talking into the phone. She kissed him on his neck. She looked up at their laptop and what she saw shook her. She left him and made a call to the manager of her company. "We found the man we are looking for, I will be right over." She took a quick shower and added a dress to her budding body. She hurriedly returned to Christian and waited patiently for him to finish his conversation. It was another half an hour before Christian joined her on the sofa. He pulled her to her feet and kissed her for a very long time.

"Have I told you how much I love you?"

"Of course, last night and this morning. You haven't told me lately." Zuri connected her eyes with his and viciously flirted with him, next, her eyes warm with love became serious as she remembered what she saw on the laptop.

"What was that on the laptop I saw?"

"My purpose in life," Christian told her and kissed her neck.

"Huh, what?" She leaned back looking at him puzzled frown on her forehead.

He kissed the frown away, "I opened my company for my architecture and computing designing. I can work at home."

"Oh, how fabulous." Zuri was over the moon and wanted to charm in and let him in on her plan, however, she knew this was important for him, she let him continued.

Christian pulled her on him as he sat on the sofa. His hands were holding hers as their eyes remained in contact. "I started it this morning. I don't have all the semantic as of yet. I'm going to do it with some, mmmm four other officers like me, engineers, I have to get the company registered and set up the whole thing so we can work at home. Two of the other officers are in wheelchairs and they are home taking care of their family. The other officer will be doing the physical maneuvering for us, he is single. Yes, they all told me they were in your program." He gave her a long loving kiss.

"Well, love." Zuri pulled herself off from his body and pulled his hand to her. "I don't have time to sit here and make love to you. I have a surprise, how about driving me to the surprise."

Christian loves surprises and was out the door before he asked her. "What, how many surprises? One, two, or three."

"This is a big one, it has to do with your purpose."

"My purpose?" He was on the main road heading to the military base.

"Turn off to the right on the road there." She pointed in the direction and stated where to go.

"I love taking orders from you." Christian guided her out of the car.

"Yes, you do." Remembering the times they made love and she guided him to her zones. She blushed.

They had entered a building and six men were there working with computers. They turned as she entered through the door. "I have the perfect solution to our situation. Here's a computer designer." She announced to them all.

"Ah, Lieutenant it's good of...."

"There will be no rank when you work for me."

Zuri turned to Christian, "we were on the verge of looking for someone to put my program in digital format, I don't have to lecture anymore or trained anyone. I would be spending very little time in counseling or training." She looked at and him than the others who were looking at them.

"Welcome aboard, Christian." They all chimed in and shook his hands.

Christian was completely taken aback and surprised that he was speechless. He had not even registered his company and he has a job. How beautiful is life!

"There's a lot of work that needs to be done before our baby is born. I want to retire with you in the woods." Zuri smiled at him with zest in her heart.

"Congratulations." They all hugged Zuri and shook Christian hands again.

"What's all this celebrating about? You should be working." Rae Jean walked into the room with a latte in her hand. Upon seeing Rae Jean she stopped and asked. "What are you doing here? You should be home with her feet up. Don't you work enough? I got this. Really?"

"Thank you. Christian will design the program. We should have a latte machine here."

"If I've known you would be here I would have gotten you one." Rae Jean replied.

"Oh no, you don't. She has to quit those and all unhealthy food for the little one, she can be born healthy."

"How you know about that, Tom?" Rae Jean wanted to know.

"I've got six kids."

"Tom, you've got to want? How the fuck you did that? You are in a wheelchair for peace sake?" Rae Jean questioned him with a puzzled look on her face.

"All the more reason. I am crippled yes, its works you know, not all of me is crippled. The kids are the results of our creativity." Tom concluded and turned back to this computer when everyone started to laugh.

"Okay, everyone back to work. Fun is all over." Rae Jean told them. She then turned to the Christian and told him. "You can take her home and start working tomorrow after you drop her off." To Zuri, "you are going home and rest."

"I am and thank you for all you do for me, Rae Jean." She held Christian's hand leading him through the door. She had informed her of their upcoming birth over dinner last week and how Christian ordered a daughter and a son. Rae Jean followed them and told them that Pong Jung is coming in tomorrow and wanted to take them to dinner. "He's spending a few nights."

"Just as well, I have to tell him about our pregnancy."

Christian assisted her into the jeep, leaving the door open, walked over to the driver's seat, and started the vehicle. Rae Jean shoved the door closed while Zuri zoomed the window down. Rae Jean leaned on the window.

"You looked tired; you know you can come in tomorrow at ten and leave early. I can manage group counseling now that Cory will be joining us. I will have him complete his application."

"On his first day?"

"Well, Christian will be working tomorrow. I bet you didn't even ask him. You shove him into it when you discovered another one of his talents."

"Oh, point taken. See you tomorrow at ten, Rae."

Christian waited until Rae Jean was out of the danger zone then he reversed and drove in the direction of their home. Zuri laid her head back, close her eyes, and rest for a few minutes.

"Christian, do you mind doing the design for us?"

"No, I don't. Thank you for asking."

"You are welcome and I am so sorry for taking you for granted. All I am thinking about is making more room in my life for you and our baby. I just was so excited that you can do the design that I never for one moment thought you might not want to do it. I am so sorry, my love."

"That's okay. We are bound to mess up with the boundaries. We don't have enough time to talk about negotiating new boundaries. There is so much to adjust to in such a short time. It takes my breath away."

"If I can sit and think……..then oh, when I sit still I fall asleep and then in my free time, I am too busy making love to you." Zuri turned and smiled, laughing.

Christian had parked the car, leaned over, and gave her a quick brush on her lips. He climbed out and went to her side of the jeep, assisting her out. Zuri leaned into him, took her time, and gave him a long loving kiss.

"The job will pay about two hundred and fifty thousand dollars a year. Since you know the owner you can negotiate for more. I must warn you, I am not going over an extra one hundred thousand dollars. That's my limit. I stand on firm ground." Zuri stamped her right foot on the ground and lost her balance doing it due to her exhaustion. Christian was amused, took hold of her in time before she hit the ground.

"One day soon we'll have all the time to work our disagreements out. I am glad you read my book on relationships. It helps that you understand and we are at the same mutual level of love. I do need to be reminded sometimes." She kissed him again, taking no notice of what just took place, and changed the topic of conversation.

"What are you going to name your company?"

They were walking into the apartment and as he closed the door went into the kitchen to fix dinner. Zuri took the plates out from the dishwasher to set the table.

"I was going to put our daughter and son's name together and form something.

Vincelette Incorporated I settled on."

"Our daughter?" Zuri rubbed and looked at her

stomach. Christian walked to her and kissed her stomach.

"Yes, we are having a daughter and a son."

"Aye aye, sir. We have to come up with two names."

"You think." Christian returned to dinner. He put two pieces of fish and two Japanese yams in the oven and heated some water to pour on top of the asparagus.

"I think for the girl we should have her named Christina Anana Vincelette or Anana Christina Vincelette."

"I like Anana Christina Vincelette. For our son?" Christian charmed in, "let's asked Pong Jung what his name is and include one of it."

"Oh, you have a point. Pong Jung spoiled me tremendously and it would be good to include him in our family. I do want to add Christian into our son's name. It is such a sexy strong name." Zuri smiled into his eyes as Christian added the leftover rice to the boiling water before straining it in the sink.

"Yes, it is. Is that what attracted you to me." He asked her as he poured boiling water on the asparagus and over it.

"No, Marine Moon."

"Marine Moon, when you said it. I wanted to know what you mean." Zuri had a seriousness to her face as she looked at him.

Christian left what he was doing and pulled her into his arms. Zuri pulled the kitchen towel off his shoulder and looked at him. He held her waist and pulled her closer to him. He said over her head.

"When I was lying in Afghanistan after the terrorists killed all my men and I was waiting for the military to rescue me, I was slipping in and out of consciousness, I saw the moon and your face was sometimes in it. I thought the moon belonged to me because I used to dream..." He moved her away from him and looked into her big brown beautiful eyes. "I used to fantasize about meeting you. I was hallucinating. I didn't know the difference between illusions, fantasies, and reality.”

“Oh, I am so glad I meant something to you then. I remember you standing watching me leave the base and my heart went out to you. Do you think that our hearts joined that day in Afghanistan? With me watching down at you standing there so alone and lonely looking up?”

Christian gave her a long deep kiss, expressing his gratitude and love. Zuri had to push him away from her to breathe. “Let’s believe that’s how we became one, visually then, presently mentally, emotionally, and physically. It’s very romantic, I think. Let’s work on our verbal communication. We have lots to do in that department.”

“Aye Aye, sir.” Zuri saluted and stepped back from him with a wide grin on her face. Christian took the kitchen towel from her as he walked away and smacked her backside with it.

“I love it when you agree with me. It’s very sexy.”

“You’re sexy, Christian. You have a hot body that doesn’t want me to leave it alone. I love touching and kissing you and ………..”

“Hang on, sexy lady. Dinner first, we have to feed you and Anana.”

“Oh sweet love and play later, me thinks.”

“So what is your real name”?” Zuri asked Pong Jung for the first time since she knew him. They were all seated in a Chinese restaurant having a variety of food.

“Why, you got tired of calling me, Pong Jung. I remembered trying to correct you as a little girl and the more I did, you continued to call me Pong Jung.”

“Pong Jung I called you, so what is it?

“Lei Chang Donghai.”

“Good Christian, we shall call our son Lei Christian Anil Vincelette.”

“Sounds good to me.” Christian leaned and kissed her hair.

Pong Jung didn’t know what to believe. He was looking

at them both waiting for one of them to explain what the hell is going on.

"We are pregnant. Christian says the baby is a girl. I don't care."

"And you want to name your son after me." Pong Jung said surprisingly.

"No, all the names are part of someone's name, a person we love."

"How far are you?

"We're six weeks pregnant. Christian hit the egg at the first go. No, I was not on any birth control pills and no, we didn't take precautions and no, we didn't plan on having children."

"Well, I'll be. You are too old for me to give you a lecture, Zuri. I am very happy that you found love. Thank you for making my Zuri happy, Christian." He extended his hands to Christian who met his hand halfway over the top of the table.

"You're going to have to tell both your family. Where are you going to live?" Pong Jong looked from one to the other.

Christian looked at Zuri, then to Pong Jong, and answered. "We are going to have to take some time off and go and see them, I guess. We are still planning things through."

"We are going to buy some land in the woods and built a five-bedroom logged cabin. Christian has, well, he's working on the blueprint of what he wanted." Zuri finished for them.

"What about what you wanted?" Pong Jung raised an eyebrow and inquired.

"Oh, that's been incorporated since in Barbados."

"What? You build a house before, anything else?

"It just happened, alright. Our relationship isn't typical. We make our rules up as we go. We are still trying to figure how, let it go, will you, Pong Jung?"

"Oh alright. As long as you both are happy that's all that matters. I do want to......."

"Oh boy, here it comes." Zuri grinned at Christian and back at Pong Jung.

"You don't even know what I was going to say."

"Yes, I do. You were going to tell us your plans about how you are going to contribute. You were going to choose your words carefully to include Christian. Normally, you would just tell me your plans and I had to follow. I usually do." Christian listening to the exchange between the two of them and knew that this was something he would not want to come between or interfered with. Besides it was all done with love, however, he turned to Zuri and asked, "Why is that?"

"Because my love, Pong Jung is an excellent planner and my life goes smoothly with his planning." Zuri looked at him, blew a kiss to Pong Jung.

"Well, since you put it that beautifully. I was going to suggest that you let me make arrangements for your family to get together, you can be there and let them know about the two of you and your coming child. Then..."

"Daughter," Christian informed Pong Jung

"Oh." Pong Jung said surprisingly. "I see." He smiled at Christian. "I would like the address of your family, Christian. Please let them know that I would be calling to make arrangements. I guess young man you have to let them know about you and Zuri. Then..."

"I already did when we moved in together. I have not told them about our unborn daughter. I agree that both families should meet, Thank you."

"ok, before we'll go see the families. I want you to show me where you want the log cabin built. I want to do it for you as a wedding gift, ah, mmm well, are you getting married?" Pong Jung asked looking at Zuri, next to Christian and back to Zuri.

Christian knew Zuri should be the one to answer; he

looked at her. Zuri leaned over and quickly leaned on the side of Christian's body. She turned to her Godfather with a sweet smile. "We settled that in Barbados. No, we are going to live together. I will add Vincelette to Curruni as soon as I have time." She turned to Christian and gave him the same sweet smile. His light green eyes turned lighter if that's possible. He grinned with love and kissed her.

"Thank you for asking me about taking my name." He said sarcastically yet charmingly.

Pong Jung seeing an opening and not a man to wait to make his plans be known, infused the other bit of news to the lovers. "Okay. Well, in that case, I want to give you both a "Living" together gift. With your daughter on her way, you both should redo your will. Anything I do for you both my grand goddaughter gets it, it is in a trust, make sure you have that clause in your will. I will let my lawyer get in touch with you and Susie."

"You still have Susie? I thought she retired." Zuri asked him, raising an eyebrow.

"Susie is my main assistant." He informed Christian and continued to fill Zuri in on the latest about Susie. "She only does my biding. She retired to the south of France with her son and family. I have Lea and Peter doing the bulk of it."

"I guess you are never going to retire? Zuri asked him.

"No, I will not. I like work and since I don't believe in marriage I had a very good time with my life."

"And God the father, I enjoyed you spoiling me, I have a very good time spending your money. You know why I have so much. I never spend any of mine."

There was laughter from the men and Zuri joined in with them. The rest of the time was spent talking about Christian's new company, the log cabin, and her arrangement of taking her program digital.

Two weeks later, Christian received confirmation on

their pending trip. He called Cory and gave him the dates that Zuri needed to be off. He then e-mailed Rae Jean as she was in group counseling with the dates. He called his parents and found out that they had already received airline tickets to travel to Austria as well as his siblings and family. Christian had to admit that Pong Jung worked quickly and very effectively.

In another two weeks, Pong Jung's helicopter landed on the pad close to Zuri's office. After meeting with several higher rank officers, Christian and Zuri joined him as they headed into Wisconsin to look at the land that Christian wanted to build their dream house.

The Agusta Westland AW 109 took five hours including a stop for fuel. The aerial view didn't say much except that it was next to a river. They found a clear spot and the pilot was ordered to land. In minutes they were out looking around not at the place for the log cabin; they were looking at the river.

There was silence from all three people looking at the surrounding filled with the sounds of animals. Zuri reached for Christian's hand and smiled into his eyes. She blushed and he kissed her for a minute, which she conveyed her approval and his happiness. Zuri realized that she has two men who loved her very much.

Pong Jung looked at them and his heart was filled with warmth and love. Zuri had found her life partner and he is part of their life. He had wished this for her ever since she was a little girl. He had wondered whether he would have been a part of her life with a partner. A heart filled with compassion as she does deserve the very best. He spoiled her not because he is her Godfather and he loved her because she had given much pleasure to others even the wild animals. He remembered the day he took her to the zoo in London when she was ten and she hated the animals all locked up with no freedom. She cried for days. He flew them to Zambia and show her that the animals do roam free. He donated a junk of change to the wildlife preserve in her honor and still does as of today.

Zuri has a heart full of love and very few knew her integrity. He is one proud Godfather. He looked at Christian and saw the same in him. Yes, they have much work to do with their relationship he agreed; he knows that they would make it. He believed in them. Besides whom would he leave his money when he dies; his grand godchildren are the only ones he will have and yes, he is going to spoil them too. He was thrilled that he will have two more people to spoil, his god granddaughter or son and Christian.

Pong Jung was a little concerned with how he would take Zuri's money and him spoiling her. He realized that Christian was not intimidated nor does he missed used her money. He's relieved; he decided he would let Christian dream come through. He would purchase all the land for them not just the land for the log cabin as he had planned. The boot camp is a great idea for him to offload some of this money. With a plan of action concerning his money, he joined the two lovers standing silently holding hands.

In the chopper once more, they headed to the private airport where his jet is waiting for the nine-hour flight to Austria for a two-week family get together. Pong Jung knew all of their families were there for the last twenty-four hours. He also knew the minute they were seated in the jet; Zuri would lay her head back in her seat and fall asleep. This would give him time to get to know Christian some more.

It was somewhere halfway into the journey, in the middle of their conversation on Pong Jung's heritage that Zuri woke up. She looked around and saw the two men she loved very much, talking. Then it hit her that she never voice, not once expressed her love for Christian since they were together.

"Oh, hell bells." She turned her head and looked out the window to the darkness that stared back at her. How can she forget something so important? What was she thinking? Every chance Christian gets he tells her and as she turned to look at him, she cannot believe that she never said "I love you" to him. She saw that they were drinking scotch and knew that this isn't a good time. She cannot go back and correct the past, she can only fix the present moment. With her decision made she joined them and sat next to her life partner.

"Oh, good you're awake, time for supper." Pong Jung rose on his feet and kissed her cheeks. "I'm going to get the hostess and let her know about super. Stay out of mischief, Zuri." He winked at her and left to find the hostess.

Zuri leaned her head on Christian's shoulders and yawned. He moved and encircled her into his arms. "Guess by the look of you, you had a good sleep. Have I ever told you how sexy you look when you sleep and how more sexy you look after you wake up." Laughing Zuri nestled into his shoulders, "I know why we make love mostly whenever I am awake, my love of my life, I am well rested to receive and perform." She turned, fixed her body to kiss him. They were still kissing when Pong Jung sat on his seat again. They were unaware of him and continued kissing. As they surfaced for air, they both realized that they were no longer alone.

"Well, as you two got acquainted, I can get back to telling Christian about my heritage."

"Did you tell him about the time you got into trouble with your grandfather because you used her karate trick to beat up a kid who teased you? Zuri asked him.

"Oh, Zuri that's a good one. I've forgotten about it." Pong Jung proceeded to tell Christian about that time in his life.

It was early morning when they arrived at the elegant

hotel in the heart of Vienna along Ringstrasse. Zuri knew to accommodate the families a floor was booked and she knew Pong Jung would put them in a suite. She had traveled with Pong Jung too many times including his and her family together in Hong Kong and all over the world not to know his behavior. She is well aware of the luxurious life he lives. She also knew that he will be paying for everything. How will Christian be taking this? She looked at him from the corner of her eyes as they were being booked into the hotel. His face was expressionless.

"Okay, we are all set to go to sleep. Everyone would be down at ten for breakfast in the ballroom." They were informed by Pong Jung as they took the elevator to the twentieth floor. "I'll go and sleep; you two can join us downstairs. I have my life partner Ana here with me; you can meet her. I figured it's time I come out and let you into my private life. We have been together for four years."

"Oh, Pong Jung I am so happy for you." Zuri threw herself into his arms and kissed him. He embraced her and they walk arms in arms until they arrived at their floor. He told her all about Ana, kissed her on both cheeks, and shook Christian's hand as he left them with the porter at their hotel door.

Christian tipped the porter as Zuri headed into the shower and turned the taps on. Christian soon found her there as water ran down her body. He felt his body sending him a message saying that he would love to explore more. He took his clothes off and let them joined Zuri's on the floor. He stepped into the shower and pulled Zuri's body to him. She laid the back of her head on his shoulders. His finger sought her warmth. Zuri gave out a soft cry of delight. His finger joined by another probed inside her, going deep and deeper. She succumbed to the liquid lounging in her veins as her heart rate hammered loud. She turned halfway and began to caress his erection. She used her nails to tease his lower manhood then traveled down and did the same before she cupped his sac. He quivered under her fingernails and cupping. He is on the verge of losing control altogether. She lowered herself on her knees as water poured between them.

Zuri's mouth opened and took his length in. His head was secured in his hands as he leaned back against the wall of the shower. The water heightened the sensations and pumped up the intensity of what was about to take place. Her tongue was lazy as she slowly used it to give his length long strokes. She picked up a rhythm as she delicately tongued the length of his head.

She gently squeezed his sac and took her two fingers and added pressure at the back in his sensors zone behind his sac; that did it for him; he lost control and shot into her mouth as she took all of him in again. He watched her swallowed and pulled her into his body. She turned the tap off and he weakly picked her up and put her on the sofa, sitting next to the bathtub. He kissed her breathlessly and toweled dry them. They walked to the bed and fell into each other's arms falling asleep within minutes. They woke to the sound of the phone ringing.

"Okay, my darling I've let you two sleep. It's time you join us here for tea. We'll see you in ten minutes." The female's voice told her.

"Mama, oh, heavens. We'll be there."

Zuri heard the shower and followed the sound. Christian was under it and she joined him to be freshened. "We overslept. That was my mother ordering us down for tea. Tea is at four in the afternoon. We sleep through lunch."

"Doctor Zuri Anana Curruni taking orders from her mother? I never thought I would see this." Christian kissed her parted lips and stepped out of the shower. She smacked him on his backside as he stepped past her.

In half an hour, with introductions made they were all sitting having tea and cakes. Zuri's dad turned and looked at her and Christian sitting together.

"I am excited that you found your true love. I have to give it to you. I was worried for a long time that you would not find a partner. I am happy it is Christian. Christian welcome to the Curruni family." Anil Curruni raised this teacup and salute them.

"Thank you, papa."

"I am in agreement with Anil. I never thought my son would be able to ever find love. Christian had pulled through a very long year and still is recovering from a....."His voice shook a little. Bringing himself under control he continued still a little shaky. "an attack in Afghanistan. I looked at my son and I am very happy to see his eyes held love and not rage." He turned to Zuri and raised his teacup to her. "Christian read all your books and I knew he was a fan. I never knew that you two would fall in love. Thank you, my dear, for what you have given my son." Christian senior smiled and sat down.

Both Zuri's and Christian's mothers stood up and looked at them. "I am thrilled that you two found each other. I know we don't see much of you Zuri. I hope we can as your father and I will be retiring in two months. We'll come and visit as much as you wanted." Jyoti concluded.

"I welcome you, Zuri, and thank you for what you have given my son. I never thought that I would ever see him so full of joy. I will forever be grateful for every......." Alana could not finish as tears flooded into her mouth. Christian left Zuri's side and held his mother until she bought herself under control. Someone had given her some napkins and she wiped the tears away. Everyone was quiet and waited for the next moment to take place. Zuri was on her feet as Christian comforted his mother and went to his father. She gave him a long hug and kissed both his cheeks. She turned to Alana and did the same.

Christian looked at Zuri and she nodded. They hadn't

planned a speech, however, she knew that Christian was going to tell them about their baby.

"Well, we are very happy to be here and meeting all of you," Christian told their families.

"Yes, Godfather, thank you very much." Zuri found Pong Jung's eyes and blew him a kiss.

"We're also happy to be in love and sharing this love with you. Zuri and I wouldn't be getting married."

"I'm going to add Vincelette to Curruni. We'll have a huge party to celebrate once the baby arrives."

"Yes, Zuri and I are ten weeks pregnant."

The families in the room uttered surprised; everyone was out of their seat giving the couple kisses and congratulating them except for Pong Jung who sat basseting in the glory of everyone. The fathers of the couple joined him and they were toasting the good future that would soon join the families.

Alana asked them if they had a name and knew of the sex of their child.

"Anana Christina Vincelette is her name and our son's name is Lei Christian Anil Vincelette," announced Christian.

"Oh, you are having twins." Sivan which meant shepherd was born in Turkey and spoke Kurdish asked in English. Sivan is the fifth in line of the Curruni family.

"Oh no, Christian thinks that we are having a girl and then he ordered a boy later on." Zuri corrected her.

"Thank you for naming her Christian, that's my middle name: Alana Christian Mary.

"I can babysit for you." Logan, the baby of the Vincelette volunteered.

" You are welcome, Alana." Zuri gives her a hug, "thank you" she turned to Logan and smiled. She turned to her side of the family as everyone returned to their seats including the various nieces and nephews. "I want to introduce Christian to each of you and you can introduce him to your family. There is Adnan, Paki, Cyrus, Tir, Sivan, Taran, Jaqson, Piken, and Nadia. They all stood up as she called their names. They introduce him to their family in chronological order. Christian introduced his family to her. There is Ryland, Charlene, and the potential babysitter, Logan. They follow suit and introduce their family to Zuri. Paki, Nadia, and Logan are single. Toasts were carried out throughout tea time. Christian never drank so many cups of tea in his life. He obliged and watched the flow of conversation between the families for the rest of the afternoon. Everyone mingled and talked right into dinner.

Red wines were served with appetizers and dinner was of European with wiener schnitzel made with beef for the meat-eaters, fish for the vegetarian, and Linzer Torte with Einspanner for dessert. They talked and laughed and talked some more, enjoying and celebrating each other. The waiters came and left and as the last dish went through the door, a band in the corner of the room started to play a tune. Music played, songs sung in various languages including both Christian's and Zuri's favorite American ones. The dance floor opened up and fathers danced with daughters, mothers with sons, husbands with wives, sisters with brothers, and both families intervened with each other, even Christian and Zuri had a few dances to themselves.

Pong Jung gave the party as usual and the flow of love poured out in abundance. As the night rolled on, nannies took the children away and the adults remained. Liqueur served and Pong Jung reminded everyone that they can drink and walk to their rooms; drank they did into the wee hours of the morning. Christian and Zuri were dancing for an unknown time when Pong Jung came and joined them on the floor. The music stopped and Zuri lifted her head from Christian's shoulder and looked to question why the interruption.

"I kept this news for the last."

"You are pregnant?" Zuri asked him. Laughter broke out.

"No, I am selling some of my business off. I can spend more time with you and I am volunteering to be the official babysitter."

"Oh, how wonderful." Zuri left Christian's arms and flew her body upon Pong Jung who welcome her with open arms. He is used to her actions; he's never tired of her hugs. "Did you get Ana's permission?" Zuri chimed in. Laughter broke out again. Everyone was congratulating Pong Jung for his new venture in life; they knew he was a workaholic, this is a huge improvement for him to relax and enjoy his life.

Christian was too buzzed from drinking the wine and liqueur to be shocked.

Tears rolled down his cheeks and he wiped them away, nonetheless, when Zuri planted a kiss on his lips moments later she tasted the tears of his joy.

7

Zuri had forgotten to verbally express her love to Christian. It came again to her in the night that she had not mentioned in the dawns that followed. She is seven months pregnant and trying to figure out how she had forgotten something so important. Upon their return from Austria, they were both working different hours. She was training other counselors to take over her counseling, getting the program digital and occupied with individual counseling with therapy. She tried to spend time with Christian, however, he became so engaged with getting his company started, working with others on her digital program, and adding the final touches to the blueprint for their log cabin that they hardly saw each other.

When they did it was usually in bed, cuddling. Most of the time, when Cory, her new assistant dropped her off at home in the evenings, Christian is not there. When she is off in the morning he is sleeping. The times they made love, which was far and few, belong to a few minutes in the wee hours of the morning when Christian rolled into bed as she woke up to start her day. The times a decision needed to be made and they had to make many were very quick conversation on the cell or text messages; Cory read her the message and replied to Christian her choices.

Christian can survive on four hours of sleep or go days without due to his Marine training, he told Anana a story of some sort before he sleeps. She heard him talking to their unborn daughter, he kisses her, pulled her in his arms, and falls asleep. He slept with one hand always on her stomach to feel Anana's kicking. Sometimes he spoke

150

to her particularly when she gives a very strong kick. Zuri would smile at his spoken words, "That's my girl, you go, girl, Anana is Daddy's girl."

In the haze of sleep, she loved him more for finding the time to be with their daughter. He stayed connected and in touch with her, regardless of what day he had or how fatigued he is from the various jobs. She, on the other hand, is having more difficulty in finding the right spot to sleep. Between Anana's activities at seven months and the short hours of counseling she still lacks a good eight-hour sleep. In between a minute here and there she would talk to their daughter, however, she would kiss the palm of her hand and rub her stomach, hoping Anana can feel her touch. The conversation between her and her daughter never stops. Although there was no confirmation on whether they are carrying a male or female everyone has settled on the child being a girl.

Zuri used to be furious with those parents who talk to their child without knowing the gender as if it was the other or who want one sex of a child and received the other. The disappointment was one thing, however, talking to an unborn unknown gender of a child can influence the sexual orientation of the child. Everything is energy. "I know our child is a girl," Zuri whispered. "I can feel the energy."

Christian knew this because she explained it to him. "Since everything is energy, talking to their child as if she is a girl when the child could be a boy will influence the character and personality. The child can be either bisexual or gay due to the energy transference." He didn't care because for one thing he has friends who are both bisexual and gay and if his daughter is, he would still love her.

Friends received emails not as often as before, while calls were returned to families between whatever free time are left. Pong Jung, Ana, and their parents will be here for the birth of their child, daughter at the end of August. Upon hearing the news, Christian had taken her home and made dinner while they caught up on each other lives. They spoke about how they would teach their daughter both of their worlds and how they will be there to guide her when she has a decision to make in her life. They both promised the other that they wouldn't be interfering parents, and allowed their children to experience life. They gave them support and be there for them when they are in pain, holding their hands until they are back on their feet again.

Discipline, manners, and independence were included in the conversation. Christian agreed to be the one to care for Anana as Zuri would have the time to train more counselors. By the time Anana was born, Christian would be working from home. They would hire a housekeeper/nanny to help them; the main thing is finding one.

Pong Jong had bought them the land and the log cabin was started to take shape. Christian had flown a few times to the site, sometimes with Pong Jong or Zuri to oversee the building. They had given the job to one of Christian's buddies who were in the Air Force, an honorary discharged veteran due to injuries and presently owned a construction company. They had hired military officers and unemployed construction workers to build the cabin as well as the other facilities for the officers who would be overseeing the boot camp.

The cabin will be ready by the time the Anana arrive in late August or mid-September. They made plans to have their son when Anana is two, closer to when Zuri would retire from counseling. She will be home with him and the children and can spend time together until they begin pre-school. They made plans without her ever telling Christian how much she loves him. She dialed his number to tell him she would be home late. Her message went to the recording. Oh, what a relationship!

"Cory, how are the two officers doing?" She was going through the closed files and stacking them in boxes for storage.

"Not good, doc, still critical. The suicide attempt was not a good job. I guessed they chicken out." Two officers had taken a shotgun to kill each other, however, they could not carry out their plan and the bullets went into their throat instead of their hearts.

"How many do we have on a suicidal watch?"

"Twenty-four. Are you ready to start? We have twenty-five worse of the worse out in the Hall waiting." Worse of the worse meant that officers are slow in letting go. They are having problems of past abusive experience coupled with war experiences that formed layer upon layer of deep-rooted anger; a double dose of Post Traumatic Stress Syndrome. It usually takes them some time to let go and adjust to life without pain.

"Send them all in. Let them bring their chairs."

"What? All of them, doc?"

"Yes, Cory, all of them and you stay and finished the files. Make sure you listen, you will know what to do with "de worse of de worse.""

Cory went out to inform the officers of the "Doc" decision. She's tired and wanted to go home to sleep. Anana seemed to agree and began kicking. Zuri's hands were upon her stomach feeling the kicks when the officers walked into her office. They all greeted her with "hi doc" and placed their chairs in front of her desk.

"Alright officers, you are going to have to help me out here. Anana is kicking a racket right now and I am exhausted. I'm going to ask questions and you're going to tell me how you feel. First of all, I want you to write your names on this sheet, I can see who is who and who is not taking part in this group counseling." Cory provided them a white paper and a pen. The first officer close to Zuri wrote his name and passed it on. An officer in the last row

asked, "What happened to the ones who don't answer?"
"And you are?" Zuri asked him quietly with a tired tone.
"Sargent Mendez, ma'am."
"Sargent Mendez, those of you who are not going to, refused to, or do not want to, will be seeing me for a longer period of time, for more intense therapy. It's your life and how you choose to live is your choice. Any more questions?" Zuri raised an eyebrow looking at all 30 officers.

Christian finished with the meeting he had with his two partners and listened to his messages. He heard Zuri's message and decided he would go over to see how her digital programming is doing. He was shattered and wanted to go home, a few minutes more wouldn't hurt him. He was glad that their offices were across from each other; he took the few steps into Zuri's office. Rae Jean says "we had enough for today and we are taking two days off. I left doc a message. Cory says there are officers on suicidal watch and the "Doc" is working late. "I called the suicidal doctor and told her to sedate the officers and told Zuri to go home." Rae Jean finished with don't question me attitude.

Christian was thrilled he wanted to kiss her, however, he said, "Thank you. I am going to pick her up and take her home. I am going to let her take the two days off and you too Cory. Thank you, Rae Jean." He was out the door before Rae Jean could breathe another breath. He was in the Hall in less than ten minutes it took him to drive there, speeding. He listened to hear if they were through with therapy as he approached the door; it was opened.

Zuri sensed Christian in the building and looked at the door as he appeared in it. "Come on in, we are almost done, continue officer." All eyes turned to see who it was and upon seeing Christian they all stood and salute him. Christian saluted them and walked to Zuri.

"Doc, we are all done for today. Go home and rest and

we'll see you tomorrow." Sargent Sanchez told her.

"No, the doc has two days off. She'll see you in two days at ten hundred hours." Cory informed them. He had followed Christian into the office. The officers picked their chairs up and as they left they verbalized, "thank you and have a good rest." After the last one left, Zuri turned to Cory with a frown on her face waiting for an explanation.

"Rae Jean called Doctor Mileson and told her to sedate the suicidal officers. She called me to have us all, even the company workers take two days off. There's a message on your phone from Doc Mileson. I guess I'll be off and see you in two days."

"Thank you, Cory. Yes, see you in two days. Have good lazy days."

"Oh, doc I planned to and you take care of yourself and Anana. Good afternoon to you both. Christian?"

"Thank you, Cory. Enjoy your days off."

Cory waved and left the office.

"Oh, help me up will you, sweetheart. Anana is kicking like hell. She'll be a stinker when she has to wait for anything."

Christian helped Zuri up with a wide grin on his lips with a "my girl" expression in his green eyes. He put his hand on her stomach to feel his daughter kissing Zuri in the process. After a little while, he reached for her purse, held her hand, and walked with her to the door into the Jeep. In twenty minutes they were home; he couldn't speed. Anana didn't like speeding and would kick a racket when he does; it was a very slow ride home. Christian helped her out from the Jeep into the apartment. "A bath is what we need. We have leftovers, Turkish."

"That's perfect, Christian. You know Anana doesn't like speeding, yet she likes spicy food. I'll run the bath." Zuri was taking her clothes off watching the water rise in the tub when Christian walked in. He went to help her and took her underwear off and held her hands as she stepped into the tub. His clothes were soon joining hers in the laundry hampered and he in the tub. There was a long silence as both felt comfortable with as words were not required. Christian washed his body first before taking the washed cloth from Zuri's hands and finished washing her body. He knew she was on the verge of falling asleep. He pulled the plug and emptied the water from the tub. He washed the suds off from him and climbed out of the water. Zuri had stood up and washed the suds off from her body. He put his underwear on, helped her out, and dried her body. She dressed; Christian held her hands as they walked out of the room to the kitchen to have dinner.

With dinner out of the way, Zuri left Christian to wash up as she prepares for bed. She was in it when Christian joined her and pulled her into his arms. She settled in and felt his warmth and love. She turned her head to face him.

He kissed her, conveying his love.

"Christian I lo …." He looked at her and she was fast asleep. He whispered, "I love you too Zuri." A smile sat on his face reached his light green eyes. He was ecstatic that she knew she never told him verbally that she loved him. She tried and that was good enough for him, at least for now. Even if she never says "I love you" knowing that she knew and does is good enough for him. He would not ask for anything more. Well, maybe a son.

Pong Jung looked at Anana and told her parents. "She looks just like me."

"Oh, Pong Jung, you'll never know how happy we are." Zuri smiled at him and then Christian. "I love you, Lieutenant Colonel Christian Andres Vincelette. I tried to say it for such a long time. I'm so sorry." Zuri was nursing Anana; Christian was sitting next to her as he watched his six-hour old daughter. Pong Jung was standing at the other side watching the bundle of joy being fed.

"Well, now I have an heir to my throne. Christian, I hope it wouldn't bother you. Anana is my heir."

"No, Pong Jung I don't mind. She's as feisty as her mother and she will manage money like her too. Thank you. Let's not tell her until she learns responsibility, integrity, and respect." Christian informed him as he looked at Pong Jung.

"Agreed." Pong Jung nodded.

Christian moved and took Anana from Zuri as she was full. He burped her gave her to Pong Jung who held her for a few minutes before returning her to Christian. "I have to go. I have a few meetings to attend. I have booked into the hotel for a month to help you out whenever you want a babysitter." Both of their parents were in the restaurant having dinner, calling all the family, and sending photographs of the newborn with her parents.

"Thank you, Pong Jung." Zuri acknowledged. He came and kissed her on her forehead, shook Christian's hand, and left. Christian pack the bags for home, turning to Zuri and his daughter; they were asleep.

In the weeks that followed, Zuri had many hands to assist her with Anana. Both grandparents and Pong Jung were there everyday, bathing, feeding, and playing with little Anana. Zuri pumped the milk from her breast when she needed to rest and sleep. They had moved into a three-bedroom single house. Although Christian was working at home, he still had time to take care of Anana, nevertheless, he left the caring for Anana to the others because they would be leaving and he would have his girls all to himself.

Zuri was counseling from home for a few hours every day. One of the rooms was set up as a conference counseling office she shared with Christian. He had set up a video feed and it worked just as good as if the officer was next to her. The officers who were in critical conditions spoke with Zuri while the others, who were on the last stage of recovery went to Rae Jean and the two other counselors who were monitoring officers and making various other responsibilities. The family came and visit in the months to come. Zuri continued to stay home and care for Anana. Christian announced that their home is complete and ready to be furnished. Zuri was shopping online when she is not nursing her daughter or counseling. Both grandparents agreed to stay on and Pong Jung came and went. The housekeeper/nanny, Martha, a female of sixty filled in when they went out to dinner.

There always seemed to be someone around and their new parents' love life went into hibernation. It was several months before Christian has the pleasure of Zuri making love to him. He had come home early one day and found no one in the house. He was dressing after a shower when he bumped into Zuri coming into the bedroom. He was about to pull her to him and gave her a long passionate kiss, however, Zuri had other ideas. She began unbuttoning his shorts; he watched her. She was in a blue dress; he unzipped and let it fall to the floor. When he saw her dress in a white lace top with a garter belt, no underwear, and stocking he lost it.

He allowed her to lift his gold mine out and beamed with pleasure as she massaged him between her hands; he began to grow strong and solid. She took the top of his manhood and covered it with her mouth. His hands were tangled in her hair holding and guiding her mouth as he watched her. He leaned his head back and savored every moment of pure delight. He felt every inch of him stretched more as her mouth covered all of him. He looked down at her and knew that any minute he would climax. He wanted to hold on a little longer and enjoy this gift that he was being given. "Oh, Zuri, let me........"

She did the unthinkable, cupped his sac, and added pressure behind his pleasure spot. She gave him a gentle squeeze and then used her tongue over the top of his manhood and pulled him into her mouth. He leaned his head back, made his music, and lost control. As soon as he caught his breath, he swept her into his arms and carried her across the bed. He laid her down gently kissed her breathlessly while his fingers played with her inner zone. He watched her closed her eyes, leaned her head away from him as musical sounds escaped from her deep within.

Zuri pushed her pelvis towards him as the sexual sensations became passionate. She had felt him slipped two fingers into her and found her inner core while his thumb bought the outer one, the clitoris to arousal. She trembled and buckled. The music became louder and she felt her whole body tingled with anticipation. She moved closer as he moved in for her kiss. She had to let go as fireworks of sensations exploded through her body and she climaxed into euphoria.

Christian played with her hair and kissed her lips as she surfaced for air. He was not done yet; he wanted more, he just gotten started. He put a knee between her legs separating them at the same time his mouth captured and nibbled the tip of her pleasure zone. Zuri back from beyond was ready for another round of lovemaking. She sank her hands in his hair as Christian made love to one breast at a time. She arched against him as he traveled up and kissed her expressing how he missed her. He was firm and so aroused that he let her touch him. The feeling of his manhood against her hand made her shift her hips to receive him. He gently bit into her lips as she let out her frustration of him not catered to her wants.

In the agony of her frustration, she couldn't concentrate on anything except the extreme electrifying sensations in her and the throb of his masculinity against her pelvis. Christian was slow and deliberate, teasing her enough and pleasing her; she would be a little content. He withdrew his lips from hers and looked at her. As she opened her eyes to investigate why he stopped their eyes met and he quickly thrust into her body. Zuri inhaled as he pulled out, lifted her hips, and thrust again. This time gently and slowly, driving deep inside her as she thrust her lips into him. Her arms slid around his neck as her legs anchored around his hips.

"I love you, Lieutenant Colonel Christian Andres Vincelette."

The dampness of their skin as smooth as his hardness move in and out of her. Upon feeling the combination of his muscled manhood with this powerful thrust as he moved deeper into her, she contracted so quickly it sent them both into a no-fly zone. This was the mark of the same day one year ago in Barbados when they made love and decided on being a couple. It was their first anniversary.

Anana was six months before they took her to see their new home. Parents, Pong Jung and Ana accompanied them on the trip. Most of the furniture was already in place and a fire was burning in the fireplace. They were all having hot cocoa when Pong Jung asked if they like it.

"Of course, we love it," Christian answered and Zuri nodded. "We are very grateful for making our dream come through."

"Oh good. I bought you one thousand acres to build your boot camp. It stretched across Ironwood passed Duluth into Minnesota up Lake Superior." Pong Jung watched shock changed into joy on every one of their faces. Zuri was the first to recover because she was used to her God father's gifts. She sat in his lap and gave him a huge hug.

Christian was next followed by his parents the Zuri's. "I wondered what you would do when we deliver your grand godson?" Zuri winked wickedly at Pong Jung.

"You'll have to wait and see, wouldn't you? I know it's Christian's dream to build a boot camp, now you can."

He turned to Christian and gave him a wink. "I believe in it too. You can have your own power and water supplies. You can build dozens of little log cabins all over the place.

"There's a town not far from here, Zuri can have her training camp there or here. You need to continue training more people. It's desperately needed. I will build a hospital in the town and make sure the schools have adequate teachers. I'll invest in a hotel so families will have somewhere to stay while their sons or daughters are in counseling or boot camp."

"This is ......thank you, Lei. I am grateful you made my dreams, our dreams come through." Christian was emotional and couldn't speak. Shock still lay with him and his parents over his generosity. They weren't used to Pong Jung and his gifts. Zuri's parents were over the shock and indulgence of him and his gifts to both them and their daughter, as a matter of fact to everyone in his family as well as theirs, over the years.

"Like I said, godfather, what are you going to do when we give you a god grandson? Buy us a jet?" Zuri wanted to know.

"Zuri, Lei spoils you rotten." Anil intervened and her mother, Jyoti chipped in. "We couldn't get you anything since Lei found out that you were his goddaughter. Me thinks, he deliberately went and gotten rich so he can give you the world."

Christian senior and Alana like their son were still in shock and it was a good hour later that Christian senior spoke. His voice shook with intense emotions of love, appreciation, and joy. "I know that I am late in saying this.......it took a while to process it all and I am still overwhelmed with all this news. Thank you for making my son's dreams come true. Zuri thank you for loving him and......" He could not continue as tears filled his eyes and choked on his words stopping its flow.

"I am also overwhelmed with happiness. Thank you."

Alana's tears flowed.

"You know, Christian and Alana you have to give yourselves credit for having such a beautiful son. What is there not to love? Your wonderful son gave me more than I ever dream of ever having. My life is complete and I have to say that you both give me that." Zuri went over and hugged everyone in the room, giving Christian a tight hug and a kiss expressing her love.

Anana made herself known by voicing her cry of hunger. They all laughed as Alana picked up her granddaughter and gave her to her mother to be fed. "You know she has my son's green eyes and I can see a bit of red in her hair."

"Yes, she does, don't you, my darling. You are going to be daddy's little girl, aren't you?" Zuri was answering and also talking to her daughter.

"How are you two going to manage with your home here and your work there?" Jyoti asked in a very gentle voice.

"Oh, we don't have the answer. The thing about Christian and I, we make it through and make the rules as we go. We have our partnership and our love secure and that is about it. We haven't had time to really chat and make plans nor do we plan. I think it will have to be like that for a while longer until I can actually give over my counseling to others and lay back. It's impossible for me to stop now. The officers are returning by the thousands from Iraq and Afghanistan."

"I am working from home. I'll take care of Anana when Zuri goes back to work. Thank you for offering to be the nanny Lei. I appreciate it. We agreed that I will be the caretaker until Zuri can leave counseling. I don't want her to leave either at this critical time. I remember lying in Afghanistan and all those months in recovery hoping nothing would happen to her, just so she can see me and take my pain away. I know the other officers are thinking the same thing." Christian concluded.

"Well, my son," Alana added. "We still don't understand what you went through. I am happy that you are here in one piece. I guess you never thought that you and Zuri would be together, much less having a beautiful daughter."

"Oh, no. I never dreamed that my dream would come true. at least never." Christian answered his mother.

"I never thought that I would see my daughter settled." Anil continued the conversation. "Alana and I always wished that she would meet someone who is not intimidated by her accomplishment and not jealous of Pong Jung." "Jealous of Pong Jung?" Christian asked.

"He spoiled her ruthlessly and they are close, more than we are with her. We are her parents!" Anil told Christian.

"You cannot live through what I have and allow jealousy to enter into life. Anger and rage were already there. No, I am very happy that Zuri is so loved. I get the benefit of that love every day." Christian looked at Zuri breastfeeding Anana who was looking at her mother smiling.

"Quit smiling and drink. This milk is not going to be there forever, you know. It goes dry and very soon to that." Zuri warned her daughter.

"Well, I guess that is enough for you, huh?" Christian took her and burped her. All eyes were following them as he walked around the room.

"I know you two will make wonderful parents. When is our grandson coming?" Christian senior asked them.

"In two years, Dad. You will have Christian the tenth."

"How are you going to work the last name?" Pong Jung wanted to know.

"I am taking Christian last name Vincelette and add it to mine and both children will have his last name," Christian informed them.

"You are taking my last name?" He raised a brow in

surprise.

"Ah, yes. I decided that when we became partners, ages ago. I forgot to mention it to you. Should I have asked, you think?" She was looking at Christian and as their eyes connected she saw the warmth of love in his eyes.

"Yes, you should have. I love you too much to say no." Christian was serious then smiled at her, letting her know that he's not annoyed that she did not ask. He looked at his beaming life partner and is overjoyed that she is adding his name to hers; he became emotional. A tear rolled down his cheek and he let it rolled. He took several deep breaths and bought himself under control just in time when Zuri pulled his neck to plant a passionate kiss on him. She tasted the tear.

Pong Jung took this time to change the subject and inform them that he will leave the chopper with its pilot at their disposal. They would be living in both places until they figure their life out. "I know Christian will have to oversee the construction of the land. There's much to do if this place is going to be ready when my grand godson arrives."

"Yes, I understand the work involved. It is something I don't mind doing. I know it will be worth the effort. I have a mental plan of what I wanted. I will make a blueprint of it."

"Well, whenever you want help that's what grandparents are here for. I am sure we can lift a log there and take it there." Anil smiled and blinked at Christian. There was laughter all around.

"Oh, we definitely want all of you involved, please feel free to come and visit. We have built rooms for your visit." Zuri assured them. Anana closed her eyes and fell asleep.

Anana was one year old. Pong Jung flew everyone to London to celebrate. Christian and Zuri had a weekend alone in Paris before returning to their hectic schedule. Since Christian was unable to return home to celebrate his thirty-second birthday due to the ongoing construction with the Boot camp. Zuri planned to take him to his hometown of Springfield, Illinois for an early birthday celebration two weeks in advance. Christian and Zuri took a week off for the occasion. Anil and Jyoti joined in with Christian senior and Alana. All of Christian's siblings with an assortment of cousins and friends were all there celebrating.

Christian never left home when he joined the Marines and whenever he was on leave he came home. There was never a desire to move out as he was away often. This is his first visit in five years, a big welcome home sign was placed on his parents' house and the lawn. Friends and neighbors who knew him lined the streets to his home to greet and thank him. There were tears in Christian's and Zuri's eyes as Christian Senior drove the car into the driveway. Anana was waving her hands to the people who stood waiting for Christian.

"Go on son, take your daughter and greet your friends and neighbor," Alana told him from the front seat as the car came to a halt.

"Come on, Anana see where I used to live." Christian leaned over and brushed Zuri's lips and wiped the tears that ran down her cheeks. He climbed out from the car, picked his daughter up, and went to say hello to his friends and neighbors.

Christian Senior, Alana, and Zuri followed as everyone gathered around them. They greet Zuri and welcome her as they chat for several hours. It was late in the afternoon before they entered the house. Christian laid Anana to sleep on the sofa and took the beer his brother Ryland offered him. Zuri was having a glass of wine on the opposite sofa when Christian joined her. He took her hand and sat next to her. "How are you feeling, Christian? This is quite a welcome. I was extremely touched, darling'." Zuri looked at him with warmth in her eyes. "I am overwhelmed."

Christian still emotional from the welcome home, smiled at her, took a drink from his beer, and brushed his lips over hers. He pulled her closer and hugged her. He needed her energy. He knew he was loved, however, he never knew how much until this day. There was love in the air and this made his journey worthwhile. This made the journey of all his men who died that fatal day worthwhile. He took another drink from his bottle and silently saluted them.

"Mom, I am hungry. Did you and Dad know about the welcome I just had?"

"No, Christian. We knew your friends would stop by for sure. They called and wondered what time you would be here. You know they are invited to your birthday party. The neighbor's welcoming home was a surprise. I am overjoyed they did and I think I will just open the party to all of them. Some of the elderly served in the Vietnam and Korean wars while some served like you in the other wars, Cold War, Desert Storms, Iraq, and Afghanistan wars. A few of them also lost their son or daughter in those last two wars. They know your story and do not blame you."

"I think you should Mom. Thanks for letting me know. I guess they appreciated what we did and are doing in the wars even if they don't agree with it. That was good to know."

"Yes, it was." Ryland patted his brother on the shoulders. "I am glad you are back. You had me worried for a long time."

"We all were worried about a very very long time." Logan chipped in. 'It made me appreciate life more."

"I didn't think you had a problem appreciating life, little brother." Christian teased him. Logan was the one who partied the most and the social butterfly of them all.

"I learned to appreciate the little things in life. I tell you, I live light and let things that I cannot control go. After seeing you lay in that hospital for so long fighting for your life, I gave up bitching." His sister intervened in the conversation. "Charlene that is fabulous." Christian rose on his feet and swung his sister off from her chair. He planted a long kiss on her forehead.

"Don't kiss me, whatever you do." Logan told him with a grin." I used to hate it when you did and all the girls saw it. You know for a very long time they thought I was gay."

"We are brothers, we were supposed to give you kisses." Ryland amusingly informed him.

"No, you don't. You did anyways in front of anyone who is looking! You know how that made me feel? Weird." Laughter broke out from the two older brothers. "We did it on purpose, just for laughs."

"You two planned it?"

"Of course we did?" Ryland admitted and Christian laughed.

"Okay boys, that's enough. Dinner is ready." Christian senior announced. Smiles were exchanged and all went into the dining room for pot roast, potatoes, and fish for Zuri. A few more bottles of wine were opened and laughter filled the air. The laughter was also in celebration of Christian being healthy from the war.

The next day, family, friends, and neighbors were all gathered for the barbeque dinner; they wait for the cake to be cut. Everyone was singing "Happy Birthday" when Anana leaned over and stuck her figure in the ice cream cake icing. She put it into her mouth, more laughter filled the atmosphere. In the corner, sat a huge pile of gifts for Christian to open after the cake was eaten.

"Thank you all very much for welcoming my family and me and for this wonderful birthday party. Thank you very much." Christian stood up and spoke to the gathering of people. After they murmured, "You are welcome," "No, we thank you" and another collection of thanks, they ate the cake and drank some more alcohol and then sang some.

It was well after midnight before the party slowly began

to break up. With the gifts opened, they all continued to party. Jyoti, Alana, and Zuri were watching how Anana laid her head upon her father's shoulders and fell asleep. Christian was talking to Pong Jung and a few friends. It was a few minutes before he noticed Anana asleep. Christian took her upstairs and put her on his bed. He changed her clothes into her pajamas, closed the door, and joined Zuri with his mother sacking the dishwasher. He pulled Zuri away from her task and planted a loving kiss on her lips. "I love you." He left to join the others who were waiting to say good night to him in the living room.

The next day, they were having a late breakfast and recovering from the last few days' festivities. Champagne was being poured and as everyone raised their glasses to toast Christian, when Logan turned to Zuri and asked, "How did you meet my daredevil of a brother, Zuri?

"Oh, I bumped into him one night while I was having a walk. I first saw him from the Chopper in Afghanistan as it was being lifted off. He was looking at it taking off and I swore that our eyes collided and it was love at first sight."

"Oh, we thought you met him during counseling." Alana sort of asked.

"No, we met before that."

"I guess you better tell us your love story. I think we have been guessing and going on assumptions." Charlene asked Zuri.

"Well, there was a fire drill and I ran out and it was Christian I was standing next to, after that, I was counseling him."

"Was it difficult to counsel my son?" Christian senior wanted to know.

"Yes, it was when I put the meeting together. I knew I had to do the counseling and not think of my feelings for him. I usually become extremely objective when I counsel, I had to do some meditation and deep breathing before I counseled Christian."

"Rae Jean noticed the energy of attraction; you know the chemistry between us and would let me know when he would be coming. I would do a-five minute mediation. I figured if and I had a tiny hope that maybe one day he would ask me out when he healed and the therapy was all over."

"Did he? Asked you out?" Ryland asked her. "No." Zuri signed. "He never did and he probably never will." Zuri smiled at Christian who knew she is giving them the very short version of their meetings. He returned her smiled.

"We never dated. I heard that she was going to Afghanistan to give the officers

an encouraging talk and I went to my Captain and asked to go and protect her. I did and she asked Pong Jung to make it okay with my captain for me to accompany her to Barbados. That was when we decided to become a couple." Christian finished for her and then brushed her lips with a light kiss.

"Oh, how romantic!" Alan's wife Senna who was half Spanish and American signed. She gave her husband a look and continued, "Alan and I dated for five years before he asked me to be his wife. I am glad you two knew what you wanted and went for it."

Senna walked to her husband, kissed him, and said, "I love you so much more now. I think we need to leave the twins with my parents and go off to Barbados for a nice romantic vacation."

"I agree. We need a break from it all." His hand went around her waist and he pulled her closer, giving her a kiss expressing his love. "I can have you all to myself." He kissed her neck and released her.

"How did you two made your relationship work, especially when you hardly work out the kinks?" Charlene asked.

"Oh, we wanted us to work. When we were in Barbados

and decided to be a couple, December twenty is our anniversary, we made that choice. I couldn't give Christian much due to my long hours of counseling and....." Zuri was cut in by Christian adding, "Zuri was overworked and overtired. I put in the hours to make it work for us and building our relationship stronger as Zuri made more free time for us. There was a time before Anana was born that we hardly saw each other. I was building our house and my business while Zuri was training others to do her counseling, that was difficult and trying times." Christian pulled Zuri's hands to his lips and kissed her fingers.

"We still have a little difficult path to work through. Christian has been the main parent in Anana's life while I try to figure out how to release myself from therapy. I want to eventually quit and spent years watching our children grow. It's not going to be like that for a long while. I guess we appreciate the time we have together." Zuni smiled at her life partner.

"We are developing the boot camp and I'll fly back and forth from Wisconsin to Virginia about twice a month. Thank Lei for the nanny." Christian informed them.

"You have a nanny for Anana?" Charlene asked with a frown.

"Yes, we do. I like taking care of Anana and when our son is born, I would do the same. Being a father is not difficult, a piece of cake. Thanks, Dad." He turned to his dad and smiled. "I have a wonderful example and I love being a dad."

For Christian's birthday, Zuri had made arrangements with Pong Jung, asking him if he can babysit for a weekend and whether she can use his plane. She wanted to take Christian to the smoky mountain in Georgia for a belated birthday. Pong Jung, Christian, and Anana are at the logged cabin overseeing the other development of the boot camp. She sat quietly in the town car that bought her to the airport. She watched as the jet landed and wheeled into the hanger. She climbed out of the car and waited until Pong Jung and Anana walked down the stairs towards her. Christian was carrying the overnight luggage as he appeared at the jet's door. Surprise was shown on his face as he saw her. She waved at him as she took her daughter from Pong Jung. "Thank You." She whispered to him.

Christian kissed her. "This is a pleasant surprise."

"Pong Jung is babysitting for us this weekend. You are I are going to celebrate your belated birthday." She watched his eyebrow rose in more surprise, she continued, "I have our luggage pack for a weekend. Kiss your daughter and let's go."

"Where are we going?" Christian asked as Pong Jung took Anana from her. Zuri watched as the luggage was taken into the plane and turn to Christian and said, "It's a surprise." Christian kissed his daughter and told her that they are going to see her in two days. She's going to be with Pong Jung. Whether or not Anana understand she nodded and leaned on Pong Jung's shoulders. Christian climbed the stairs to the plane where Zuri waited for him. They waved to Pong Jung and Anana who continued to rest her head on Pong Jung's shoulders.

"This is the second time you have been away from her, Christian. How are you feeling?" Zuri asked as she bucketed herself into her seat.

"A bit sad and a little empty. I know she's in good hands and loved. This is the second time I have been away from her. Where did you say we are going? This is the best and longest celebration I ever had for a birthday." His green eyes lit up with pleasure as it met hers; he grinned.

"I didn't say where." Zuri smiled and grinned at him. "It's you and me all alone for a long sexy weekend."

"Can I start now, you know since it's my birthday present and all?"

"No, you'll have to wait." Zuri leaned over and gently

squeeze his manhood. They were buckled in the seat as the plane was taking off. She let go and felt him became hard. "Good." She leaned in for a long loving kiss. She moved away from him and watched his flushed face. She wickedly and playfully kissed his ear and then whispered seductively. "I have on a purple teddy and garter belt and............" She ran a red nail over his bottom lip.

Christian laid his head back again on the top of the seat and was lost in his thoughts for a long time. Zuri watched him as he brought himself under control. He opened his eyes to see her looking at him seductively. "I am going to get you for this."

"I am hoping you would, Lieutenant Christian Andres Vincelette. I am ready to rock and roll with you all weekend long." She ran a red nail on his lower lip as her tongue followed.

It was all Christian could take. He closed his eyes and rested his head on the seat. A frustrated sound came from deep within his throat. Silence beheld both of them as the jet climbed above the clouds. Zuri was so caught up in her thoughts that she was not aware that Christian was unbuckled and stood up. She sensed him and her eyes flew open and mated with his warm ones. He unbuckled her and picked her up.

It was her turn to be surprised as Christian walked with her to Pong Jung's office. He closed the door with his foot and put her to rest on the desk. He unzipped his jeans and let them fall. He pulled her to him and kissed her passionately, urgently, and madly letting her know that he is ready to be released. In the meantime, his hand had pulled her dress up and entered her. Zuri shivered and upon feeling her, he too shivered. He put his hands on her backside and picked her up, quickly and swiftly with one push, he entered her. The tip of his erect staff brushed against her belly and she groaned withdrawing his hands from her steamy center she grabbed him by the hips and he boosted her up to perch on the edge of the desk, placing her in a perfect position to receive him; his body was ready for release as he clasped himself in a position for the final claiming. He pulled her off the edge of the desk.

Zuri slid onto him in a deep smooth stroke, so perfect she might have been made for the moment, wrapping her legs around his hips and drawing him even more closely to her; he thrust deeply into her and she cried out as her most sensitive knot of tiny nerves banged against her pelvis. She dunged her red nails into his shoulders as he gently put her down to sit on the desk. His hands held her waist and he drove himself deeper into her. She arched her back to him and he buried his lips into her neck. She gave her pelvis muscles a quick contract; her head fell back as Christian pushed further into her. She let go a sound of a new joy as Christian not only joined her and fused their sound together; he emptied himself in her.

Unknowingly to them, their son Lei Christian Anil Vincelette's seed was planted and watered with the music of pure love before the planned two years.

Christian had not seen much of Zuri since the dawn of four days ago. He bathed Anana, fed her, and put her to bed. In a few days, they would be celebrating her birthday. Christian Senior and Alana are arriving in a few minutes to babysit for them.

Zuri had not been feeling well and he hoped she went to the doctor for a check-up before their up-coming trip to Barbados. She has been occupied with counseling more hours again while she trained others to do this particular type of technique for officers who are suicidal. It seemed the officers have not developed any trust with the other counselors and Zuri had been working with them for the last two months.

Rae Jean had been taken over the bulk of training and group counseling. Once a week Zuri, Rae Jean, and the other counselors would meet and discuss the latest development. The digital program is completed and implemented. A veteran technical was hired to do the job and all questionnaires and assessments of each class were collected and went through Rae Jean who managed the less serious cases while Zuri managed the serious ones. The workload was lifted a little with more weekends here and there for them, nonetheless, Zuri still has a long hull of challenging long days ahead for her program to be where she wanted it to be, successful.

The boot camp is an ongoing process; most of the groundwork is in development. The construction manager oversaw the entire project, therefore Christian does not make as many trips there as he did in the early stages.

The cabins are rented as soon as they are built by the officers. Many set up camp around the river while the small little town and incorporated village supplied them with food and other necessities.

The biggest project is fencing the area from the other lands that bordered the camp. The wild animals are tramping the fencing down and other people are entering the camp. This is a constant problem and there seemed no solution in sight. A thought popped in and he called his manager and told him to put two feet of the concrete wall and then used barbed wire on top of the fencing. He was deep in this discussion when the doorbell rang. He hung up and answered it.

"Hi, son." Christian senior greeted Christian junior as he hugged him. Alana followed her husband and did the same, kissing him on both cheeks.

"Zuri is late and Anana is asleep."

"That's okay, son. Your mother and I need a cup of coffee and we are going to bed. We can't handle traveling as we use to, plus we were up with the neighbors as their son came home from Afghanistan.

"Mike came home?" Christian asked.

"Yes, honorary discharged like you. He lost a leg. He spoke highly of Zuri. He is very happy for you both." His father concluded. The door opened and Zuri walked in. Hugs and kisses went around before she said, "It was a horrible day; we lost an officer. She had enough and took her life." Christian took her hands and pulled her to sit next to him. There was silence for a while; after Zuri received her comfort and energy boost she turned to her in-laws and asked. "Thank you for coming. How was your trip?"

There were underground in Harrison's Cave, four days into their two weeks vacation when Zuri reached for her lover's hand. The last time they were on the island, Christian and Zuri didn't venture out to see anywhere. The days were spent making love and building a relationship. On this trip, however, they included exploring a little of the island. On Zuri's birthday, they told the cook that they would be cooking the meal. They were in the kitchen with a bottle of wine open, fish with breadfruit, and a rum fruit cake for the celebration.

Zuri gave Christian a card. "Well, open it. Go on." She watched his expression as he broke the seal of the envelope and pulled the photograph that was on a card out. He looked at the photograph of a magnificent dawn capture perfectly. It took his breath away. He turned it over and read the words by Ibn Abbad, "My night became a sunny dawn because of you." "I know it's my birthday and we are celebrating me. I am celebrating you. That's my birthday gift to me."

Christian grasped in involuntary surprise as his reaction sparkly with electrifying sensations that spread warmth and love throughout his body. He reached for her and pulled her ever so gently onto him as the pressure of his pleasure searing through her short cotton dress. She felt his excitement and she quivered in anticipation of his every move.

The energy that shuddered between them was the highest vibrational lovers can possibly experience. They have lost count of the number of times they had given each other pleasure, how many exciting waves of freedom they released upon the other body which was so often forgotten in their hectic lives. Wrapped in the throes of each other passion, excited to be here, celebrating all outside them were forgotten as Christian undressed Zuri's dress. She watched him drinking in his aroma as her hands traveled to explore the well-known contours of his semi-tanned muscular body.

Zuri's dress followed Christian's clothes and all were left were their naked body. Green and brown eyes mated as he picked her up and took her to the sea of love. The wind was blowing slightly and it was a hot night. He walked through the surf as it roughly tried to take them down. Upon reaching smoother water closer to the shore, and feeling the seafoam around his ankle, he gently let go of Zuri's body to slide sensually down his and held her as her pelvis touched his and settle there for a few minutes as she kissed his chest. He held her strongly and slowly continue the journey, waiting until her legs were securely touching the wet sand. His arms affectionately molded her to the muscled curves of his body. He lay in the sand pulling his lover on top of him. The night air filled with languages of the night creatures calling out to be mated with the sound of music in the distance.

Zuri laid lightly in his arms as her arms hugged him around his neck. Christian moved through the surf on the beach coming from the ocean circulating his body to claim her lips with a mating ritual of lovers. For the first time since Christian picked her up his eyes left her as he kissed her lips conveying his love for her. It was a kiss full of love, spilling his feelings to his lover. She received it and returned her feelings of love until both withdrew for air. He looked up at the moon and whispered against her ear, "Marine Moon" and as Zuri move onto her back to look up at the moon, Christian quickly move on top and entered her. The impact took her by surprise, however, the sensations it uprooted was one not to be forgotten. He moved his body against hers as their passion intensified, sending them into an orbit of ecstasy.

They felt the spar of this intensified passion flickered rapidly in their stomachs and hearts as the pressure boiled to a maximum. Hands explored the skin, as Christian rolled onto his back, pulling Zuri to sit her on him. She felt him in her as his lips kissed her neck, teasing her ear. Her hands moved to his neck as she pushed him back and took a nipple then the next and back to his mouth, teasing and caressing his body. Shivers of sweet electrifying fervor ran from one body to the next, circulating as they teased, caressed, and kissed each other. Fingers threading through the loosened thickness of black and red hair as eyes flirt with each other. Laughter filled the air for a very long time as they nourished each other, taking their time.

In the heat of exploration, the lovers who chose each other to be life partners became still as their laughter lingered combined with ocean breath and the scent of the sea in the air. As the laughter died on their sun-kissed lips, hands, and lips involuntarily moving to their rhythm moved and became as intensified as their kiss and energy.

The rhythm that was once slow began to pick up a faster beat as Christian tasted one breast then the other, enjoying the swelled of Zuri's nipples that became firm as his teeth played with them. The sparks of this mutual awakening surged with intensifying passion and surfaced in their merged bodies through the fusion of their romance, laughter, and breath of the ocean. They leaned together as his lips covering her breasts and her lips nibbling on his nipples, leaving a trail of kisses along their necks, lips, and ears. The feeling of sensuous love splurged into their core as his firm maleness kindling a tender mating out of her core as fulfillment rose to engulf them. Arms that encircled their damp mating bodies tightened their hold on each other as together their impetus arousal flooded into one massive explosion that rocked their world.

In the middle of the early morning, as dawn was beginning to emerge, Christian woke and went for his birthday gift again he had made for Zuri. He kissed her lips and then trailed more kisses down to her stomach. He felt her hands in his hair keeping him there as her laughter sang an early morning tune. "Good morning to you my wonderful lover." She raised her head and looked down at him as he worked his way down to her core. She watched him as his tongue circulated her hot spot. The sensations send her head back into the pillow, her music that came from within lay in the dawn that was rapidly changing.

Christian responded with a double pleasure as he slipped two fingers into her with his tongue on her core made more music for her to sing. Within seconds they had a beat that Zuri was arching and dancing to the rhythm of immaculate electrifying of pure pleasure. A few moments later, what was supposed to be his birthday gift to her was all forgotten as Christian lost control and entered her. He rocked them into oblivious bliss from beyond the ocean of love. An hour later, their bodies were warm with love and breathing was normal. Christian picked up the gift he had intended to give her before he woke her up and was carried into the sea of love.

"Good morning, my sweet Zuri, here is your gift." Christian gave her a package wrapped in his favorite purple colored paper.

Zuri removed the wrapper and looked at the five by eight inches of art that were before her. It was a moon shining upon two lovers enwrapped with each other on the beach as the surf rolled over their bodies. At the lower corner was the inscription of "Marine Moon, Lieutenant Christian Andres Vincelette." Tears of joy rolled down Zuri's face and she buried her face into his chest. Christian arms circled hers as they laid in silence drinking this moment of sharing and caring. Suddenly, Zuri rose and pushed her body in front of Christian. Alarm with her sudden moment his eyes sorted her in questioning as he silently waits for an explanation.

"I have to tell you something. Oh, I been meaning to, and …….oh Christian we are pregnant!" Zuri launched at him and watched his face lit up as he processed the information. "I found out the day your parents arrived. We are ten weeks pregnant. We conceived in the jet on your way to celebrate your birthday."

Christian gently leaned into her as he kissed her stomach and then her. He was speechless and his kisses were expressing his contentment and excitement. "We are early, do you mind?" He had to ask her.

"No, I didn't plan anything, you are the planner and the one giving orders. I wish for a boy, Christian. I'm happy with another girl, are you?

"Oh, darling, I love you and our daughter and I would be happy with another daughter. I haven't been disappointed with us or our work or our family. I enjoyed the moment we are together and I am concerned when you work those long hours. It would get better. It's all towards us being together. Neither of us saw how long it would take for you to be able to make the time."

"We are going to have to choose another girl name, Christian."

"Ah, we can wait until we know what gender our child is going to be. Let's enjoy these precious moments we have together and go and have lunch at Sam Lord's castle.

"I love you." Zuri looked into his eyes and whispered.

Four weeks later, Christian senior and Alana along with Zuri, Christian and Anana were having dinner celebrating the fourteen-week pregnancy. Christian's parents had volunteered to stay due to the pregnancy as Christian was helping Rae Jean with another digital program for addiction and suicide victims which are almost in conclusion. They told her parents and Pong Jung who will visit later. He's tied up with business in Japan. Her parents are on a cruise in Alaska.

"Well, I have good n...." Zuri had begun to make the announcement of the gender of the baby when Anana interrupted and pointed her fork saying, "Look! Rae Je, mom." All eyes turned in searching for the physical evidence of Rae Jean. Upon spotting her, Christian and Zuri gasped in surprise to see who she was with, her partner Air force pilot Captain David Jordan who was kissing her.

"Kiss Rae Je, dad." Anana was dancing with excitement and wanted out of her high chair. "Up, up." She begged. Christian stood and took her out of her seat, wiped her hands and mouth. He set her on her feet and they watched her run to where the couple sat.

Christian sat down while Zuri stood up and followed her daughter who was calling for Rae Jean. It took Anana touching Rae Jean's lap before she was noticed. Rae Jean made roam for Anana on her lap as she searched the room for her parents. Zuri was upon them in less than a minute smiling wickedly at Rae Jean. "It took this meeting for me to meet you." She told Captain David Jordan. "It's a pleasure."

Captain David Jordan was on his feet the minute Zuri joined them. He knew who she was and had met her before when his crew went to her for counseling. On one of those occasions his eyes had fallen upon Rae Jean and he was hooked on true love.

"Good to see you again, Doc. I didn't know you were not informed about Rae and me. I thought everyone knew."

"Maybe everyone knew. I was kept in the dark deliberately. "She," nodding to Rae Jean, "wanted to keep me guessing.

"Hello, Rae."

"Hello Doc, so now you know who my secret lover is."

Upon hearing the word "lover" Anana tried to say it and came out saying, "looff." Laughter broke out as Zuri told her time to go and her daughter responded with a "No." shaking her head in that physical form of communication. "Stay with Rae Je, mommy you go."

"Please let her stay, after all, she is my goddaughter and I don't see enough of her."

"All right." Zuri smiled at Captain and her daughter. She joined the others and said to them, "I couldn't believe that romance was blossoming under my nose and I was blinded to it all."

Christian put his arms around Zuri. "You were busy with all of us Zuri. You hadn't the time to think about yourself much less anything else. There were lots of things you missed, you have to, otherwise, you can't give that much to us who are desperately in need of you and what you are offering."

"Point taken, Christian. I'm missing out on our daughter as well and I don't like it."

"Zuri, think forward to a year from now. All of what we are doing is for that time when we can spend the next few years watching our children grow up."

"Oh, honey I know. Thank you." She brushed her lips across his arm, "You are going to have your son."

A gasp came from the grandparents as Christian pulled her and planted a long passionate kiss on Zuri's lips. Grandparents waited until they were parted to give them "congratulations."

"You know if you two want us around to help we would gladly stay," Alana informed them.

"Oh, thank you. We are going to take you upon it. Please stay as long as you can. I am grateful. I have a feeling that Lei Christian Anil Vincelette is going to knock me off my feet just like his dad did."

"I did, didn't I?" Christian wickedly grinned and pulled her closer to him.

"Yes, you did, Christian, and I have to say I am so happy you did. I was going crazy with trying to figure out how to seduce you."

"I was only hoping to be there for you. I never imagined that we would be in love and having children."
"Well, I am happy that you found each other and it all worked out." Christian senior commented.

"Yes, all of our children found their partner and we are blessed with wonderful grandchildren. I will call Cory to set aside some time for us to go shopping." Alana was waiting for approval from Zuri.

"Please do. I think I found a suicidal counselor who is doing a terrific job. He was once suicidal and asked me to train him to be a counselor. He is doing a fabulous job. I should have some free time coming. The doctor says I am going to need a lot of rest as I am too tired and overworked. My body is back to normal as can be after giving birth. He is concerned about the overworked part of me."

"Well, you can hire someone to do the cleaning, cooking, and laundry, can't you?" Alana suggested.

"You know, Zuri I think Mom is right. We should have a housekeeper for both homes and keep Martha as a nanny for both children. The cabins needed cleaning after someone leaves as well as while we are there. This home here does as well and that would free up some time for me to help Rae Jean with the final touches of the counseling program project."

"Thanks, Mom. Let's do it. You can help Christian choose two housekeepers." Zuri agreed.

"I'll take care of my granddaughter while you lot sort things out." Christian senior chipped in.

"Oh, thank you, Dad. We are fortunate to have so many people helping us. You know that Pong Jung will be making a new will and he is going to pay for the children?" Zuri looked at Christian looking for any objection.

"You know I haven't any objection when it comes to Pong Jung. He had a difficult life and when he told me how much you mean to him after he was named your godfather as well as Anana's grand godfather, he can move in if he wants to."

"I know he did have a horrible life." She agreed and then turned to Christian senior and Alana and said, "his father, Jin Su disowned him because he refused to marry a girl they chose. My parents invited him to come and live with us, his father tried to have our parents throw him out. They disagree with his father who went to his father Jin Lee, Pong Jong grandfather to get my grandfather, Ahmed to get my father to kick him out.

"When nothing worked, his family abandoned him. I was about two years old and I would follow him everywhere. My parents asked him if he wanted to be my god-father. He was twenty-two and was honored. My three older brothers took their savings and gave them to him to invest in the stock market. It played off and my brother quit their jobs and breeze through college without ever having to work. They paid for Pong Jung's degree in business and the profit he made off from their investment he was buying a failing business, build it up and sell.

"I was about five when I took my savings and give it to him so I can become rich. I had ten dollars. He would take it and about a month later he would double it and give it to me. I then kept half and give him the other half. It went on for years like that until I was sixteen and found out the truth. He had just finished making his first million dollars."

As if reading the others' thoughts, Zuri concluded, "No, his father never forgave him. He still secretly sees his mother and sisters and grandparents whenever he's in China. Sometimes they would come and visit with our family telling the father that they are going on vacation but not with whom."

"That is so sad. You have to forgive otherwise you suffer so much anger." Christian senior contributed.

"Yes, I have forgiven Bush for sending us to fight those useless wars." Christian intervened.

At this very time, he heard, "Daddy." Two tiny hands came and rest upon his thigh as he hauled her up to sit on them. Anana looked up at him and he kissed her head. She was smiling and beeping with love for her father.

Introductions were made, Rae Jean and Captain Jordan joined them in celebrating their pregnancy.

"Who is going to be his godfather?" Rae Jean asked.

"Good question since we haven't got one for Anana. One day Zuri and I will figure it all out. In the meantime, we are going to have fun."

"You mean work and try to squeeze some fun in." Zuri charmed in.

Three months into work, twenty-two months pregnant, Captain Jordan made the call to Cory. "Send Christian home to get a bath ready for Zuri. One of my men just ...." He couldn't finish the sentence because he was too emotional to spill the words out. It stuck in his throat. "It's bad, Cory. There's blood everywhere .... all over her. I'm taking her home now with an MP."

"Acknowledged." Cory closed his cellular phone and opened it again. He punched the one-digit number on speed dial to Rae Jean who went in search of Christian upon hearing the message from Cory. She found him in the editing room with the project manager.

"Christian, you have to go now. Zuri is covered in blood. We lost an officer and his blood is all over her. I will call your parents to leave and take Anana to the park. Go Now." Rae Jean told him.

The bathtub was filled with water when the doorbell rang. As he answered it, he saluted the two officers and took Zuri who was wrapped in a blanket from them. The MP, military police spoke, "put all her clothing and the blanket into this bag. I'll collect them later. Call his number." Although Christian has sixteen of his card and knew the drill well. It seemed for the last eight months this was a random act. He took the card and nodded to them.

Zuri was trembling profusely. He guided her into the bathroom and took her clothes off and put them into the bag. He laid it to rest on the tiled floor as he helped her into the shower. He took his clothes off and then proceeded to wash all of the blood off from her body.

He partly lifted her into the tub where he joined her. He pulled her back into his chest and held her there until her body settled into calmness. He unplugged the water, rinse off the suds from them both, and guided her to sit on the edge of the bathtub while he tried them. He put on his underwear and then dressed her in one of his t-shirt that read Marine. He put her into bed and held her close until she fell asleep.

It was his position that Alana found them. She would normally knock, however, she knew what her son would be comforting Zuri. They are well aware of the sixteen times that Zuri had experienced officers' suicide. Christian had called her the first time as soon as Zuri fell asleep. He asked her advice on how to be there to comfort her, to guide her, and to be there for Zuri. She had told him until Zuri says how she wished to be comfortable, hold her in bed, and wait until she pulled herself through the whole experience.

Christian senior would answer the phone and when he heard what took place he would give his wife the phone. He never became involved with the mother and children relationship as he had developed a different one with them. As soon as Christian saw his mother at the door, he rose from the bed, pulled a t-shirt and shorts out from the closet, and left the room.

"Zuri will sleep it off. Rae Jean will come by later and they would go out to dinner. She'll be back to normal by morning. Where is Anana?"

"I put her in the bathtub and your dad is watching her."

"Oh good. I think we have some leftover..."

"Yes, we do. We picked up hamburgers and fries."

"Oh thank you, Mom." Christian hugged his mother and then went in search of his daughter. Alana went to put the bag of food into the oven so it can stay warm. Ten minutes later, they were having dinner when Zuri joined them. She took a fry from her daughter's plate and put it into her mouth.

"Mine, mummy mine," Anana informed her. She bent and kissed her daughter on her head. "I go and get mine. I love you this much." She opened her arms wide and showed her. Anana smiled and returned to her food.

"Here you are, love." Christian senior had risen, took Zuri's hamburger and fries from the oven put them into a plate, and place them on the vacant chair next to Christian's.

"Thank you, dad."

"Couldn't sleep?" Christian asked Zuri.

"No, I tried and dozed off for a few minutes. Rae Jean is picking me up in two hours. I would be back to normal by the time we talked about the incident."

"My heart goes out to you." Alana smiled at Zuri.

Anana is listening, however, not quite understanding the content of the conversation. "My heart mommy, heart." She pointed a finger to her heart. Laughter broke out in the room and lifted the tension that was stored in Zuri.

In forty-five minutes, Rae Jean and Zuri were having red wine as they talked about work. It was two hours later that Rae Jean turned their attention to the suicidal incident of the past and present moment.

"You know, I knew I would lose some of them, I never dreamed that I would be having blood all over me. I don't know how I could have coped if I didn't have Christian. This is so new to me and I thought that I have managed all of the past suicidal incidents. I have not and they keep piling up."

"It's not easy and there's no easy solution of releasing any of it. I suggest you get up early in the morning and do your meditation until you release it."

"Yes, I will do just that. I have enough guilt for not spending more time with Christian and Anana. I feel I am missing out on her growth and the things she says.”

“You better do another meditation on those guilty feelings also. I feel moving forward until you retired from counseling and therapy you should be up early and do some meditation to help you cope with your day.”

“Yes. I have to get back into the meditation routine. There’s much to do that I feel tired all of the time. Now with Lei, I feel I am neglecting him. I have not spoken to him in days and I sure don’t want him to start to accumulate my tired energy. I want my son to be born healthy and strong and handsome like his dad.”

“Well, you’re going to have to cut back on your time more and give the responsibility to others.”

“And Rae Jean, how do I do that?”

“Hire more people, we can do with at least four more counselors. Instead of training them from the beginning, let’s hire two addiction and two suicidal specialists. We can let them work with us and slowly let them loose on their own. The minute they can stand on their feet, we train more, and in this way by the time Lei’s here in November, you can be there with him and your family.”

“I agree with you. I want in the end to show up only in an emergency and whenever I feel like it. No more overseas trips and not so much involvement.” Zuri informed her of her plans.

“Christian and I had planned to retire into the camp with the children and spend time with them for the first five years. Then we plan on traveling the world with them.”

“You still have time to do it. We have to get organized because Zuri, I too want to start a family. I would need someone to take over my job.” Rae Jean smiled at her and beamed with happiness.

“Oh heavens, are you two getting married?”

“Yes, in November and I am also pregnant.” Rae Jean informed her.

“Oh congratulations, Rae. I am so happy for you. When

are you due?”

“I am only four weeks pregnant to your twenty-two weeks. May sometime.”

“I think we should have to hire and train more people to do this job we are doing, Rae Jean. First, we should hire two more assistants apiece. We can shovel all the bits and pieces to them. Let our assistants be there for us. Let us train four counselors, two apiece to do what we are doing. They wouldn’t get tired and overworked.”

“Let’s hire two males and two females and pair them up. In case the females become pregnant the males can continue with the work.” Rae Jean added. The waitress appeared to see if they needed more wine and appetizers.

“No more wine for us, one glass is all we can take. We would love some more salsa and chips, please.” Zuri asked their waitress, Agueda.

“I’ll leave the bill ladies. We are closing in about thirty minutes.”

“Thank Aqueda. Como esta usted?”

“Bien and it is good to see you two again. Take Care.”

“Rae Jean, I think you and I should be coming here every Friday night and talk until we can have counseling running without us,” Zuri suggested as she dipped the last chip into the salsa. “I have a contract from the military to afford the expansion.”

“I agree. Oh, great, no worries on the hiring. When I think of the hours we have put in to get here, it makes the hours we are going to put in easier. It would give us something to look forward to when we lose an officer to suicide.”

“Yes, I couldn’t believe how creative they can be when they want to take their life. This officer used the nee.....”

“Oh no, I don’t want to know. I don’t think it is creative.” Rae Jean stopped Zuri from her description.

“It’s a negative creativity.”

“You know it was her choice. I guess she just couldn’t wait.”

"There was more than what she witnessed in Afghanistan. She carried some childhood abusive experiences with her. It just sits and builds until it exploded in her. All she could see is pain and even the medication didn't work. Her physical body was numb; she was emotionally shut down and the only thing left was her vision. She couldn't shut it out." Zuri explained to Rae Jean.

"I know when they get into that stage it's trial and error, it becomes difficult to reach them. They made their choice and decision." Rae Jean comforted her.

"You know while I was counseling Christian I was so scared that I would screw up. I would let my emotions get the best of me. I never dreamed that I could do it. My stomach would be tied up in knots. The one person who I wanted to help the most, I didn't believe I could do it."

"You did, Zuri. Look at him now."

"I know. I keep discovering how talented he is every so often. He drew me a beautiful card for my birthday. I have it framed and put it on my desk. You must come and see it, whenever you have the time."

"Whenever I have the time." Then a thought popped up and Rae Jean continued, "You can take a photograph with your phone and sent it to me."

"I will do that."

"Doesn't it bother you that Christian makes decisions without telling or consulting you?" "No, I love a guy who can take charge. Christian has a very strong persona and whatever he does he does it with passion. I love that about him. I have met my match because it takes a very strong male with a passion to match my own."

"He hasn't told you about what happened to him in Afghanistan?"

"No, one day when we retire he will. It's not important now. The most important thing is me being stress-free so

Lei can be mentally, verbally, emotionally, and physically healthy. I really don't want him to be picking up my stress before he's born."

"You lean on Christian a lot, don't you?

"Oh, yes. He's my rock. Our relationship is successful because of him. I haven't contributed much in maintaining it. He knew that coz we discuss it when we first got together in Barbados."

"Oh, I thought you two gotten together in Germany?"

"Yes, we made love there. We became a couple in Barbados. The little time we had we spoke of what we want and Christian took it from there and built it into what it is today."

"I guess I better let go of the control if I want mine to work." Rae Jean signed.

"Taking and being in charge is not control, Rae Jean. It's trust. Control is ego and has no trust between partners. Taking charge is trusting your partner to know what's best for both of you. It's true love between two people. It's intimacy."

"How did you and Christian get there?"

"It just happened. Our attraction was not only physical. It sank deeper than that the first time I saw him looking at me in Afghanistan and the two times when we bumped into each other. Something clicked between us and we acknowledged it. We control it until Christian was free from counseling and healthy. Let it flow. We haven't spoken of it because we silently knew Christian was not in a place to have a relationship. When we were in Barbados I told him I was not in a place to have one either.

"Christian knew what he was getting involved with and to what extent. I didn't. We have the same integrity in our values and foundation and that's what makes it work. Sometimes for weeks, we do not make love. We do a lot of flirting and cuddling. Oh, we are forever kissing.

"It took me a long time to tell Christian I love him,"

Zuri admitted to her.

"What? Really!"

"Yes, first I couldn't give him love when I didn't feel it. When I realized that I needed to say it to him. I kept forgetting or I fell asleep. I had to kinda make an appointment with myself to tell him. Sad as it is, that was how it happened. Let go of the control, Rae Jean and let David in. Let him take charge and quit fighting with him. Why don't you take a nice long week off? Go to Barbados. I can have it arranged."

"Oh, I would love that."

"Good. Ready to go." Zuri took some bills out and left them on the table. "Sent me the dates and I will arrange it all for you both."

The next two months and thirty weeks pregnant, it was hectic with hiring other counselors and assistants. Zuri had taken the morning off and works from one to eight in the night. She was home in time to read Anana a story and kissed her goodnight before she fell asleep.

Christian had more time as the housekeepers in both homes took care of all the things he would normally do. He traveled to the camp once every other week and spent the weekend with Anana there. Zuri had time for herself and Lei. Pong Jung of course came and go in whenever time permitted. Rae Jean and David were in Barbados. The digital counseling program is ready for a trial run as soon as Rae Jean returned. There are about forty officers and civilians signed up for the program.

It was September and a lovely day when Zuri woke. She heard the shower on and rolled out of bed. Anana was with Pong Jung for the weekend. She had a few hours until she goes to work and a wicked thought, actually a wonderful one as she joined Christian in the shower. He turned and pulled Zuri to him the minute she stepped into the shower. Lei had stretched and grown strong as Christian's hands covered her stomach and his unborn son. He bent and kissed him and told him not to listen to what they are going to be doing.

"Oh, you think he would listen?" Zuri leaned into him and kissed him passionately.

"Mmm, what did you say?" Zuri didn't answer and slowly lower herself on her knees. She took his length and played with it in the palm of her hands before lower her mouth over the top. It had been a long time since they had made love. Christian leaned against the wall and began making music as Zuri's tongue give his emotions, exquisite pleasure. He can feel her hand moving along the length of his erection as her tongue kissed the top. Her other hand cupped his sac and put pressure into his zone. He lost control and let loose the last three months of sexual pressure in him. He watched her swallowed his release and pulled her up onto her feet slowly. He kissed her as his hand sort her zone. Finding it he played with it as she sank her face into his shoulders.

Christian was listening to Zuri making music of her own. He turned the tap off, held her hands, and guided her to the bed. He lay beside her as they touched and kissed and looked deep into each other's eyes. With bodies still wet he rolled her to her side with her back to his chest. He moved her legs so he can maneuver his manhood, he entered her.

Zuri found a comfortable position on her side as she felt all of Christian in her. She buried her face into the wet sheets as he moved in and out of her. His hands stationed her hips; he can have a smooth ride in and out without her uncomfortable. The music of love became louder as Christian slowly and gently continued his strides as they moved to their personalized rhythm. He felt Zuri's body tense then picked up the intensity; he was ready for her. He moved as fast as he can and within seconds they were rocking to the ecstasy of their own making. Zuri rolled on her back and turned to her side to see Christian who leaned into her and kissed her. "Damn it, Zuri it has been a long while since we make love."

"I know. I missed you. I keep thinking of the time the children are grown and we have the time to stay in bed and make love all day long."

"Zuri, that sounds promising."

"It's a promise then. I love you...." She didn't finish as Christian kissed her deeply ad silently for a long time. He watched her breathing became normal before he said, "I've waited so long for you to tell me you love me, I never thought you would. I don't think I hear it enough. I know you do love me Zuri, my wonderful love. It's damn good to hear you say it." Zuri's eyes still connected to his smiled a smile that touched her heart and his and onward to their eyes. They lay like this for a long time, drinking themselves drunk on pure love. It was Christian who broke the silence and changed the subject to their unborn son.

"I have a feeling that Lei is going to have dark hair and brown eyes like his mother."

"Lieutenant Christian Andres Vincelette I learned a long time ago not to ever argue with you. Offensively, you have too much time on your hand I need to put you to work."

Christian laugher rang into her heart. "Are you thinking of having more children?"

"Oh no, I can't find the time for the ones I have and even when I have the time I want to spend it with them, I fall asleep. After they grow I want to get old with you."

"Alright. I'll go along with you. If you ever change your thoughts, I am gamed."

"Christian I was thinking of having the doctor tied my tubes or whatever it is they do for the latest birth control in surgery. I would not have to be on "the pill" or have any more children."

"Are you sure, Zuri?"

"Yes, I am sure about this and I want you to be okay with it, too."

"I am, really I am. I understand your view and I know our relationship has been an unusual one. I am happy that you took my name even though I would have loved to marry you. Are you aware that we are the only ones in both families that are not married?"

"No. I never thought about it. If marrying you means so much then I would marry you tomorrow."

"It did at first. It doesn't mean a thing anymore to me. All I wish for is what you wish for us to do, spend more time together."

"You know if the need ever takes place for more children we can adopt a few more. There are many unwanted children that it kills me to see them when I used to travel. I used to give my money away. That's why Pong Jung rarely gave me cash. I have a card with money on it to spend. I wanted to take care of all the children who have no one."

"Really? Pong Jung did that?"

"Oh Christian, he truly instilled in me that doing something is better than giving where the money is concerned. He said that I cannot solve the conflicts, however, doing a bit is better than giving lots of money. When I visited a country I would go and see what the orphanage needed or the school and purchase it for them. I would buy food and take it to the homeless children."

"You know we should think of setting up a charity foundation and donate some money to it or have others donated to it. We can keep this Boot camp going. It would take millions to keep it running smoothly."

"Tell me about it? Are we broke?"

"No love, our money was barely touched except for household stuff. Pong Jung gave me every month. I get a big fat juicy check from him, deposited into my account. His accountant balances my checking account, pay my taxes, and anything to do with money goes to the accountant."

"You know he's like that. He doesn't give him money unless he believes in something. He has about 20 charities going. He makes more than he can spend. I think he is getting tired of it. Ana told me he's working less hours these past months and making all the arrangements to spend a few weeks with us for Lei's birth."

"I figure he would."

"It's only a matter of time, I guess. A few more weeks and Lei would be here. I can't wait."

"Aren't you glad that we bought this six-bedroom house?"

"Oh, Christian that was a good idea. I guess christening it will be in order since it has only been three weeks since we moved in."

"Yes, it is perfect timing. We have to thank our parents for chipping in when we need them to and Logan and Jaqson and Pike."

"Yes, I don't know how my parents did it with so many of us. They are forever visiting one of my brothers or sisters or us and still have time for cruises."

"It was easy for my parents. My mother only worked during the day as a part-time doctor's nurse while my dad was a full-time architect. He loved to design and build things."

"Oh, I didn't know that. You got that from him?"

"Yes, I used to watch him, design, and build whatever we want. We rarely bought anything only what he couldn't build. I consulted him on this cabin."

"I hope you teach our children the same, my love, they can be useful to the world one day."

"Oh, I think they would with both of us and Pong Jung, they wouldn't have much choice.

"Are you ready for another round of some serious lovin'?" Christian asked her as he kissed her breast and plucked at a nipple.

Zuri pulled him to her and planted a kiss on his lips. "I do love ... yipes! Our son is kicking." She pulled Christian's over to the spot to feel their son kicking.

"Yes, my...our son is strong......"

"And handsome as his father with a tan like his mother." Christian grinned at her as his son threw another kick into his hand. Zuri looked at him as she felt the kicking of their son and Christian receiving it.

The fog had lifted and dawn broke through the mist of sun rays when Lei shoved his way onto Planet Earth. It was the age of the dawn of a beautiful fall morning when their son, Lei Christian Anil Vincelette was born. Any moment, he would break through out of the dark and into the light of dawn. Lei let out a long scream the second he entered and let everyone know that he didn't like being out of his cocoon.

An hour later, Christian held his son who was tiny and light and kissed his forehead passing him over to his mother for her to nurse him. As Zuri fed him, she reflexed on the three months rest the doctor had ordered for her after the last suicidal experience from the officer who was scheduled for therapy. She had her usual checkup and was immediately put to rest, otherwise, she would lose the baby due to stress. Christian took her home and put her to bed. He called her parents and asked whether it's possible for them to stay for a few weeks; his parents fill in the last few weeks leading to Lei's birth.

Zuri had to scale back on the individual therapy and forcefully and regretfully hand over the counseling to two of her top counselors. Doctors Aiden McAuther and Clova Melingtish who she was training before she had joined the military. They usually have conference calls on each officer in the afternoon before they see them the next day. Most of her day, however, was spent sleeping or reading a book. Christian kept an eye on her activity and made sure that she didn't overdo herself. She spent time with Anana, watching a cartoon, reading a story every day curled up together in bed, and sometimes they had meals there. Zuri enjoyed these moments and cherished them.

A cry came out of Lei when she pulled her breast out of his mouth to switch him to the other one. Christian took him and waited until Zuri was ready and laid him back with his mother. They were alone as their parents along with Pong Jung and Ana went to informed everyone once again of the new addition to the family. Anana was quiet because she didn't quite understand the dynamic of what was going on except she has a brother.

Pong Jung had taken her hands and let her out of the room. As much as he wanted to stay, he knew Christian and Zuri needed time alone and privacy. Besides, Anana needed some time of her own to adjust as well to want ever she is trying to understand. This would be a huge adjustment because she has to share the time she usually has with her dad and mother with another little person. It's too much to ask of her, therefore letting her know that she is still loved by others would help ease the burden of any jealousy arising.

There are enough adults around to make sure that this doesn't happen to Anana. He will see to it that she is not forgotten when Zuri and Christian both are preoccupied with Lei. He had taken a month of work to spend with the Vincelette family. Zuri had added Christian's surname to hers and that was a party in the making. He had flown everyone even Rae Jean and Captain David Jordan into Barbados with a few of both Christian's and Zuri's friends to witness the ceremony. He had planned the whole thing as usual. Anything in Zuri's life that was known and her Godfather would be involved, This was no different than the other events he had planned. Pong Jung smiled with honor to have her in his life as well as the rest of the Currunis, Vincelettes, and Donghai's family. Since his father died, his family can freely visit each other and travel wherever they desired; he visited them at least once a month for a few days.

Pong Jung looked at his life partner Ana and her interaction with Anana. He was honored to be alive, rich, and in love. He had come a long way in the making and he had much support throughout his life, never mind his father and his traditions. He had sole off a large portion of his worldwide enterprise, for him to have more time to settle in one place for more than a week. He had moved into his apartment in New York permanently as his home base. From there he supervised the reminding of his engineering business particularly the section of the military. Anana jolted him out from his thoughts. He opened his arms to her and gave her a huge hug and proceeded to kiss her forehead.

"Jun' hungry food pleas'." She looked at him with her light green eyes smiling at him with a frown of hunger.

"Here is your hamburger, my sweet lov' and fries." They eat in silence watching the ducks with ducklings swimming in the lake and birds flying or lazing in the trees above. Ana had spread a blanket on the grass and they were all sitting enjoying the weather. Pong Jung's thoughts return to the day of celebration. It was a bright sunny day and the couple looked smashing. Christian wrote a black slack with and white shirt while Zuri's dress was a simple light yellow silk strapless gown that hung to her pregnancy and fell to her ankles. The cake was a simple rum fruit cake with white icing and a man representing Christian behind his pregnant wife with his hand upon her stomach. Zuri's hands were on Christian's and next to them were a little girl in a short yellow dress represent Anana. The meal was Zuri's favorite, flying fish, bake breadfruit, mixed steam vegetables with cornbread served with a mixed salad and coleslaw. Everyone partied till the wee hours of the morning, lazed all day on the beach, and all week they continued the party before they left for their respective home. Christian and Zuri stayed for another week.

"Christian, you know it's a good thing this happened now."

"What happened now?" They were in the suite of the hotel that Pong Jung booked for everyone after the ceremony in St. James.

"That I added your name to mine."

"Why?" He asked with a frown because he couldn't see the logic. He was taking his jacket off and turned to look at her.

"Oh, how beautiful!" Zuri exclaimed, a low sound came from her throat and her head was back against the door of the patio. She was still fully dressed, however, her shoes were off. One hand rested over her swollen stomach where he can see his son kicking up a storm saying "hello out there." The sound from her and the visual excited him more and he covered the distance between them. He found her lip, kissing her until she pushed him away.

"Look!" She exclaimed breathlessly. They watched the dawn bloomed together, his arm around her and her head resting lightly against his shoulder. Over the ocean, colors raised from the horizon bleeding into the early morning sky, tinting the silvery-white that clouds low over the sea. The sand blushed white to pink and then deepened to pink before the sun slowly gilded it golden. "I am happy to add your name to mine. I didn't want to wait till Lei was born. I was afraid that we would be too busy and time would pass."

In another few hours, the baking sun would leech the color out from the landscapes all around the island. These two lovers have enjoyed celebrating with family and friends, kissed in the hushed moment that dawn is breaking. Christian heard Zuri pulled him into the suite from the balcony and walked to when the sun was rising. They thudded against the door oblivious to the sound of animals calling in the early morning. He undressed her slowly, one piece of clothing at a time, which was not much, dress, bra, and underwear, his eyes held hers. She undressed him, one piece at a time; his shirt, this slacks, and underwear, her eyes never leaving him.

"I love you." she reached out and very tenderly stroked his cheek. He turned his lips and kissed the palm of her hand. Imagining his lips and tongue against her skin she wanted to taste him instead he helped her found a comfortable place on the bed and they fell asleep.

Upon arrival to the island, Anana was with her cousins who were cared for by a few nannies. They were free. Christian was on the balcony admiring the view when he was joined by his lover who had a short blue dress covering her pregnancy. He was well aware of his desires to take her into his arms and taste her as he kissed her. Wrenching his mouth away, he walked to the door with Zuri and took her hands, lifting them high above her head, his fingers searing between her zone, removed his finger and pinned her roughly to the door. Her cry of passion found no mercy in him and he pulled her up on to tiptoe till her mouth was on a level with his; the action caused her full breasts to rub with exotic voluptuousness against his chest.

Christian moved his hands downwards over the soft swell of her stomach down to where black curls covered the "v" between her tights. He bypassed the temptation to kneel and buried his face within; instead, he stroked her inner core. His breath quickening and her legs moved far enough to accommodate him, giving him easy access to her most intimate places. He had enough and wanted to taste her this minute; he led her to the bed. He kissed his way to her zone; his tongue found her core. He tasted her for a long time working his way in as his thumb played lazily with her outer hot bud. His tongue probed everywhere and had the pleasure of exploring uncharted place it never landed before this very moment. He never knew there were this many hot zones on Zuri's body.

Pregnancy worked wonders on her. It seemed that more of these hot zones his tongue is probing is giving her more "gs" to make new melody because for the life of them being together he never heard that note before since they became a couple. He loved listening to her response to his tongue and lips, fingers, and manhood. In seconds, Zuri was making music that sent out a melody of pure stupor that he knew well. Her hand throbbed on his body echoing his wishes which she was determined to grant him tonight. The second she leveled her breathing, she took him in her mouth, and soon he too was making music. This was the last time they made love and would be for a while after the birth of their son.

Zuri smiled at her life partner. "I think I need to sleep. We still have to see how Anana is taking all of this in."

"You rest my love. She is with Pong Jong and Ana. Our son is fast asleep. I think I'll have some sleep myself." He took Lei from his mother and put him in his crib next to the bed. He turned to look at Zuri who was fast asleep. The bed looks inviting; he took his shoes off and moved towards the bed. He lifted her and moved her to her side and slip into the bed. He molded their bodies together and fell asleep. This was how the nurse found them. She smiled and left because she knew their son would wake them letting them know he is hungry. True love counters all, remembering her husband and son waiting at home for her.

Three months after returning to the reality of both working, making love was put on hold. Zuri worked at home in the afternoon counseling the serious officers on the net and taking care of her children in the morning while Christian was working on his company. It was not easy even although they had help from the housekeeper, nanny, Pong Jung, and the family she was still in need of sleep.

Lei nursed and she read to Anana, nonetheless Christian was still in charge of much of the responsibility. He has this boundless energy and never seemed to be worn out on any task. She, on the other hand, was easily tired and cannot get enough sleep. She started to go to the office once a week for an hour, two weeks after Lei was born. In four weeks, it began to be two hours twice a week and before she knew it she was back to full-time for longer hours after three months. Christian saw what was happening and confronted her about the situation. It was eight in the night and she had finished nursing Lei when he approached her. He took Lei from her, kissed his son, and put him in his bed with some soft music to sleep. He returned to Zuri who was in the shower and waited until she was dressed pulled her onto the sofa in the living room. All was quiet as Anana was asleep and the nanny was retired for the night.

"Oh, hell Christian! What did I do now? I feel like you are about to reprimand me for something that I don't have the fuckest idea what I did?" Zuri frown at him with sleepy eyes.

"You didn't do anything, wrong love. I am very concerned about you and your health. You have given birth three months ago and you are back working full time. You have to give yourself some time to allow your body to adjust. You can't do it all." He held her close and brushed his lips on hers.

"Oh damn it all. Here I was thinking that I have to do it all. There is so much that is new for me; that I've never experienced before, sometimes I am so overwhelmed. I don't know what to do." She admitted to him.

"I realized that; that's why we are having this discussion. I've noticed you think you feel obligated to the officers. Even if you are paid you are not and there is only so much you can do." He pulled her closer and gave her a tight hug."

"I guess you know me pretty well, huh?"

"Yes, I do and I love you. It's one of the reasons why I fell in love and still in love……..more in love with you today than when I first saw you in the chopper."

"Really?" It was what she wanted to hear. It perked her up and she pulled herself away from him and looked at him fully taking him in as if it was the very first time she noticed him.

Christian let her processed what thoughts that is being transpired in her brain. He watched her looking at every fragment of his face and love it when she took a big gulp of air upon seeing the two days old scar under his chin and the month, an old one settled on his cheek. He smiled at her waiting for her to kiss them. What he didn't expect was her pulling herself up and moved away from him. He was surprised, however, he felt it best to wait it out. Waited he did and watched her space the wooden floors for a good hour. Suddenly, she climbed on top of him and cried. He held her for another two hours as she cried and cried, empty her frustration than to his dismay, his wonderful lover fell asleep. He picked her up and put her to bed.

After his shower, he checked on the children, fed his son, and climbed into bed with her molding her to the curve of his body. He held her till dawn broke loose and he heard his son crying for food from the radio beside the bed. He bought Lei to her and she fed him. Christian made coffee and breakfast for both of them. It was Sunday, the nanny day off, and Zuri's. Anana would sleep till nine and Lei being feed and change would go back to sleep for a good three hours. He trained them; he knew how it works. Listening to the officers who are mothers and fathers helped more than those books. Firsthand experiences were the best and what he knows, he asked his mother and Zuri's. The rest was from trials and errors.

In the process of his investigation, he found out Zuri's

mother worked from home when the children were born; the children constantly saw a parent. She and Anil were fortunate that they could afford such a large family. They made the rule that one parent would always be visible to the children to teach them to be independent and to discover their truth. When they fought they never intervened nor take sides. They had to find a solution to their conflicts. Zuri never could find any solution; they told her to go and take communication, sociology, philology, and psychology classes. Pong Jung encouraged her. She came back to them one day and told them that she developed her own program and have solutions to every one conflict. They had asked her about her conflicts and she merely laughed and mentioned that she does not have any. Anil had looked at his wife and asked, "we have a perfect daughter?" She had replied, "I guessed we made a perfect daughter." She had proceeded to give him a kiss and then she added, "until she finds out she is not; then my perfect husband we have a problem....mmmm a very unusual situation.

They had taught the children that there are no problems only conflicts. When they addressed the poverty in this world, it was a conflict of interest that people who have money are in conflict of helping the less fortunate. Although each of them has godparents, Zuri's godmother was Anil's sister Sira who died when Zuri was ten at childbirth. The child, Padmini is a parent herself and is Zuri's godchild. She was happy to see that Pong Jung always sent for her whenever there was a celebration. Although each child was born in a different country and knew the heritage and spoke the language, it was crucial that they also learn the language of their native country.

She and Anil had chosen that particular country to give birth because one day they wanted that child to help develop it. They had to give back, therefore choosing a country that is poverty sicken was essential. They chose

China for Zuri because of Pong Jung who was going through such a difficult time with his father. He and Adnan were best friends and often joined them for dinner while they were working in China on a bridge. Adnan taught him English and he taught Adnan and Zuri's Chinese, really Mandarin.

Christian loved talking to Jyoti and Anil about Zuri and all the funny things she did because it helped him understand her and support her in times of need, like last night. He picked up the tray and took it to her. Zuri smelled the eggs, biscuit, and coffee long before her lover entered with it. She had lain awake after she fed Lei, who lay next to her kicking his legs and talking his own language. She was thinking about last night and felt empty, a slight void with a yawning to retire early; she can watch her children grow up with Christian. She allowed her thoughts to drift back to the day she was eight months pregnant and they had flown to the cabin for a week's rest. The truth of the matter was that Christian had some construction work to oversee and he also wanted to keep an eye on her taking a rest as the doctor had ordered. She knew he had a daunting feeling she would overdo it with the counseling and therapy, regardless that it was through the internet.

Anana was outside and Zuri was lying on the lounge chair reading a book. Christian was inside on the computer working while the nanny Petra was out walking. She told her daughter to stay there while she goes to get some cookies. Upon returning she was shocked to see what her daughter was holding and who sat there watching her. She yelled for Christian. Her daughter was sitting right where she left her and she was holding a baby snake in her hand. The mother of the baby snake was charging towards Anana who stood fearless talking and betting the snake. Christian seeing what was happening pulled his gun from the hiding place and fired a shot at the mother snake. She stopped and realized that she was not dead, started to charge again.

Christian took the snake from his daughter's hands and set it free. He held Anana's hand with his right and gun in his left-pointing it at the mother snake. The snake lowered her head and waited for her baby and together they happily went off into the woods in the opposite direction. Anana confused, looked at her father than her mother. She had seen her father hold snakes before, what is the problem with her holding one. She had also seen him shot one. She had seen him using the "bang-bang" many times. Her mother and father looking and talking to each other using words that she doesn't know or understand.

"Yes, she saw me taking the snakes to the woods and yes, I have used the weapon more than once with her. You know I wouldn't put her in danger. I keep the gun on the top of the kitchen cupboard unloaded."

"No, I'm not angry with you, love. I was concerned about her knowing and not understanding the danger of snakes. I knew you as well as the officers have guns here. I also know that I trust all of you for being responsible with them. The only time I have a conflict with guns is when it belonged to the responsible idols out there and that no one is doing anything about the excessive illegal weapon on the streets."

"Ok." Christian didn't know her feelings on either the snake or the gun.

"I think you should tell Anana that snakes are out until she learned which ones to play with from the ones she cannot play with. Christian, all snakes are poisonous. We have a bit of the antidote for the less poisonous ones and none for the most poisonous ones. Let her spray vinegar on herself when she goes outside, it would keep the snakes away and bugs too. How you teach her I would be interested to know. I'm going to lie down a bit. Your son is kicking a racket." She had left them and forgotten to asked and realized rarely does she ever check back with him how things went. Guilt was her enemy these past months. She was busy formulating a plan to retire when her handsome hunk lay the breakfast tray on the bed.

"Good morning love." She leaned in to be kissed.

"Good morning to you Zuri. How are you feeling this morning?"

"Oh heaps better from last night. Crying works wonders on me soul, my handsome hunk." She bit into the biscuit and took a forkful of eggs.

"You can cry on my shoulder anytime." He proceeded to take his shirt off for Zuri to have a look and sat opposite her deliberately. She looked and he continued, "I have strong broad shoulders and I am a handsome hunk." He waited until she lifted her eyes and looked at him; he grinned and gave her a wink.

"My my my, you handsome hunk, what else do you possess that me might be interested in?" She flirted with the idea of climaxing with him. It had been so long since that moment in Barbados when they celebrated her adding his name to hers that she had forgotten what it was like to make love to her lover. Months had passed and many nights she settled for Christian climbing into bed at all odd hours cuddling her. She was beyond exhaustion for being a part-time mother, therapist, and partner for any loving.

She quickly finished her breakfast and watched him eat his as if he had a plan of some sort of action. He did, he read her thoughts and he was gamed. He put the tray on the floor, pick his son who is asleep in his bed in the next room, and closed the door shut. He pulled his jeans off and she merely touched her fingertips against the hot swollen manhood that stretched in his briefs and made him shuddered with pleasure; his whole body was trembling. The intensified sensations echoed through his body into hers and the feelings were making them feverish and dizzy with excitement.

She was thrown back onto the bed as his hands roughly stripped away from her panties. He straddled her. He took the brown tip into his mouth and gazed with his teeth on each. He began wildly kissing her, he parted her legs with his knee. He pushed into her as she arched right off the bed in ecstasy as she received the throb of his body. With quick fierce thrusts, he drove deeper and deeper as her head thrashed wildly on the bed. With a snivel, he fell upon her thrusting her hand away and urging his titanic passion into the hot wet sheath that eagerly awaited him. She accepted him with another voluptuous arch of her back her legs lifting to wrap high around his waist. They made music together as he sank even deeper into her core enclosing his hardness in its satin residence; a residential place from which he apprehensively never want to leave.

Christian gripped her backside drubbing into her rapidly. Her thighs still drawn up beside him tightened over his waist hold him enough. There were feelings of love pouring and the longing coupled with needs felt entirely complete. He felt the walls of her vagina gripped him again suddenly making gentle spasms as he obliged with a quick slide in and out of her core. They were moving again, picking up a faster rhythm. A sharp sound came from Zuri and he felt her gripped him inside again and again. They picked up a rhythm and he knew she had climax; he released in her after a few more jabbing thrusts, he spurted everything from him shooting out, taking his breath with them. She clutched his arms and watched the passion on his face as they explosion into each other, her second orgasm. Heart rate normal and his breathing improving, Christian was on his back verbalizing his thoughts.

"Oh Zuri, would we ever get tired of making love. It gets more passionate with time. I never knew how exciting it would be to make love to you. I love it and I look forward to learning something new."

"I know. Sometimes I find my thoughts randomly drifted to making love to you, like just now. I didn't think it would happen. I guess you read my thoughts, huh?

"No, are you kidding? I can't read your thoughts. I felt your energy, your sexual energy, and I got turned on so fast I could hardly swallow my food." Laughter broke out and did a cry from Lei demanding attention.

"Oh just in time," Zuri announced and hopped off the bed looking for her clothes. Christian did the same and they hurriedly walked to the children's room. Christian picked Anana up and took her to the bathroom while Zuri took

Lei changed him and sat in the rocker cuddling him.

"Love, how did you ever taught Anana not to pick up the snake?"

Christian grinned and was happy that she remembered to follow through, never mind it was months later. "I never did. I called your mother and asked her. I figure she would know more than mine because of the places you all lived and she had to teach you all so many different things, the proper procedures in managing dangerous situations. She said spray vinegar on my body and let Anana watched and then spray it on her. Make it an outside activity so she has to do it otherwise she cannot go out."

"Mmmmm, that's simple huh?

"Yes, that's simple." Holding Anana in one hand, he leaned into her over the rocker and gave her a kiss. He was through the door when Anana told him, "Me kiss mummy, daddy." He turned around for his daughter to kiss her mother.

Zuri was very occupied with her retirement plan. She had a three-day meeting with all of her top executive officers in her company. Rae Jean is her second in command and almost due with child agreed with her choices and decisions. This was planned and ready to be executed. They had met previously and she had outlined her plans for her and the executive officers. By the time they were through, they were ready to announce to the others; the three days meeting was invented. From this day onwards, she and Rae Jean would be there for questions and support because in a few weeks Rae Jean would be on maternity leave for three-plus months.

The officers and counselors were nervous; they were reassured that they were not completely on their own as of yet. They have a few weeks to get their act together and move forward with the program. They were also informed to choose two others, one military, and the other civilian to train them to do what they are doing. They have a year to train the new counselors and then they can have the freedom to take time off as required. Zuri had planned to go into the office as usual to support the counselors and answered any questions until she felt confident, she will hand over the reins of her company to others. Rae Jean was working less as delivery was falling upon her. Today, she called Zuri to let her know she is too exhausted to work and will be in bed.

"Oh, I know that feeling. I am sending over the housekeeper with food for you. Tell her what to do and then meet me at six for dinner at the usual place."

"Oh yes, just like old times. I need old times in my life. See ya."

The hours quickly flew; Zuri met the very much pregnant Rae Jean who was ten minutes late at the diner in town. Rae Jean was on maternity leave and lived in a townhouse with Blake. She still oversees the counseling at the military base, however, it's only on an emergency basis. Since the program is digital, it's easier to maneuver and required as much personal counseling. The officer has to complete the digital program first before personal counseling begins and Zuri had trained twenty-four, twelve civilian, and twelve military officers, both males and females to manage the overflow. Any complications or conflicts of interest are directed to Zuri and Rae Jean who usually solve them over conference calls. They rarely venture onto the base.

As the counselors become confident, the conflict of interest becomes less and less. Zuri usually visited the military compound once a week or as required, however, recently it had been once every two weeks. She hoped it would be once a month and then occasionally or when she chooses to and not required. Exhaustion still plugged her and missing out on the growth of her children filled her with sorrow. Rae Jean saw the agony that emitted from Zuri of missing out on the growth of her children, promise that it would not happen to her; she trained three counselors to do her job. Blake will start his vacation in a week; he has three months of accumulated vacation to help with the delivery of their son.

Zuri raised her head and saw Rae Jean pushing her huge body through the door. She pulled herself onto her feet and crossed over to the other side of the table and pulled the chair out for her. Rae Jean grinned and offloaded her body weight into the chair.

"Thanks."

"Ah, you're welcome. You look like you could do with some sleep?" Zuri laughing told her. "Not that I would know anything about that."

"Right. Food. I am so starved. I want two hamburgers with fries."

"No kidding. You are acting as if you've never eaten. I know you have, a few …two hours ago."

"Zuri, do you remember those times when you were pregnant and you were always eating."

"No." Zuri flat out deny with a twinkle in her soft brown eyes.

"You had every officer bringing you food." Rae Jean reminded her.

"No. You have too much time on your hands to remember so much. Maybe you should go back full time to work." Zuri teased her.

"Ok. I got it. I teased you so much that it's your turn. Isn't that revenge anger?"

"No."

"Is that all I am going to get out of you?"

"No." Out came the laughter from them both. The waiter arrived and two burgers with everything and a fish dinner were ordered. They sipped on ice tea, talking endlessly about everything and nothing.

"Do you miss the counseling, Zuri?"

"Yes. I do. I did it for so long and for so many hours that I kinda feel naked. I am getting used to the time off little by little. The first week was horrible and I didn't know what to do with the children. Christian didn't say anything only gave me lots of hugs. He let us, the kids, and I figured it out.

"Anana gave me funny looks and asked, 'Mummy work?" when I said no, she asked, "Mummy sick," and when I said no to that she looked puzzled and walked away. She's not used to us doing anything together."

"Oh, dear. It will get more rewarding when she realized that you are not going anywhere and she can trust and relied on you."

"I hope so."

"How's chunky cheese?" Rae Jean picked up the habit of calling Lei that when she lifted him for the first time in the hospital on day one.

"He's nursing as ever. He laughed a lot. I know he's a happy one. Anana wanted to change his diapers and Christian let her help him. He told her when Lei is a bit older she can do it all by herself. He is so kind and gentle with them and he knows the right things to say all the time."

"Blake has been reading books."

"You know I think it is up to us to let them in. I read so many times that the men felt left out or jealous when their partners are pregnant and more so when the baby is born." Zuri seriously admitted.

"I know that. I think it is up to the mothers to let the fathers in. Were you ever jealous of Christian?"

"No, I was overjoyed that he did what he did. I was not in a place to do much. I was fortunate to have such a wonderful partner. You too, Rae Jean." "Oh, don't I know it! Blake was wonderful when I told him that I was pregnant. He said not to worry that we don't have a Pong Jung to make life easy for us; he is superman." The old friends were laughing. "He has organized for our parents to be here for the birth and I have him for three months then each of our parents would be here for a few months then our brothers and sisters who are single."

"Oh good. I will contribute a housekeeper so…"

"What? Oh, Zuri thanks you very much. I am so grateful."

"You are welcome. You deserve it because you worked all those long hours too. I couldn't have done it without you. We both have come such a long journey in life."

"You don't say? It was worth it. I guess you were correct in saying that what you deposit in life is what you will be receiving."

"Yes, I've forgotten about that. Besides Pong Jung have deposit an awful lot these past years, I say."

"I only started when we team up for counseling and therapy. Then again I am younger than you." Rae Jean grinned.

"Thanks for the reminder. You have to deposit more than that. Count the years as a military officer and the wars you fought. You joined the military to fight for our freedom. The two wars, Afghanistan and Iraq were not about our freedom and it was not what most of the officers signed up for, however, you contribute anyways and that's what counted."

"Thank you for saying that. I think us officers like to hear that."

"Sad as it is Rae, so does the other countries and their officers that were lied to. We tend to forget about them."

"I know and that is sad. I remembered fighting with the Aussie, French and Danish officers. How come that idiot Bush is not being held accountable for war crimes?" Rae Jean wanted to know.

"It's politics. Rae, There are more death threats on him than anyone else, I am sure. I bet you that every country who went to war and fought alongside you have put a bounty on Bush's head."

"You have a point. I know they are mad as hell to believe the lie Bush told them." Rae Jean felt a kick and put her hands on her stomach. Zuri was out of her chair and touch the spot that was shown to her of the presence of life that made himself known.

"Oh, that was strong." Zuri was laughing and began talking to the unborn child. The rest of the meal was spent talking about babies and strong kicks and shopping for clothes, breastfeeding, and the lack of sleep. All in all, they were both in bliss talking into the night. It was another three hours before they left the restaurant with a promise to meet again in two days. Blake would be home in a week, it's their time together.

The girls met again for the next two months before the baby was due. Actually, it was on one of those days that they were having dinner that Rae Jean water broke. "Oh get the waitress, will you. We need to bag this and take it with us to the hospital. My water broke."

"Oh hell, what now! Couldn't he wait!"

"Thanks a lot, Zuri. Breath and quit panicking."

Zuri hails the waitress while calling Blake to meet them at the hospital. It took them twenty minutes to get there with contractions coming rapidly for Rae jean. Blake met them as they pulled up at the entrance of the hospital and took over from the frantic Zuri. She called Christian and told him, who left the children with the nanny and was on his way. He had one of the officers drove him the twenty minutes it took to the hospital as Zuri had the jeep. They waited together for the delivery and saw the Jordan family before leaving for home.

Life became hectic for Zuri due to Rae Jean being on maternity, she had to manage all the extra emergencies and a few extra travels to the base to secure the counselors and therapists to smooth out the conflicts of interest. It seemed when she is home, she is always on the cellular phone. She began to resent it because many times she is nursing Lei when there is a conflict of interest that required her attention. On several occasions, it took more than thirty minutes to sort out the conflict itself than to create a solution.

During the week, they spend near the base and on weekends they are at the cabin. Tomorrow she has to fly to the base to have an all-day meeting with all twenty counselors with their assistants. She went looking for Christian who was making a birdhouse for Anana. Lei was sleeping. She stood and watched Anana giving her father a piece of cut wood.

"In a minute love," Christian spoke softly to his daughter.

"Minute?" She asked him looking into a replica of her own eyes.

"Mmmm two minutes."

"Two minutes." Anana held up two fingers showing her father who nodded his head in agreement.

"You are so smart." Christian smiled at his daughter who became aware of her mother. She yelled to her saying, "me very smart. Mummy daddy says Anana very smart."

"Oh, of course, you are." Zuri laughed at her daughter

and down on her knees and stretched out her hands to welcome her. Anana seeing her mother's position ran into her arms and took her kisses. Christian seeing this gave a hearty laugh and covered the short distance between them. He picked Anana up in his arm and pulled her mother up with the other. He kissed his daughter and then one for his lover. He immediately felt the sadness and knew she had to leave. He held her and pulled her towards the table that held the unfinished birdhouse. Together they worked building and filling it with bird feed. They took Anana to choose a tree to hang it. Christian lifted her while Zuri gave her the house. They stood back watching and waiting for birds to visit. They didn't have to wait long as a flock of black and white birds of the swallows bred came talking to each other in their tongue. Silence followed as they watched the birds until the sunset upon which they went in for dinner.

For the next three months, many dawns gave way to Zuri's constant traveling between her home and the military base as she handed over the reins to four doctors and the director of operations. The journey took a toll on her as she left her newborn son without a mother for a week at a time. Although she pumped milk for him to be fed it was not the same as holding and feeding him. Anana was quiet as she watched her mother go, always holding her father's hand as if she's afraid that he would go too and leave her. Christian would hold her for a long while before she goes whispering in her ear "soon" giving her comfort. On the days she returned, she would lay in Christian's arms for hours, pulling on his essence, hoping it would wash away the little bit of guilt she felt, however, she missed her family, greatly.

Today, she returned in the early hours of dawn, her son's fourth month. Christian met her as usual at the helipad with open arms and a long passionate kiss that took her breath away. He saw the stress and knew she is going to cry; he led the way to the path to the house.

Zuri took a shower, kissed her daughter who sleepily whispered "mummy" as she whispered, "I love you." Christian watched her as she observed their daughter sleeping, he pulled her away to their son's room. As if he knew his mother was home he was kicking and smiling with baby sound waiting for her to pick him up.

"Oh, my love did the chopper woke you up? It didn't do a thing to Anana. Com' let me hold you. I missed you." Christian left them and return to bed. He knew Zuri treasure these precious moments with their children and he gladly gave them the privacy to strengthen their bonding.

Many dawns he would be awakened thinking she was home only to realize that she was not; he comforted himself knowing she would be home soon, retired from counseling and they would be together in the months to come. He secretly counted down the days when he can wake up with her every day in his arms. Oh, he missed her presence and the days seemed long without her. He had plenty to do regardless of the help he has from the housekeeper, nanny, and officers from the camp, nonetheless he planned that he would be occupied, and missing Zuri would not hurt so much.

He knew it hurt her to leave them as much as it pained him to see her go. It has become a standard-issue not to talk about it. The few times he did, Zuri spend the night crying that he can predict the times she would and tonight is one of those nights. Grant you, she would wait till the day passed as the mornings were spent with the children. They didn't foresee the difficulty of their separation, otherwise, he would have hired a manager for the boot camp. He had an advertisement out for two months with no response. The few hours they have for themselves before the children demand breakfast would be spent in each other's arms, kissing and hugging.

Making love became memories and when it did take place, it was short and sweet, however, rare.

Zuri entered the room and settled into Christian's opened arms. As they cuddled and curled their bodies into a single side position, molding themselves as one, tears fell from her and Christian tightened his grip. In a few short minutes a voice from the door whispered, "Mummy are you home, I dreaming? Christian lifted his head and motioned his hand for their daughter to join them. Zuri was wiping the tears and trying to gain control so her daughter wouldn't see her which didn't work. Anana ran to her side of the bed instead of her father's as she usually does and saw her mother's tears. She stood for a minute watching her mother clutching her teddy bear Tiger tight in her arms.

Christian kept his observation silent as Anana peeked at her. "Mummy why are you cryin'?"

Zuri stretched her arms out and Anana climbed into bed with them. "I am sad that I have to leave you, Lei, and Daddy. I missed you guys so much that it hurts so I cry."

"Does it help to cry?"

"Yes, it helps me to let the pain from missing you, daddy and Lei go away a little bit."

"How Mummy?" Anana moved from the curled position she has taken refuge in from her mother to sitting on the edge of the bed. Seeing this, Zuri moved on her back and held Anana from falling, however, Christian stayed on his side of the bed.

"When you let the tears flow it helps take the pain I feel from missing all of you away. It feels as the pain washed away the hurt feelings I can't express, talk about goes away too."

"Oh. Daddy takes the hurt away when he holds you like me, mummy?"

"Yes, does daddy take yours away?"

Anana nodded her head and leaned over and kissed

her mother; she climbed over her mother to her dad and threw her arms around his neck and kissed him. "I love you, daddy."

"Why? Thank you, my gorgeous daughter."

"You took mummy words. She called me gorgeous and Lei handsom'." Anana giggled and climb off the bed running to the door. She was out a second before she ran back and stood at the door looking at her parents. "I am hungry, daddy."

"Mummy will fix you something to eat."

"Mummy come, me and tiger is hungry?" Anana announced looking at her mother's teary eyes.

"Gave me one second and I will be there, gorgeous."

Anana giggled upon hearing her mother called her gorgeous. It sounded different from when her father, who usually called her "pretty lady," says it.

She doesn't know why nor does she care. They both loved her.

Zuri joined her daughter in the kitchen, the table was set and Tiger was seated next to Anana. Who set the table? She looked up as Christian entered, reading her thoughts and seeing the surprise mixed with wonderment in her eyes, she whispered in her ears as he passed her into the fridge for the milk, "Anana did."

"Thank you for setting the table, Anana." Zuri walked over to her gorgeous daughter and kissed her head.

"elcom' mummy." Anana happily giggled.

She and Christian made a peanut butter sandwich with warm milk. They chat about everything noticing the silence in Anana.

"Anana love, what is the matter?" Christian asked her

Ignoring her father she turned her blue eyes to her mother across the table. She had Tiger in her arms. "Mummy, can I cry with you next tim'?"

"Oh, darlin' of course." Zuri opened her arms the minute Anana left her chair running to her. She held her as tears flowed, working into a bawled. Tears soon followed from Zuri. Christian watched mother and daughter holding each other and crying. He pulled himself on his feet, clear the table, and washed the dishes; his tears began to fall.

10

Zuri woke to the cool air and the light of dawn, which painted the sky with brilliant colors of scarlet and gold. She closed her eyes for a few more minutes and smiled as she looked out the window into the dawning of a new day.

Finally!

This is her life, spending days with Christian, Anana, and Lei. No more long days of therapy or being exhausted and desperately in need of sleep. These were her days of rewards for planting seeds so many years ago and more than anything, having a wonderful godfather who makes her life worked.

Anana was a little over two years while Lei is six months old. They are outdoors children, spending most days outside. Anana takes private lessons in music and ballet from the officers with children. There is a nursery and pre-school in the camp managed by the officers who are mothers. A few pre-school teachers were hired to guide the program into production. Anana attends in the morning hours, five days a week.

Lei nursed and sleep. She usually has him on a blanket outside. He looked at the sky and clouds talking up a storm. On occasion birds flew over he would become so excited kicking his little feet and scream with joy. She loved watching her children playing and growing.

Today is Saturday and she slept on and off for two days. She and Rae Jean had visited the spa for a day. Rae Jean and David are parents to twin girls. They had to postpone their wedding until the girls were at least a year old. Zuri turned over and fell asleep for another few hours. It was late in the afternoon before she left her bed and came in search of Christian and the children. She found them in the living room. Lei is in Christian's arms and he had his hands in his mouth. She guessed he is on the commence of teething. Both of them were looking at Anana, who was outside with Casper the German Shepherd.

"Daddy."

"Yes, darling."

"Come and get me," Anana told her father as a wicked gleam of mischief surface in her green eyes.

"No, not now Anana, time for a bath and dinner." All eyes were on Zuri as she entered the room.

"Can we play that game tomorrow, Anana?" Zuri asked her daughter.

"No." Came an angry reply from Anana. A frown stuck on her forehead and blue eyes demanded to be obeyed. She stumped the ground with one foot as she pronounces the "no."

"Anana in the house this minute," Christian ordered her in. Anana signed and walked into the house as Casper followed.

"Go and wash up for dinner. Now Anana."

"Yes, daddy." She put her head down in disappointment for not being able to talk her father into playing. How come it worked for her friend Missy and not her? She knew that voice of her fathers and don't like it much. He meant he is serious and not joking or playing. She wanted to listen because it meant later he would play with her after Lei is in bed.

Christian brushed his lips as he passed Zuri. "I am going to wash this fellow up, why don't you go pour us some wine?" Zuri nodded and head into the kitchen. Something wonderful was coming from the oven. She stopped for a minute and inhaled. "Ah, pizza for dinner."

She pulled the half bottle of red wine from the kitchen counter, took two glasses out from the cupboard, and poured wine into them. She took a sip of hers and set the table for four. She was pulling the pizza out of the oven when Anana walked in. Upon seeing what was for dinner, she began dancing to the table singing. "Pizza for dinner, pizza for dinner, I'm having pizza for dinner." She changed her language and started singing in Chinese. She and Zuri were having a conversation in Chinese when they were joined by Christian and Lei.

"I didn't know you speak Chinese, Zuri." Christian was astonished and shocked at the same time.

"Ah, my love." She reached up and kissed him. "It would be interested to discover each other hidden talents, wouldn't it, love?"

"Yes, I can't wait to discover you all over again." Christian had put Lei into his seat and looked at Zuri with his flirting green eyes.

"Oh, darling. I don't think I am going to be bored!" She grinned at him.

Christian put a slice of pizza on each plate and proceeded to cut Lei into smaller bits mostly cheese who would play with it in his mouth until it is soft and then he would swallow it as he was taught to do by his father, also there was some sweet potato with chicken blended for him. Christian seeing Zuri's hands emptied, pulled her into him and nibbled on her lower lip. He worked his way down to her neck and spent some time there. He moved his hands on her backside and pulled her into him. Zuri felt his arousal and she moistened more as her hand went down his jeans and she gently squeezed him. Christian had to pull away from her to maintain control. As his eyes mated with her, he grinned. "I have the children trained. Once they are down for the night, they would sleep through till the morning." He flirtingly told her.

"Oh, Good. I guess I can have a good long sleep." Zuri grinned at him.

"Oh." His face was serious. "Are you still tired?" Zuri mischievously grinned at him. Christian had a puzzled look on his face as he tried to comprehend her expression.

"Mommy more pizza please," Anana asked.

It was in the early hours of the morning that Christian felt a hand on his manhood. He relaxed and enjoyed the sensations that are beginning to stir in him. This is one of those moments he will hold out as much as he can because when he came to bed last after showering, Zuri was asleep. She looked so sensuous he wanted to wake her up very slowly. He let her rest because he knew she would pleasure him later. He began to make music as her tongue circulates over his erect length. His hand moved through her hair and anchored her head into place. "Oh yes, darling, stay right there for a little while longer." The tension was building into fiery sensations that quickly traveled to his heart. He was going to lose control. He pulled her on top of him and pushed her down on his erection. "I want to release myself in you." He whispered on the tip of her nipple. "Oh, heavens, how I missed you." He went to the other nipple and next to her lips. His hands were holding her hips on him as Zuri tried to find her groove.

She was well aware of the sizzling vibrating passion rapidly building in her zone rushing to her heart. She sensed the change due to their breathing and the quickened pulse beating in them when she found her groove on his pulsating erection in her. She picked up her tempo and rock and roll on him. Christian stretched out and switched on the bed lamp. He had a desperate need to see her. He picked himself up and sought her mouth with his own as savoring sensations began to slowly explode and melted their bones into a sweet smell of true love. Zuri looked at Christian dizzily, her brain refused to think. She felt every fiber of her emotions of passion, love, pleasure climax into her heart. She kissed him and gently bit into his lower lip and his neck. She contracted her muscles and pushed him down on the bed. She took his hands and pin them down by the side of his head.

Zuri held the contract and let the sensations dominated her body. Soft sexy brown eyes lit green eyes as the intensity built. She let go of the contraction and watched as Christian let out a breath. She followed and contracted her pelvis again. He was waiting for her and he did the same. She felt the powerful ache of excitement increased as she breathed in his masculine scent. She let the contraction go and felt the pressure of his hard thighs behind her as he turned her over onto her back. Her legs went to rest upon his shoulder as he pulled out and entered her in one swift moment.

"Oh, Christian."

He was so deep in her that she let go of all time and day as the music of love flowed out of her. Christian was riding the ocean of intensified exotic sensations that washed over them, drowning them into an escalating feeling of ecstasy. "I love you, Zuri."

A week later their lovemaking improved and they were out of hibernation. Christian and Zuri were discovering how to adjust to being together every day. They had to learn to give the other privacy and space to grow and nourish themselves. They didn't make love every chance they had because that would not permit the intensity to build and their lovemaking would become ritual and boring. Instead, they flirted and played with each other. She had begun leaving love notes for him after the birth of Anana and became so occupied that she had stopped; she continued. Christian, on the other hand, became spontaneous with his foreplay. It kept the energy of sexuality burning.

The nanny went on a long overdue vacation for a

month. They took the children to school and picked them up. Lei went for a few hours for social development. The children also were adjusting to having mommy home. They were so used to Christian attending to their needs that they never turned to Zuri. She gave them time to adjust as she too understood this new role they had to work through.

Zuri spoke with her siblings, long lost friends, and all her family she had not maintained many contacts with since she began counseling the military officers. They had agreed not to have anyone visit for a month as this would give them time to work through their kinks in adjusting to family life. She spoke to Pong Jung every day. Twice a week Ray Jean and she would Skype sharing the latest on the children. They would meet up once a week for grooming and dinner. It took Zuri and Christian about three months to adjust to a new life. They planned events and activities for the children and took part in the other officers' family activities. They were less challenging days as Zuri let go of the old life and let in the new family one. Christian released some of the family responsibilities to her as the children realized that she is not going anywhere. They were merging into a family, finally. Activities became hectic as families began to visit them.

Pong Jung resumed his monthly visits and took Anana away for their usual weekend to someplace or the other. Lei enjoyed using his teeth with the new dog, Champion they chew on everything that looked feasible. A big birthday party was in the works for his first birthday. They didn't travel as Zuri wanted to feel completely at ease with her new roles as partner and mother. She wanted both children to be potty trained before traveling anywhere and Lei to appreciate the new places as Anana. They added two more rooms to the cabin and in the process built a paved road for easy traveling. They begin having a shrimp and fish farm as well as growing organic vegetables. The officers at the Booth camp did most of the farming. Zuri and Christian continue to manage their companies and had decided to hand over the reins soon.

The hospital was being built in the village that fell on the other side of the camp. They had interviewed doctors for the various jobs and staff for the hospital. Rae Jean had trained counselors for the center to oversee later by Zuri. Life was no longer a challenge, however, it was occupied with daily decisions. It seemed that she or Christian was always on the internet or mobile phone talking to someone or the other. They had agreed that neither of them would work the same hours in case of an event of the children surfacing. Christian worked in the morning and Zuri in the afternoon.

As the weeks passed, the managers of their company were given more responsibilities leaving room to change their schedule. Christian and Zuri kept occupied for a few hours a week, not more. They take on projects that they can share together and with the children. Christian had a new hobby of building electrical control planes. They all chipped in to be his assistant. This was where they were gathered this fall afternoon.

" 'ere dad-a, 'ere." Lei extended his hand to his father as he gave him a piece of something to fix the plane that Christian was building. He was almost one and spoke a few words his sister taught him. Anana loved to teach him things.

"Thank you, son." Christian looked at the piece and realized that he was not ready for it, smiled at this son. He hid the part among some others lose unknown pieces on the table as he continues assembling the plane.He watched with Zuri as Lei went for another piece that lay on the blanket they had set out with various parts of the airplane for the purpose that the children can help. Lei dropped the part on the grass and ran to his sister who was looking at the rabbit drinking from the stream.

Lei's hand went into his sister's and he looked up at her with adoring eyes and smiled. He pointed at the rabbit and mumbled some words that cannot be understood, however, his sister did and nodded her head in answering him. Anana held his hands and gave him some attention as she watched the rabbit hopped away making room for some dears.

"Oh, Christian look at them together!"

Christian looked at his children and kissed their mother passionately. He was emotional, therefore speechless. Zuri seeing his expression became emotional with him. He wiped her tears away and pulled her back into his chest as they watched their children together arm in arm, in loving silence. Finally, his emotions somewhat control, he whispered in her ear. "These are the moments I want to remember when I sit in my rocking chair holding your hands."

"I think my handsome hunk, we will have lots of those moments. I have much photographs and videos; they will last another lifetime. This moment I can't capture on anything. It's only worth experiencing."

At that moment, the father dear sensing someone watching looked up and began his journey where Anana and Lei were standing. Upon seeing the dear coming towards them, Lei let go of his sister's hand and bolted for his parents. He started to cry. "Dad-a." Lei shouted with fright. Anana looked at the dear and said, "go away." She yelled and realizing that the dear was doing no such bidding she too began to yell.

"Daddy."

Christian picked them up in his arms as the deer stopped, looked, and turned back to his family. Zuri's eyes danced with laughter as they met Christian's. They had to control their amusement and comfort the children. Lei was passed to his mother as Christian comforted his daughter. The laughter surfaced again much later as

Christian lay with Zuri in his arms. They fell asleep with the laughter on the incident ringing in the air.

A week later as the years of tiredness disappeared from Zuri's body, she began to explore the campgrounds. She loved to walk by the stream that flowed through the acres of land into Lake Superior and enjoyed the beauty of the wild animals. She saw Christian picked a snake up and took it deeper into the woods. How brave is her handsome hunk? She had asked Christian about the snakes the first time she saw Anana has one whether they were dangerous and he had mentioned "yes." He was careful not to explain to Anana that when she is older she can remove the snakes and put them in the woods. He made sure that Anana put some vinegar on her body so the snakes would ignore her. She had a spray bottle sitting on the patio, each time she goes outside she sprayed some on her body. He had put snake pellet all around the house and toward the pool and stream.

Today, sprayed with vinegar she ventured out further enjoying the afternoon sun. It was a beautiful day and Zuri was so taken up with her enjoyment that she strolled upon a dirt road and decided to follow it. Christian probably took the children for a walk. "I think even Lei knew his way around there more than I do," Zuri whispered to herself, more on the lookout for snakes and wildlife than Christian and the children. Fifteen minutes later she stumbled upon a large cabin with the word "Pub" written on it and decided to enter it. She opened the door, stepped into the cabin, and saw it crowded with officers. Everyone's eyes were on her as she stood with her hand on the doorknob wanting to flee. The silence was found everywhere and even the animals stood still. It was several minutes before Zuri stepped inside and looked all around her eyes searching for Christian and the children. Upon finding none she said,

"Hello." In a minute she was greeted with "hello doc"

and everyone resumed what they were doing. An officer walked up to her and asked, "would you like to join us, doc?"

"Oh, you are so kind, yes I would, thank you."

Zuri was well aware that although the officers were carrying on with their business they were conscious of her and what she was doing in the pub. She was also aware that she probably counseled many if not all of them and she is clueless as to who is who. She wondered if she should say something as the officers made available a chair for her.

"I am sorry that I don't know any of your names." She accepted a beer from an officer, who had poured it into a mug for her.

"That's okay, doc. We know yours."

"And you are?"

"Lieutenant Anderson." The introduction was made and then Zuri asked, "Do you know where Christian and the children are?"

"Probably fishing further up the creek." Officer Peterson answered.

"Doc, how come our names, ranks, and what happened in the war, you never asked us?" Sergeant del Cargo asked.

"Because it would have been too much and too long therapy. I hadn't the time to sit there and listen to you when long lines were waiting for my attention, every day. I had to make choices about what is the safest quickest therapy for all of you. Your name, age, and most of the information was for your release. All I looked at your answers to the questionnaire and assessment you filled out upon signing up for my program and how deep-rooted is your pain. I didn't have time to be your friend or get to know any of you." Zuri was aware that there was silence once again.

"Do you know how many of us you counseled in the

years before you retired?" Officer Sellers asked.

"No, I lost count at the first ten." Laughter rang out from the cabin.

"Hey doc, thanks for building this camp for us and our families. We thank the Lieutenant already." An officer in a wheelchair came forward and extended his hand. "Sergeant Matterson" Zuri spent the next hour shaking hands and being introduced to the officers. She answered their questions and comforted them. There was laughter upon hearing some of the replies and this was what drew Christian into the "Pub." His eyes lit up upon seeing the scene in front of him. Zuri was having a beer with officers of the camp. They had formed a circle around her and laughing. It was quite a sight as he lowered Lei from his shoulders and set him on his feet. Soon a path was made as the children were noticed, as they made their way to their mother. Christian stood there looking at Zuri and greeting the officers. A little hand was rested upon Zuri's thighs as she acknowledged her son.

"Lei." She picked him up to sit on her lap. Anana joined her and stood next to her. Zuri put an arm around her daughter and kissed her head. Her eyes searched the crowd for Christian. She saw him talking to an officer. Sensing her, he turned and smiled; a smile that touches his green eyes that travel from his heart. Zuri received and returned the warm loving smile to him. They stayed there for another two hours with a promise to visit more often. After dinner, they read the children a story before they settled into the sofa and shared their days.

"I think I am going to call our mothers and do some shopping in New York. We all can do with some more clothes, especially the children." Zuri sipped her wine and waited for Christian's answer.

"You should. I spend more of your money than you ever did. Have you ever spent your money, Zuri?"

"No, only Pong Jung. I always used it. I wouldn't even know how much money I have or what to do with it. I don't even know where my ATM card is. I really don't know. Pong Jung always took care of my money."

"Well, I know how much you have and it runs into the millions and I can give you the card. You can use yours and Pong Jung. I will give you a list of things I want and you can ship it here if it is too much to bring."

"Christian I think we should buy some more land and built an airstrip, we can go and come as we like. I want to have the freedom to travel and move as I please. I enjoyed the free days at the spa and going to the bookstore and the coffee shop." "You should do all the things you did before you went into counseling and met me."

"Yes, I should, and thank you Christian for mentioning them. I am a mother now. I have a family to include in some of those things."

"Those things like what?"

"I would like to take Pong Jung's yacht and go sailing in the Caribbean when winter becomes unbearable. The officers told me to be prepared for the winter as it can become nasty. I think we should have a generation for this camp, for the winter months."

"A generator, mmmm Zuri that's an excellent idea. I'll get one installed before winter arrives."

"I was thinking about a food store too; the officers can bottled food for winter and keep it in the store. The vegetables can be frozen with the fruits and we can bottle some of the spring water. We have to create jobs to keep the officers busy as well as have food for them."

"I do want to make it easier for them." Christian mentioned thoughtfully.

"Yes, it was nice to chat with them this afternoon. I still wouldn't remember their names. I can't figure out who is an officer, a sergeant, or a Lieutenant. They still address each other by rank."

"Yes, once we get to that rank we will continue to address each other by rank. We errand it, you know. I think it is my right to be addressed by it. It's a military thing, a respect thing."

"Really, I didn't know you feel that way, Christian."

"You turned me on when you say the whole name including rank."

"Well, what do you know?" Zuri gave him a flirtatious smile.

Christian leaned into her flirtatiously and lightly brushed his lips on hers and then nipple the low one. Zuri's hand went out to take hold of him and spilled the wine on Christian. He felt the cold liquid hit his erection and jumped. Zuri realized what she did and started to laugh. She pushed herself on her feet and extended a hand to Christian who took it. She pulled him into the bathroom and turned the shower on to be heated.

"It's been a long while since we had a shower together." Zuri took her clothes off and stepped into the shower turning the tap to warm. Christian was behind her in a very short time, kissing her neck. Zuri's back was resting on his chest as she enjoyed the sensations of the warm water etching with Christian's kisses upon her body. They touched and kissed and touched some more before they bathe each other. It was a good half an hour later they were lying in bed, kissing and touching and laughing with each other.

Zuri's tiredness was slowly leaving her as they nourished each other's essence. This was a different kind of making love, the kind that keeps a relationship going for a long time to come, a loving that added the romance spurring into maturity. This is the true essence of what they want to do for so long and they never had the time to do, nourish the essence of each other. The whispering "I love you" fed into their hearts were waiting to be conveyed under these circumstances, exactly this way.

The touch that they gave each other was one of tenderness and truth of their love for each other. Zuri's touch sought the secrets of each scar on Christian's body, his touch found new meaning as he explored the silhouettes of every curve even the little rise on her stomach of carrying his children. He bent and kissed the high rise as Zuri's watched him and laid her head to rest on the pillow, laughing. She waited until he kissed every inch of her body and did the same to him. It was his turn to enjoy the sensations as Zuri explored his scars and kissed each one of them.

"I am going to go and have more scars."

Zuri lifted her head and smile at him. She leaned in for a kiss and he pulled her onto his chest, giving her a breathless kiss. As she surfaced for breath, he turned her over and pulled her hips to his waist. His hands gave her a gentle spank on her backside and he quickly entered her. She whispered his name into the electrifying air filled with their warmth of love. Christian heard her and pushed further into her core. In seconds, they picked up their rhythm and dance to their music of true love.

Christian and Zuri had started a charity organization after the children were born sharing the same name as the camp, Ana Lei. They began to develop the cause and investigate which other organizations they would contribute to and support. Many of the officers Zuri counseled including friends and family had donated and Pong Jung had double it. They expanded the camp to all military officers and families around the world. They hired military officers to manage the organization, however, decisions were made by a board of directors which included Christian and Zuri. It was one of these meetings that Christian was attending while Zuri was home with the children. The meeting was held in the village at a restaurant. Christian would be home in time for dinner, which Philippi would be preparing.

Lei is five and a half years, while his sister is seven years. Zuri had left them having breakfast while she spoke to her mother on the portable house phone. After hanging the phone on its rack, she called to the children.

"Anana, Lei where are you?" Zuri called and listened for their answers.

Upon receiving none she walked outside into the heat of the morning looking for them and calling their names. They knew that they were not permitted to wander off anywhere without letting Christian or she know where they were going. "Now where would those two run off to?" She wondered as she went in search of Philippi in the kitchen. "You haven't seen the children huh, Philippi?" She spoke in Chinese.

"No. I heard them giggling and the door close to the front." Philippi mentioned to her in English.

"Thanks," Zuri replied in Chinese. They had agreed for her to speak Chinese and Philippi to speak English to improve hers, the language would not die and the children would not forget it. Zuri walked outside again after picking up her mobile phone. She walked along the path into the wooded area calling their names. She turned around concerned for their safety in regard to the wild animals. She knew they were not lost because someone would have spotted them the minute they entered the wooded area. It was half an hour and no reply from the children, where are they? She has opened the front door when she sensed someone was there and turned to acknowledge them. She opened her mouth to voice greetings and was astonished to see her children.

They were silent and looking at her. Lei held on to his sister's t-shirt and he was looking at her expression and was Anana. She wanted to laugh and taught better of it. This is a huge joke to her and no doubt to their father, however, she has to let them know that she is crossed with them for not telling her where they were going.

"In the bath you two, now!"

They both ran past her so quickly she smiled. She sniffed the air and said, "Vinegar?"

"Yes, mummy. There was no more vinegar, we used mud. The snakes wouldn't get us." Anana found the moment she wanted to break the dreadful silence and laugh. She didn't. She knew how Christian would manage this situation because he taught his daughter and she is teaching her brother. What she is not sure of is how to manage it? She took her phone and captured a precious moment.

"Of course not. What happened to it?" As if she didn't know. Their daughter emptied it for her to do what she wanted. Lei looked at his sister and his mother; all he wanted was someone to smile and he would know he's not in trouble. When no one did, he ran to the bathroom and showered. Anana followed and did the same, hoping all would be well if she washed off the mud from her body. Zuri turned to look at Lieutenant Anderson who bought them for her. "What got them so dirty?"

"Doc, they were playing marines in the woods. They dug into the mud and put them on their clothes and the skin that was exposed." Lieutenant Anderson smiled at her, white teeth shone through black lips.

"I don't believe this? Marines, is that a game?"

"I guess it is now."

"What am I supposed to do with them?"

"Laugh. I am."

"Oh, it's not the game I object to, Lieutenant. It's the fact that they did not let me know where they were going."

"Oh, that would make me mad."

"Do you have children?"

"Yes, doc. Two teenagers who lived with their father down south. We are divorced and the kids come and see me whenever they can, mostly the holidays."

"How are you doing with your relationship with them?"

"I realized that I am not a mother to them. I missed that opportunity when I was stationed in Afghanistan. I am more a friend which is better than nothing. I am grateful they still wanted to know me after I got back. Thank you for helping me through my challenges. I always wanted to say that to you."

"Oh, you are welcome," Zuri said surprisingly.

"I know you don't remember me and I don't expect you to. It's okay. We are having a little group meeting every Wednesday at twenty hundred hours. You are welcome to join us anytime. We would love to have you."

"Oh yes, please include me. I would love to join you and the others whenever Christian is home, that is." Zuri said eagerly.

"Good. I would tell the others just show up at the pub."

"Thank you and see ya." She waved at Lieutenant Anderson and turned into the house.

Off to her children; this was the first time she would be disciplining them without Christian and his guidance. Zuri took a deep breath and went to the living room contemplating what she should do when her son appeared and ran to her. "I lov' you, mommy." Lei climbed into her lap and kissed her checks. Well, doggone it, that did it for her. She looked at her son; she can still see mud on his neck and behind his arms. She was about to tell him to go back to the shower when Anana joined them.

"I am sorry to upset you, mommy. I was teaching Lei how to play Marines."

"I am upset because you did not tell me where you were off to, not for playing marines."

"Oh." Anana was surprised and speechless.

"Next time please let me know when you choose to leave the house." Zuri wanted to laugh and kept a serious face looking at both of them.

"I will promise mommy." Anana was relieved.

"Will too, mommy." Brown eyes looked into hers. Lei had brown eyes and curly dark brown hair with a little bit of red that glows in the sun. Anana had straight light brown-reddish hair with the lightest green eyes. They both had light brown skin that is easy to tan.

"Alright off you go." They both ran off toward their playroom, relieved on their faces. As usual, after the children were tucked in for the night, Christian and Zuri were cuddled on the sofa, sipping wine. Christian proceeded to fill her in with his meeting and decision made on the other charities their organization would be supporting. They chatted about the different topics that were discussed in the ongoing projects.

"Besides the officers donating money into the organization, other people are as well. Pong Jung continued to double it and others he associated with, are doing the same. Zuri, a huge sum of money is going into the organization. We have a full time accountant!"

"Oh good, Christian, we can do much more with the money. Let us send some counselors over to Africa and India and grow food. We can hire some of the military officers to deliver food. We can get the female to the school in India. There is an orphanage there that I usually donate money to that Cyrus is in charge of. "

"Good idea, Zuri. How was your day?"

"Oh hell bells, Christian, do you really want to know?"

Christian broke out in laughter after Zuri told him about her experience with their children. "That was the mud on Lei's body I washed off after dinner?"

"Yes, I realized later that sending him to wash it off was a mistake. He is only five, I left it. Oh, Christian, Marine of all the game you had to teach them?"

"It had nothing to do with mud on their body, Zuri. I taught Anana survival skills, how to live in the woods, and what to eat. I don't know how she got the mud going. I am going to ask her about that."

"Maybe she saw the other officers doing it."

"I wouldn't doubt it. Some of the children in school fathers are active Marines, who knows. You did great with them, my love."

"Thank you. Lieutenant Colonel Christian Andres Vincelette."

"You're welcome, Captain." Zuri roared with laughter.

"You know I was shocked to see you standing wet. I guess you didn't know that your clothes were soaked and I, also the drill sergeant can see right through you. I was turned on and hope no one noticed."

"No, I didn't pay attention. I was furious."

"You looked sexy, all wet and serious. It was the talk in the mess hall all week."

"What? Are you serious?"

"Yes, that's not the only time the conversation turned to you."

"Really Christian, tell me more." Zuri wanted to know. "I didn't think people talked about me so much."

"Yes, during recovery, I bought your books. Well, dad went shopping and bought them for me. He and mom would take turns and read to me. Soon the other officers started to listen and they got their own books or we share, passed them onto others. We would ask questions on what you meant and discussed what you wrote. Some of the officers started betting real money on what you meant on certain topics. You start changing our words to yours and our communication became effective. It kept us going and wanting to be healthy."

"Oh, love that's so sweet. I am happy that I was spoken of and in that manner. Thank you for sharing with me."

"You know even in Afghanistan some of the officers had your books and those who returned had taken your class told the others about you. I guess we were all praying that you would be there for us. Some of us were so tired of the wars that we wanted to be hurt and be discharged.

Many knew they would not, they hoped anyway. After I saw my whole unit blew up to bits I wanted to die too. I kept thinking of you hoping to see you. When the pain hit I didn't want you to see me like this, I felt guilty for being alive.

"In the end, before I was rescued, I saw the moon and asked it to shine its light on me to heal me for me to see you. I saw your face in the moon and would go in and out of consciousness. It was hell. In the weeks that followed, I became impotent and all I wanted was for you to take the pain away. I didn't even want anything else. I didn't feel like a man. I was dead. I had given up hope. That night I was crying asking the moon to shine its light and fixed me. I had made up my mind not to see you and it saddened me deeply. The next thing I knew I was looking into your eyes. I thought I was hallucinating as I've gotten my fantasies, illusions, and reality mixed up.

"Then I saw your tears and all the sensations that splurged between us kept flowing as we looked into each other's eyes, I came alive and felt my erection. I spontaneously kissed you, in some way it was a thank you. By the time I left, I couldn't sleep, I went to the roof of the bunker and waited for you to walk to your office. I came alive again and knew I had to see you." Christian looked into her eyes searching for understanding, compassion, love anything. What he found was the essence of what a lady should be, he found it all in Zuri. He passionately pulled and held her to him for a very long time. "I am overjoyed that you are here. You made me realized how beautiful my world is today. Thank you." He whispered in her ear.

Zuri was speechless for a long time as silence stuck them into a comfort zone of understanding that was private between two people. They let it ride out its course before Zuri added her feelings to her lover's. "I was not bargaining on falling in love. I was exhausted and desperately need some TLC. That's what I was looking for when I saw you standing there watching the chopper go and something clicked in me. You were the only one watching us go."

"Really?" Christian raised an eyebrow looking at her. "I was watching you not the chopper." He saw Zuri checks turned from brown to red in an instance. He beams with love because he can make her blush.

Zuri blushed some more if that was possible. She ignored his beaming and continued, 'I fell in love with you that night you cannoned into me."

"I cannoned into you?"

"Huh, of course, you did?"

"I think we bumped into each other." He looked into her eyes daring her to doubt him. She did not and instead blame it on the moon, "Marine Moon."

"Oh no, not my moon," Christian exclaimed and bed over and kissed her for a very long time; he held her.

Zuri let him kiss her, hold her, let him seek his comfort from her, and let him feel safe and secure as she had done many times in the past. This is what true love is about, caring, and sharing. They had worked their relationship against the norm and odds for survival. It worked for them even in the darkest of moments, true love had kept them anchored until they had worked out the kinks and have a partnership. This day's dawn was breathtaking for two people who won the struggles of life's challenges and found themselves in the process of loving each other.